FOCUS, SAM

FOCUS, SAM

ROHIT GORE

Rupa . Co

Published 2011 by
Rupa Publications India Pvt. Ltd.
7/16, Ansari Road, Daryaganj,
New Delhi 110 002

Sales Centres:

Allahabad Bengaluru Chennai
Hyderabad Jaipur Kathmandu
Kolkata Mumbai

Typeset by
Mindways Design
1410 Chiranjiv Tower
43 Nehru Place
New Delhi 110 019

Printed in India by
Nutech Photolithographers
B 240, Okhla Industrial Area, Phase I,
New Delhi 110 020, India

To authors who have inspired me.
Especially Stephen King,
Nick Hornby and Elmore Leonard.

Contents

Acknowledgements

Thanks to

My wife Pranita, who told me to get my act together and start writing. She believed in me when I didn't. It was her encouragement and constant support that made me write.

My parents, Mrs Varsha and Mr Dilip Gore, who encouraged me to read as many books as I can. My in-laws, Mrs Seema and Dr Sunil Pathak for their blessings and support. My brother-in-law Nikhil Pathak, for helping me with many aspects of this book. My sister Deepty Gore, for her good wishes.

My editor, Vineetha Mokkil, for believing in this book and making my dream a reality. My super agent, Kanishka Gupta of the Writer's Side Literary Agency. Ujwala Samarth, for helping me in improving this novel immensely.

To my friends who betta read my writing – Deepa Aithal, Subhabrata Ghosh, Shruthi Krishnamoorthi, Abhijeet Kothiwale, Shalabh Maloo, Himanshu Jain, Vinay. Nayak and Heena Makvana.

To all the authors I have grown up reading.

Chapter 1

I DIDN'T REMEMBER THE ACCIDENT. THE DOCTOR SAID THIS wasn't very unusual. Our brains often block out memories of unpleasant events. Calling my accident an 'unpleasant event' was like saying WW II was a skirmish. My ankle was broken. My left shoulder was dislocated. There were many visible and not-so-visible bruises; some of them had been dressed by a very stern-looking nurse who smelt of coconut oil.

Many people visited me in the hospital and asked the only question I had no answer for: How had it happened? The first few times, I said that I didn't remember. After a while I just shrugged, which was even more painful since I am a left-shoulder-shrugger.

We all have accidents. What made my case unique was that I had an accident *every year*. It didn't happen on the same day every year, but if you added the number of years I had spent on this planet, (twenty-nine), and divided it by the number of accidents, you would get a fraction very close to one. I had a limp in my left leg, something I had learnt to live with and even hide. There wasn't a single day the bloody leg didn't hurt.

My mother never missed an opportunity to tell the story of my first recorded accident – how she had dropped me when I was just a two-year-old. She had been trying to do the impossible – balancing a baby while riding pillion on my father's Vespa scooter, the 1978 model with its rear seat inclined at a treacherous forty-degree angle. My father had had a devilish urge to rev up the engine of his new toy (this was the time when a Vespa scooter was his greatest guilty pleasure) to a speed of sixty, and my mother's sari had fallen off her shoulder. Like any ultra-self-conscious Indian woman who can never let *that* happen, she had promptly clutched my father's shoulder with one hand and adjusted her sari with the other. That had left her with no hand with which to hold me.

My mother laughed every time she told this story, especially when she described how I had wailed and how long she had cried. I couldn't be faulted for howling after bouncing on the rocky road like a bloody human tennis ball. She said it was a miracle that I had survived. It was a painful story, and it became even more so when she told it every Diwali to her four sisters. They laughed and reminisced about the number of hours she had cried after letting me slip.

Since then the accidents had happened almost every year. I remembered everything before and after the accident. It was just those few crucial minutes that I blanked out. People did fill me in later, but it wasn't the same. It was like missing the most intense scene of a movie. Like missing Lauren Bacall say, 'Steve, you know how to whistle, don't you?' Like missing Gabbar Singh say '*Kitne aadmi the?*'

✧

'This is the twenty-eighth one, right?' Jai asked.

I said nothing. Counting my accidents gave me the creeps, but Jai Deshmukh, who claimed, and rightfully so, to be my best friend, had a fetish for it. He had all the details about my mishaps stored in his accountant's brain. When they had happened, what I had broken, what caused them, how long it had taken me to recover. He always said after the tally: 'It wasn't your fault.'

He said it now with a little smile.

That's what I loved him for.

I closed my eyes.

'Oh, please, don't get into the crybaby mode.'

For a best friend, Jai was lousy at reading my thoughts.

'I am on heavy-duty painkillers, you moron. They are making me dizzy. I stopped crying after the tenth.'

'Like hell you did. I still remember the ruckus you made after the thirteenth. The whole hospital visited you for three days just to see the kid who could scream like that.'

Bloody accountants!

'Can we talk about some pleasant memories?'

'Sure we can,' he said and adjusted his owlish glasses, 'What happened between you and Maya?'

'I said *pleasant*, Jai.'

'What can be more pleasant than Maya? More so when she wears that little pink dress.'

'Excuse me, but last I remember, you used to call her bhabi. And that pink dress isn't little. It's a full blown salwar kameez for god's sake.'

'Oh, come off it. Beautiful women aren't anybody's bhabis.'

I shut up. After a long silence, Jai patted my hand.

'I think there is something seriously wrong here,' he said in a grave tone. I had never heard him use that tone before.

He flapped his hand as though my body was some inanimate object beyond his comprehension.

'You know, I've been thinking since your latest accident. You need to see someone.'

'Someone?'

'Yes. There's this man . . . People say he is the re-incarnation of Nostradamus.'

'What?'

'Nostradamus. The man who saw tomorrow, remember that movie?'.

'Jai, I know who Nostradamus was.'

'Yeah, okay. So this man is said to be the modern N. He has predicted many terrible events which actually happened. Like the Tsunami, 9/11, the Iraq war, President Obama's election . . .'

'How is Obama's election terrible?'

'It must be for some people!' he said impatiently. 'Focus, Sam, focus. The point is, he is one hell of a soothsayer.'

'And I care because . . .?'

Raising his hands in theatrical exasperation, Jai said, 'He can predict your next accident! He can tell you when and how it's going to happen. Then, you just have to avoid stepping out of your house on that day. Heck, you avoid stepping out of your bed that bloody day. Simple.'

'What if he tells me that the ceiling fan above my bed is going to fall on me?'

'How many times have you heard of that happening . . . Are you mocking me?'

'No.'

'That sounded like mocking with a capital M.'

I said nothing.

'Fine. You take care,' he patted my hand again and stood up.

It was an unwritten pact between us. He visited me after every accident. He lived thousands of kilometres away but never missed being beside me when he got the news. Perhaps it was this sudden upsurge of emotion for a loyal friend that made me say: 'Wait. Tell me how we can contact this man.'

Brightening up, Jai said, 'Oh, don't you worry. It's all been arranged. He's visiting you tomorrow. I've already paid his fees.'

'Fees?'

'You think predictions come for free?'

'You didn't have to do that.'

'No worries, dear friend. I used your ATM card for the cash.'

'Jai, how the hell do you know my PIN?'

He squeezed my hand. 'You haven't changed your PIN for the last ten years. See you tomorrow. I will come with Babaji at eleven.'

I seethed for a while and then I laughed. I would live to repent it all later.

✧

When Jai had said Babaji, I had imagined a man with an unruly beard wearing bright saffron clothes. He would have a vermillion smear on his forehead too. The Babaji who sat next to my bed was a young man, perhaps not older than me. He was wearing a shirt and a natty tie.

Steepling his fingers and rubbing his thumbs, he sighed and said, 'I have seen your *kundli*, Sameer.'

I was mesmerised by his voice. It was as if an eighty-year-old man had spoken.

'Your accident happened because you dropped your pen while boarding the train, didn't you?'

I was speechless. Although I didn't remember anything about the accident, I did recall that the Parker pen, gifted to me by Maya on my twenty-ninth birthday when we were still madly in love. It had slipped out of my shirt pocket. I had tried to catch it, fumbling like a novice juggler, but it had fallen on the filthy

Mumbai railway platform. Maya's disappointed face had flashed in front of my eyes – her bee-stung lips twisted, like a broken rose petal. I remembered that I had jumped, forgetting that the train had assumed significant speed by then. Everything went dark after that.

I must have gaped, because Babaji's smile widened. Perhaps he was used to gaping mouths.

'You have no memories of your accidents, do you?' he asked.

I shook my head.

'But I know how each one of your accidents happened.' He leaned back on the chair and proceeded to tell me about them, including the Vespa scooter one.

I couldn't move for a long time. There have been very few moments in my entire – some would say entirely inconsequential – life when I have felt completely awestruck. In fact, there were just two. The first was when Maya and I became an item, as in the moment when we both realised that we were sure about spending the rest of our lives in the 'happily ever after' mode. The second was this.

'Babaji, how can we get Sam, I mean Sameer out of this accident-a-year routine? Is there a curse on my friend? Has someone cast a spell on him?'

The soothsayer leaned forward and looked at me with the kind of grave expression meant for terminally ill patients.

'Yes, there is a curse on this young man. It can be lifted only by a woman.' And he nodded as though agreeing with himself.

'Okay. Which woman?' Jai was doing all the talking on my behalf.

Babaji closed his eyes and said nothing for several minutes.

'I don't know,' he finally said

'You don't know?'

'I have tried to see it. But there is something in my way. This young man will have to find that woman for himself.'

'But can you give us some kind of direction? I mean she could be anyone! Also, while we look for her, can you tell us when his next accident is due?'

Babaji steepled his fingers again and said, 'Exactly one year after this one.'

'See! I told you,' Jai crowed triumphantly, 'Now, just don't step out of the house on that day!'

'He will have to step out of the house. But there won't be another accident.'

'Great! You mean the next one will be his last?'

'I mean the next one will be *the last*. He will die that day.'

✧

The modern Nostradamus had left three hours ago, but neither I nor Jai had spoken a word. It was raining hard. I jumped at every clap of thunder. It wasn't even evening yet, but a pall of gloom hung over us. The hospital setting and Babaji's *last words* made the atmosphere morbid. As if on cue, my left leg, the one with the ancient limp, was aching.

Although Maya would disagree, I'm a very level-headed man, yet how was I supposed to react when someone who seemed to know every detail of my past had predicted that I would be dead in a little over a year? I was big on science. I had a degree in chemical engineering to prove it. The 'science' guy inside me, who had once spent three consecutive sleepless nights pouring over the class topper's notes to escape flunking organic chemistry, wanted to kick my ass for even listening to Babaji. But how I could disregard the words of someone who had revealed the colour of the sari my mother had worn the fateful day when the streak of accidents had started? It had been purple. Nobody knew that apart from my mother, my father and me. She had never worn it again, blaming it for almost killing her only son. She had told me so.

I mulled gloomily over what Babaji had said about my curtailed future and the way around the curse. Although there was something blocking his vision, he could clearly see how I needed to go about lifting the curse. This is what he had said: 'You need to find every single woman you have been in love with. The woman who can rid you of this curse is one of them. And you need to do it within a year.' I had listened, appalled. He told me what I would have to do to save my life once I found these women.

'I'm sorry, Sam. I don't know what to say. This was a very bad idea, wasn't it?' Jai said. I wanted to tell him it wasn't his fault. I said nothing.

'Do you even remember who all you've been in love with?' he asked sceptically.

'Let's hope I do,' I said.

'Why don't you make a list and I'll start catching them one by one?'

'Babaji said I need to do that myself. *And* I need to find them one at a time.'

'Yeah, but it will take you at least three months to get back in shape. I can do the leg work in the meantime. I mean, I can get their addresses and stuff, make it easier for you.'

'I don't think that will work, Jai. I've been thinking about it for the last few hours since he left. I need to make this journey, this quest, myself.'

'You sound scary,' Jai said, his voice quavering. I knew he wanted to undo some of the damage that he thought he had caused.

I smiled. 'I know. I'll need your help. Let me get out of this damned hospital bed and let's meet after three months and try to save my life, what say?'

Jai tried to smile too. 'That's a deal.'

We were quiet for a long time after that.

'Are you going to tell Maya about this?'

I shook my head.

'That's the right thing to do, I guess,' Jai said and sighed deeply. 'We will save you, my friend. We will find this woman. It'll be a breeze, you wait and see.'

The way it turned out, he couldn't have been farther from the truth.

✧

It took me three months to recover. The twenty-eighth accident was the worst, as if something evil was telling me how it would feel on the twenty-ninth. Just like on all the previous occasions, my parents were right by my side. They had agreed to leave only after I refused to eat if they stuck around for any more time.

I did the following things during those months:

1. *Cried for more than five minutes.* Jai would've called me a wimp, but it is difficult to control your tear ducts when you know you are going to die in a year. I had that crying spell after Ms Coconut Oil, the nurse, had cleaned up my wounds. The futility of it all struck me: Perhaps, in a year's time, she would be participating in my autopsy.
2. *Fretted for approximately twenty-three hours every day over whether to tell Maya about it or not.* She was the only person in the whole world, apart from my parents, who knew my most intimate secrets. My parents claimed they knew my secrets, but she was the only one to whom I actually told everything about myself. After the first month in the hospital, I had decided to tell her. Jai, who called me every day, persuaded me not to. In the second month,

I decided not to share this terrible news with Maya. But Jai had had a change of heart and tried to persuade me to spill the beans to her. In the third month, we both agreed that we shouldn't burden her with the knowledge of my impending death.

3. *Worried about my bookshop.* It had once belonged to my uncle, who, to my everlasting surprise, had bequeathed it to me in his will. I worried because I had left the shop in the care of my two employees, Pinky and Baki. If ever the Booksellers' Association constituted a 'worst assistant' award, these two would be the undisputed joint winners.
4. *Made a list of all the women I had ever fallen for.* Of course, the biggest question buzzing in my head was – would all the women on my list consider my life worth saving?

Although my shoulder and the ankle still cried for a pain-killer every few hours and a couple of bruises were taking longer than expected to heal, I was, at the end of my three months in the hospital, largely mobile and ready to start on my quest. Jai called it 'Saving Bookseller Sam'. When he had used this expression the first time, I had thought it was catchy, but had had an uncontrollable bout of shivers nevertheless. I visited the local Ganesh temple and sat on the cold marble floor for a while. It is said that you should start any quest with Lord Ganesh's blessings. I needed Him on my side.

✧

Chapter 2

THE FIRST NAME ON MY LIST WAS MADHURI JOSHI. SHE WAS also the first girl I had promised to marry. We were both seven then. I had no idea how to find her, but the logical place to start was my school in Akola, a small, sleepy town right in the middle of the country.

My mother's reaction when she saw me at the door was the usual.

'Sameer! Why so long between your visits?'

My parents had returned to Akola after tending to my wounds, just two weeks back. It had become a sort of routine for them every year. But that little fact didn't matter. My mother still had to ask me the question.

'There was nobody to look after the bookshop, *Aai*,' I mumbled the set reply.

This was a little play that had been going on for far too long. I'm a good son, at least I think I am. But there was always a little extra, that little delta which was missing in all my attempts to be so.

There was the expected commotion in the house at my arrival. My father folded the newspaper and gave a hint of a smile. He came over to me and slapped my back twice. Another ritual that had gone on for far too long.

'*Aai, Baba,* I need to ask you something,' I said as I sipped the sublime tea my mother had made.

'The answer is yes!' my mother chirped.

'What?'

'You two are made for each other. She makes really bad tea, but she will learn. When do you want to do it?'

My father sipped his tea and grunted. That was the highest approval anyone could get from him.

'Who are you talking about and what do I want to do when?'

'Maya, of course, and your wedding.'

'I . . . no, no. I wanted to ask you something else,' I said, avoiding their eyes. 'Do you remember a girl called Madhuri Joshi?' I blurted out the question before they could ask me anything more about Maya.

'Of course I do. There is a wonderful photograph of you kissing her,' my mother said, smacking her fingers.

'What?'

'It was your birthday party. Your fourth, and all the children were at our house. Madhuri's mother was standing very close to me, holding her in her arms. A week after your birthday, when we got the photographs, there was this picture of us mothers holding you children, and you two merrily kissing each other.'

'This is weird.'

'No, it's not. It's cute. Don't you recall this picture? You used to look at it when you were a little boy. Let me get it for you,' she said, rising from the sofa.

My father cleared his throat. They constantly sent private messages to each other. The very obvious throat-clearing meant that my mother should bottle up her largely infectious, (but at times almost unbearable) enthusiasm for sharing the smallest of details. She sat down again and said, 'Anyway, why did you mention her so suddenly?'

'I need to find her,' I said, still avoiding their eyes.

A concerned look passed between my parents.

'Don't worry, *Aai, Baba,*' I said gulping down the scalding tea, burning my throat. 'I just met someone in Mumbai who knows her and who wanted me to give something to her.'

It sounded unforgivably lame. But my parents, by then experts in catching my lies, were also experts in indulging me.

'The Joshis moved away from our colony some twenty, twenty-two years back, I think. To Mumbai.' I felt miserable about going back to Mumbai. I had thought that all the girls I had fallen for in my childhood would be in Akola. The thought made me smile. Maya would've called it the classic Sam thought process. *'The focus of the universe is the desires of Sameer Sathe, and the universe shall make everything the way he wants it.'*

✧

When I returned to Mumbai and the bookshop, it felt as though I had returned to my lair after years. Bakthavar Singh Rathod, my assistant, had decorated it with red ribbons saying, 'Welcome back, Boss.' Although his name made you think of a dacoit who was seven feet tall, with a big, bushy moustache and a massive pot-belly, Bakthavar or Baki, was the antithesis of this image. Barely five feet tall, he had the mannerisms of an elf, and had proclaimed himself 'the greatest living JRR Tolkien devotee'. I very much doubted if he was, but I never said so. Baki was a sensitive man.

'Welcome back, boss!' he said pointing at the ribbons that said the same thing.

'You didn't have to do it,' I said sinking down into a chair behind one of the counters. The smell of old books hit me. It never failed to give me a strange buzz.

'Oops, sorry I am late!' Pinky Patel, my second assistant, called out as she walked in.

'Boss, this is becoming a pattern here,' Baki said.

'Hey welcome back, boss! And don't you start complaining as always,' she snapped at Baki.

Pinky Patel, twenty years old with a few hundred piercings in her body, had answered to an advertisement I had put up in the shop about hiring an assistant. In fact, she was the only one who had applied. She had walked in making metallic noises. They sounded bizarre, coming from a human body. She had told me she was the only daughter of a famous stockbroker who was a regular 'investment advisor' on many television channels. She wanted to be 'independent' and did not believe in the way her father earned his millions. It was rip-off money according to her. This girl, with kohl in her eyes that made her look like a beautiful raccoon, wanted to be an author one day and what better job than being an assistant at a bookshop? She had said she would work virtually for free. The only condition was that I had to allow her to read as many books as she wanted. I had agreed at once, a decision I sometimes regretted.

'You take five whole minutes to drag your ass from one end of the shop to the other!' Pinky had a gift for exaggeration.

'Oh yeah? And I presume you dust all the books every day and clean the store and . . .'

'Folks, can I have some peace, please,' I interjected.

Pointing at me but looking at Pinky, Baki said, 'Yes. Peace. Do you understand what it means?'

'It means you keeping your bloody mouth shut,' she said, putting her finger on her lips.

'God, you two are impossible,' I said and did what I had always done in the past -- changed the subject. 'How were the sales in my absence?'

'Not much, boss,' Pinky said throwing up her hands as though I was a little slow not to realise there was no reduction in the number of books on the shelves.

'People are just not reading enough nowadays,' Baki complained.

I didn't know what to do with these guys. I was sure half the people got scared by Pinky's appearance. The other half got bored by Baki's soporific voice.

I tried once more. 'Guys, bookselling is not like selling saris or groceries. You have to . . . Educate customers, understand their choice of books and offer a wonderful world in a book for them to get lost in,' the two of them completed my sentence.

'We know, boss,' Pinky said, biting her black lips. 'You've told us a million times at least.'

✧

I sat there for a long time wondering how to find Madhuri Joshi, the first girl I had ever kissed. Maybe I would get lucky and she would be the woman who could liberate me from my curse.

'How do you find people?' I asked aloud.

'Google them,' Pinky said, without lifting her eyes from the task of applying dark brown nail polish.

I looked at her incredulously. Sometimes you are so close to the problem that the most obvious solution evades you. I went to my old computer and logged on to Google. I typed 'Madhuri Joshi' in the search window. It threw up a few thousand hits. I tried Madhuri Joshi Akola. This narrowed it down to less than a hundred. Incredibly, the first item in the search list turned out to be the right one. Later, I wondered if I had exhausted all my luck in that instant.

Madhuri Joshi was a divorce lawyer working with a big law firm in Mumbai. Her brief bio on the law firm's website told me that she was twenty-nine years old and had 'first-hand' experience of how divorce proceedings worked as she was a divorcee herself. I thought it was a rather cheesy way of presenting your credentials. But my judgment of what is right or wrong has often been called into question.

I dialled her office number, disconnecting before it could be picked up, feeling like a fool. What was I going to say to her? 'Hey, I'm your first kisser and I need you to help me in lifting this curse?' I was sure she wouldn't remember me. I decided to visit the offices of Pestonji and Shah Associates, Attorneys At Work For You.

I had to wait three long hours for 'Missez' Joshi, as the peon in the legal office referred to her. Every few minutes I had to suppress an overwhelming urge to bolt. I questioned my sanity. What was I doing waiting for a stranger who would in all probability have me arrested for harassment? What would be the first thing I would say to her? Why was I pursuing something that a hack had told me to do? I remembered the sombre face of Babaji and the way he had described each of my accidents. There were things that even I had forgotten about those mishaps. I shuddered at the prospect of begging Madhuri to do what Babaji had told me to ask of every woman. She would definitely either ask me to get the hell out of her office or worse, get me beaten up. I looked around the office and wondered if it was a wise thing to mess with lawyers. My left leg, with a bloody mind of its own, was throbbing non-stop. It did that every time I was wrestling with tense thoughts.

After three hours, I had to pee and I looked at the peon who was approaching me. I was about to ask him where the loo was when he said I could meet Ms Joshi.

'Have you told her who I am?' I asked him.

He made a vague, dismissive gesture. Everybody is a smartass in their own territory.

I knocked on the door of Ms Joshi.

Madhuri Joshi waved me in and raised her index finger to prevent me from speaking. She was talking, more like screaming, on her mobile.

'You tell that bastard the next time he comes within three kilometres of you I will personally make sure that his balls are chopped off his wife-beater's body! Stop crying, stop crying! Don't be a wimp. What are you, some 70s movie heroine?'

She went on admonishing the caller for a while, giving me a chance to control my breathing, get a hold of what I was going to tell her and take a long look at a pissed-off woman.

She was slightly overweight in an alluring sort of way, reminding me of Sridevi, the legendary film actress. Her large eyes were spitting fire. After a few more minutes of rebuking the caller, she ended the call, slamming the mobile on the table.

'Bloody idiots,' she said and closed her eyes for a moment, trying to snap out of her anger. 'Yes?'

'I am sure you haven't recognised me,' I blurted, immediately wishing that I had said something else, something more assertive.

She said nothing, but her eyes narrowed a little, trying to place me. I felt stupid. She was a lawyer, meeting hundreds of people like me every day. I was sure many people started their conversation with her that way and it was probably her favourite 'to-be-dismissed' first line. And I wasn't exactly a Brad Pitt look-alike that women would want to remember.

'No,' she said and leaned back in her swivel chair.

'Sameer Sathe,' I said and waited for a few moments, hoping my name would jog her memory. When it didn't, I was completely at a loss about what to say next. The way it had panned out in my head was that I would say my name if she hadn't already recognised me, she would hold my hand, I would tell her my plight, she would do the thing Babaji had wanted her to, and my curse would disappear. In reality, the plan was unravelling at the first step and it struck me that I had no back-up.

'I . . . uh . . . I believe we were each others' first kissers,' I said, not believing what I was saying.

There was a stunned expression on her face. I braced myself for a scream calling for security to kick me out. To my surprise, she burst out laughing. It was the best sound I had heard in months. She tried to suppress it with her hand, failed, threw her head back and laughed again. I couldn't help but join her, mostly out of relief. My laughter sounded like hiccups.

'Sameer Sathe! How have you been? This is a stunning surprise!' she said after a while.

'I am so relieved. I thought you were going to scream bloody murder,' I said a little sheepishly. The plan seemed to be back on track.

Just then her cellphone rang. She cut it off. These were all good signs.

'Don't tell me you've come here for a divorce?'

'Nope. Not married, yet.'

'Ah!' she said. We exchanged updates on the past twenty-two years, about our parents, some kindergarten friends we both remembered and after about five minutes we had pretty much reached that awkward point in the conversation when the two protagonists are trying to gauge what the other is thinking.

'I know this is a little strange, but there is something I need to tell you. It's a matter of life and death,' I said, clenching my fists. Everything depended on what she would say next.

'Okay, I am listening,' she said.

I told her about my accidents. She was shocked. I told her about my latest one which had left me bedridden for three months. She made horrified sounds. Then I told her about Babaji and his prediction.

'You've got to be joking, right? How can you even waste time with such charlatans? You're an engineer, for god's sake!'

There was this little man in my head who screamed exactly this, several times a day.

'He knew each and every little detail about those accidents, Madhuri,' I said, oversome by a strange urge to defend Babaji.

She was quiet for a few moments.

'Why are you telling me all this?' she finally asked.

I told her about the woman, my saviour, who would liberate me from the curse.

'Madhuri, this is very difficult for me to say, but I need your help. I need to spend two weeks with you, living with you in your house, being with you virtually twenty-four hours a day. You could be the woman who could save my life.' That's what Babaji had told me to do – spend two weeks with every woman. Make them realise your life is worth saving, he had said.

She looked out of the window for a long time and finally spoke without looking at me.

'This is perhaps the most bizarre request anyone has ever made to me,' she said.

'I know. And you don't have to do it. I mean you can always say no. It would probably kill me, but now that I have heard myself saying it out aloud, it does sound totally out of line.'

'Okay,' she said abruptly.

'What?'

'I said okay. I don't want to carry the guilt if something happens to you after I say no.'

This was proving to be a piece of cake. I smiled at her.

'You'll have to put up with somebody though,' she said leaning towards me.

'No problem. I'll occupy the smallest corner of your house.'

'No, you don't understand. I'm living with a man right now. And he's the jealous, possessive type. I'll talk to him tonight and try to explain. Hopefully he'll agree to have you over,' she said, avoiding my eyes.

I thought I saw a sudden, but startling flash of vulnerability in her eyes. I had no clue what the circumstances of her divorce were, neither did I want to know. I just wanted to spend the next two weeks shadowing her and hoped the curse would be gone by the end of it.

✧

I called Madhuri the next day and got her voicemail. I called again after a while. No luck. I left her voice messages in increasing degrees of panic. *She must've thought it over the whole night and with every minute the entire thing must've felt increasingly intrusive, then irritating and finally downright ridiculous. She must've doubted my intentions.* The only thing going for me was the bizarre nature of the request. You can't walk up to a woman and tell her such a story just to get into her house and ultimately her bed. She *had* to give me the benefit of the doubt.

I went to the bookshop in the afternoon and told Bunty and Bubbly (or Bonnie and Clyde) that I might be gone for two whole weeks.

'Boss, you all right?' Baki asked me, deeply concerned.

'I am fine. I just need to take care of something,' I mumbled.

They looked at each other.

'Okay you two, don't pull that mom-dad act on me. That's how my parents behave when I tell them something perfectly normal. Don't look at me as though I'm walking into the Valley of Death,' I said pointedly, looking at Baki.

'We heard some strange things,' Pinky offered. This, coming from a twenty-year-old who wore torn clothes just to spite her father and pierced her body every two weeks or so.

'What have you heard?'

'You've been behaving quite . . . differently . . . of late,' Pinky said.

Raising one eye-brow I said, 'Glad that you guys notice my behaviour. I used to think I was a pesky inconvenience in your world.'

Baki laughed. It sounded like a series of sneezes.

'Excuse him, boss. How-to-react-to-sarcasm is a few years away in his delayed growth plan.'

They started quarrelling. I tuned them out for a few minutes, making a mental list of all the things I needed to do before I took the first step in my quest. I had to stop the newspaper, tell the milk-man not to deliver milk for two weeks, make sure these two creatures took care of pending bills. It was then that the thought struck me: There must have been very few people in the history of mankind who had been in my position – people who knew when they were going to die. This list-making activity could be a sinister training to prepare for the real deal – the final list I would make before D-Day. I wondered what kind of lists people before me had made. It made me shiver. I must've made a scared sound because the two children stopped quarrelling suddenly.

'You okay, boss?' Baki asked.

'You ask me that once more and I am going to smash your teeth!' I shouted, temporarily forgetting how sensitive the elf-man was to my words. He recoiled as though I had actually hit him.

'I'm sorry, I'm sorry,' he said in near panic.

A few customers walked into the bookshop. Baki approached them like a little puppy running towards its owners after being bullied by a stranger. I went back to my chair and rubbed my forehead.

A book was slammed on the counter. It was *Brothers in Arms* by Lois McMaster Bujold.

'You might've forgotten the pact, but I haven't,' Jai said.

I looked up and smiled.

'Don't you give me that indulgent smile. I am pissed off. You want me to remind you of your exact words? "It's a deal", he said, trying to mimic me.

'You're a pathetic mimic, Jai,' I said.

'And you are a pathetic friend! Why haven't you called or taken my calls for the last two weeks?'

'I have to do it alone, Jai.'

'I'm an accountant and for me a deal is a deal.' He whispered fervently. 'I am in this with you, brother.'

'Don't be melodramatic.'

'I'm not.' Jai said, slightly offended, but resuming his normal voice. 'Now tell me, what all have you done till now?'

I told him about the list I had made. And about Madhuri Joshi.

'Why didn't you find all the women when you were in Akola?'

'Babaji said . . .'

'To hell with Babaji! We can't be wasting time.'

'Jai, either we do this the way he asked us to or we wait for my death. And he said that I must find one woman at a time.'

He was quiet for a few moments.

'What can I do?'

'Go back to Delhi. I'll call you every day,' I said, although my heart wanted him to do exactly the opposite.

'Can't. I've taken a year's sabbatical to be with you,' he said nonchalantly.

I was stunned. There aren't many moments in life when you truly thank god. This was one such moment for me. I thanked Him for giving me a friend like Jai.

'Will they take you back?'

'Nope. The bastards already got a replacement who is cheaper and works harder. I'm worried I may not get the job back after a year.'

'Jai . . . '

'You don't have to feel all that mushy. I'm sure you would have done the same.'

'Yeah. Hm . . . perhaps,' I said.

'Let's work it this way,' he said. 'I will be very close by. You won't see me, but you will feel me. If I sense you're in trouble, I'll jump in.'

'You sound like the sidekick from a noir novel.'

'Since you want this to be your exclusive story.'

'Not me. Fate.'

Just then, my phone rang. It was Madhuri Joshi.

'There's one big problem,' she said.

✧

I sat in front of Madhuri and a man who wore an angry frown. It was a beating-will-start-any-minute kind of expression. He was a bear of a man with an overgrown beard.

'Sameer, this is Pratap, my . . . We're engaged,' she said in a soft voice. The man didn't take his eyes off me. I could almost hear his thoughts and none of them were pleasant.

'I told Pratap about, uh, your situation and he doesn't believe any of it,' she said.

Gone was the voice I had heard in the law office. Her transformation was bewildering. From what I had gathered about her, she was a tigress in the courts, ripping apart the men who were harassing their wives. Here, sitting in front of me was a woman who couldn't possibly be the same Madhuri Joshi I had heard about.

'I think this is all big bunkum,' the bear said in English.

My fear for the bear ratcheted up a notch. Someone who uses words like 'bunkum' in real life must be feared. I said nothing. Everyone is entitled to their opinion. I didn't think any kind of cajoling would help.

'But Madhuri thinks she has to help you with this lunacy,' he said. 'Now I don't know what your true intentions are, but if they are even an inch outside of what Madhuri has told me, we are going to have a different kind of conversation.'

'You don't have to worry, Mr Pratap. My intentions are absolutely noble. It's a former boy scout's promise,' I said with my fist on my thudding heart.

'You seem to be a smart-ass. I don't like smart-asses,' he growled.

'Me neither,' I said.

'Guys, can we please have a civil discussion here?' Madhuri intervened. 'I've thought this through carefully. Please come to my – our – house tomorrow morning.'

I didn't look at Pratap. This was going to be fun. My left leg agreed with its non-stop throbbing.

◇

The next morning sharp at eight, I knocked on Madhuri's front door. She invited me in. It was a small apartment, like all Mumbai apartments. I could sense the violent intrusion of a man in her house and I didn't mean myself. She had lived alone for a while, shaping the house the way she wanted it. The house would've been her own canvas. The strokes of her brushes were gentle but colourful. With the grand entry of the bear, the canvas was in disarray. It was evident in many things. There was an ugly, sooty ashtray right next to a beautiful vase. One of his shirts was on the divan, its bright green clashing with the beautiful blue. His soiled shoes were flung carelessly on a tasteful carpet.

'Coffee?' she asked.

I nodded and she disappeared into the little kitchen. The bear opened the bedroom door and lumbered towards the sofa.

'Good morning,' I said.

He ignored me.

Madhuri entered with three cups of coffee on a tray.

'Unfortunately, this is a one-bedroom flat. You'll have to make do with the sofa here,' she said.

'Thanks. Sofa is just fine,' I said.

The bear snorted and harrumphed. This time, I ignored him.

'We need to leave, I've got to reach office at ten,' she said and made for the door. I followed.

✧

'Come on, say it,' she said as we were sitting next to each other, hip to hip, thigh to thigh, shoulder to shoulder in the human meat box called the first class compartment of the Mumbai local train. I would've enjoyed this very pleasant sensation in any other situation. She smelled wonderful, even in the train's sweaty, suffocating environment.

'Say what?' I said.

'You and Pratap were getting along like a house on fire,' she said with a sarcastic twist to her mouth. 'He's told me his views about you. I want to know what your views about him are.'

'Madhuri, I understand his unease. I would have reacted in the same way,' I said.

'I don't mean that. You must've seen . . . felt the relationship between us. And I know you know about my divorce.'

'Actually, I don't. And your personal life would be like a sacred place for me. I won't enter it with my condemned soul.'

She laughed.

'You could always make me laugh, Sam. Even when we were seven-year-olds.'

'Did it have anything to do with the way I looked back then?'

She laughed some more.

'I met Pratap when I was going through a very bad phase. My father died a few years back, suffered a lot, cancer. Pratap is a doctor. He was with my father when he died.'

I generally squirm when people tell me their intimate secrets. Maya called it Sam's 'want-to-piss-but-can't' movement. I couldn't squirm then. There was no space and perhaps Madhuri would've got a wrong signal.

'You know, I married when I was just eighteen. It was just crazy,' she said with an embarrassed smile. 'I had met this guy at the National Law School and within no time he got me pregnant. My father wouldn't let me have an abortion and really, there was no other option but to marry.'

I remembered her father. A domineering man who never smiled and made his family's life miserable.

The train stopped at a station. Like the waves of an angry sea, people flooded out of the compartment and flooded right back in.

'God, I haven't told this to anyone for a long time,' she said.

'You don't have to,' I said.

'We had promised to marry each other, hadn't we?' she said, turning towards me.

That was the strongest memory I had of our time together.

'I am sure I didn't understand what long-term commitment meant then. And thankfully you rejected me,' I said.

She smiled a sad little smile.

'I miscarried. Tough luck, eh?' she said.

For the next few minutes we listened to the rhythmic thud of the train interspersed with the chatter in the compartment.

'I . . . I don't know what to say, Madhi,' I said, using her childhood name.

'The last person who called me that was my father,' she said.

Her father was dead. Good analogy there.

'We'll be getting married soon . . . Pratap and me,' she said.

It must have been the childhood bond we shared that made her tell me those things. Later, I felt she shouldn't have told me. Knowledge is a deadly weapon. And at times the burden of truth can break you.

◇

For the next one week, I stayed with Madhuri Joshi and the bear man. We fell into a nice rhythm. I was with Madhuri the whole day. She told me I didn't look my age and would easily pass off as a college kid, so she introduced me as a college intern who had been assigned to her. I didn't know if she also included my intellectual being in the 'don't look my age' part.

The bear's hatred increased with every day and by the end of the first week, we had managed to blank each other out from our main and peripheral visions. I could have been looking at a view with his ass right in my face but I wouldn't have seen it. The only thing I was worried about was his threshold. I had sensed a growing hostility with every passing day and I knew it might turn rapidly into something ugly. I mentally urged him to hang in there. Just a week more and I would be out of his hair, Madhuri's house and their lives.

They had a strange relationship. Outwardly, it never showed, but she was subservient to him. I didn't have a clue as to why she was allowing him to bully her. He didn't seem all that busy for a doctor either. At that time, I didn't know what I learned later – that he was serving a temporary suspension for negligence.

Madhuri was very defensive when she told me about it, though I hadn't asked specifically. All I had observed was that he seemed to be there when we left in the morning and also when we returned in the evening. More than a couple of times, I had heard them quarrelling late at night. It had been loud enough to wake me up. Madhuri never spoke to me about anything apart from asking me for breakfast, lunch and dinner. I supposed she too was desperately waiting for the two weeks to get over.

On the seventh day, I saw a little bruise on Madhuri's face.

'Something scratched me,' she said, turning away.

'Looks more like someone to me,' I said and regretted it immediately.

She didn't talk to me for the rest of the day.

I wondered how she was straddling the dichotomy of her professional image and her relationship with the bear. It was a bit like reading Somerset Maugham and Mickey Spillane together. Or listening to Guns 'n Roses and Norah Jones at the same time.

On the eighth day, Madhuri burst out of her office, running madly towards the exit. I was just outside her room and ran behind her, secretly hoping that bear man had met with an accident.

'Hey, wait up! What's happened?' I called out.

She didn't answer. Her eyes were blazing, her face was drenched in sweat. She was clenching and unclenching her fists, a sign that someone was in trouble. She hailed an autorickshaw. I jumped in beside her before she could ask me not to.

'Mhatre hospital, Ghatkopar,' she said to the driver. I said nothing throughout the journey wondering if my wish had suddenly come true. I hated myself.

'Padma Kore. Which ward?' she asked the receptionist at the hospital, barely pausing in her stride.

A bunch of people were surrounding someone lying on one of the beds. They parted when Madhuri arrived. On the bed was a woman who was burned beyond recognition. I stopped in my tracks.

'The *harami*?' she asked an old woman who was sobbing softly. The woman nodded.

The anger drained out of Madhuri's face. Her eyes filled with tears. She held the woman's hand with a tenderness I hadn't thought she possessed. The old woman started whimpering loudly. The woman on the bed stirred and looked at Madhuri. Her face was a terrible mass of burned flesh that was visible through the bandages.

'I am so sorry,' Madhuri said in a whisper.

After a few minutes Madhuri got up from the bed and walked out of the ward. She leaned her forehead against the dusty wall and cried. I stopped a few feet away from her.

'It's my fault. I told her to fight back. Not to give in,' she said, her voice unrecognisable through the sobs. I could guess what had happened. After a few moments, she got herself under control.

'I am going to make sure her bastard husband rots in jail forever,' she hissed.

We stood outside the hospital, silently, for a long time. At last she said: 'Look what my facade has caused today. I sit on my ass the whole day in that office telling people to be something that I am not.'

I nodded.

'I have no moral right to do that, do I?'

'The way I see it, you've got to choose,' I said quietly. 'Do you like being Missus Pratap or Miss Madhuri Joshi, the best divorce lawyer in the city?'

She was quiet for a few moments.

'I've always made the wrong choices, Sameer. I want this one to work out.' She looked at me pleadingly.

'I guess righting a wrong choice involves discarding the wrong choice,' I said.

'So you mean I am destined to keep making these stupid choices and keep discarding them?'

'No. You need to get one right. The rest will follow. If you ask me, I think being the best divorce attorney beats the hell out of the other choice,' I said looking into her eyes.

✧

It happened on the twelfth night. The final showdown.

The bear man walked up to me and said, 'I told you not to deviate an inch from what you had told me.'

'As far as I recall, I told you nothing,' I said.

The blow that landed on my face was from a man who weighed forty kilos more than me. I staggered back. I had not expected the blow and it made me a little groggy. Madhuri ran into the room, jumped between me and the bear man and screamed at him. I was too dazed to take in what she said.

The bear man walked out of the house, banging the door loudly. 'You know what the upside of all those accidents is? It makes one quite resilient,' I said through my throbbing pain.

She laughed and hugged me fiercely.

I still slept on the sofa for the next two nights.

'How can I thank you?' she said on the fourteenth day.

'By being there for me a year from now,' I said.

'What?'

'You might well be my saviour a year from now,' I said.

'Do you really believe that man's words?' she asked, a little incredulous.

'Have to,' I said with a shrug.

I walked out of Madhuri Joshi's house the next day and went straight home, hoping she would still be around when D-Day came.

There aren't many things in the world that are more pleasurable – or taken more for granted – than the simple act of being able to sleep in your own house, in your own bed. I was in my bed pondering this simple truth after spending two weeks on Madhuri's sofa. When the doorbell rang, I didn't want to get up to open it. It rang a couple of times more, and then I heard the door open. That could only be one person. I didn't know if I should jump out of bed like an excited puppy or ignore the situation completely.

Maya stood at the bedroom door, her arms folded, leaning on the door frame. It was a sight I had once hoped to see every morning for the rest of my life – minus the clothes on her, that is. I still didn't get out of bed.

'How are you?' she said.

'Alive,' I replied, immediately regretting the unnecessary sarcasm in my tone.

Of course, she was wearing the perfume I loved on her.

Letting out an almost imperceptible sigh, the kind that was once accompanied by an indulgent smile whenever I said something that irritated her, she said, 'There are a few things of mine I need to take.'

'You could've taken them when I was in the hospital, on the verge of dying,' I said.

'I didn't know a dislocated shoulder could kill you.'

Then, biting her lips she said, 'I'm sorry. That was insensitive.'

'What? More insensitive than you not visiting me more than seven times in those three months?'

'I didn't know you were counting,' she said.

After a few moments of trying to stare each other down, she looked away and said, 'I see you've got some company on the bed.'

There were things on my bed that wouldn't normally have been there – a few books, (okay, quite a few books), some CDs, my iPod, amongst other stuff. It was the side she used to sleep on.

'What were you expecting? A naked girl?'

'It would've been far better, yes, than those things.'

When I said nothing, she turned around and walked into the kitchen. I knew she was going to take her Garfield coffee mug. It had been gifted to her by her dad. When she had brought it here a year ago, she had said it looked better in my kitchen.

I got out of bed.

'Why don't you take all your things once and for all?' I said, standing in the kitchen doorway. I was on a roll. Someone had to stop me before I hurt myself.

'Where have you been for the last two weeks?' she said ignoring my question.

'Trying to save my life.'

'Will you stop being theatrical for a while?'

'Why do you care anyway?'

She stared at the floor for a few moments. I stared at her. I couldn't remember when she had looked more beautiful. There was a glow on her face that I had not seen for a long time. I wondered what or *who* had caused that glow. That radiance had been pissing me off since the moment she had walked in.

'Have you found your cup?'

She nodded. 'I'll leave my key here today.'

'No, it's okay,' I said a little too quickly, 'I mean, it's okay either ways. You can keep it. If I ever lose mine, I know whom to contact.'

It sounded pathetic.

'Okay,' she said. She was about to step out of the flat.

'Who is it?' I barely recognised my own voice.

She chuckled. 'I was waiting for that question,' she said as though relieved that I hadn't let her down. 'Anyway, why do you care?'

And she was gone.

This may sound corny, but the entire house had seemed to come alive for the time she was in it. I missed her. Her smile, her perfume, her laugh, the way she cooed when she saw cute dogs and babies, the way she sometimes danced when she thought nobody, including myself, was looking, her frustrated groans when she worked late nights, the way she made tea (which was, quite frankly, lousy).

I was back to being lonely in the house my uncle had bequeathed to me along with the bookshop. Suddenly I didn't want to be there anymore. I picked up my list of potential saviours. The next woman on it proved a lot more difficult to find than Madhuri Joshi.

✧

Chapter 3

'I DON'T KNOW HOW TO FIND HER,' I SAID TO JAI AS WE sipped beer in a shady neighbourhood bar. Harish Bar beat the hell out of any five-star place for its service. Harishbhai, who was the waiter, cook and owner, knew each patron's choice. You needed to go there just once. If you ordered Johnny Walker Red Label with three cubes of ice, you wouldn't see the fourth in your glass the next time you walked in.

'I can't go back home twice in one month to find out about these women. They'll think something's terribly wrong. I remember she was in school with us only for a few months. Her father had a government job and she lived in the government quarters.'

He nodded. He remembered Anjali Warde too.

All my sleuthing came to a dead end when I couldn't find Anjali in the directory or on the internet. I had tried to find Ramakrishna Warde's phone number in the phone book and had found a few people with the same name, none of them Anjali's father.

'Isn't this the part where the sidekick comes up with a brilliant idea?' I asked.

'The sidekick is scratching his head and thinking of something important to say, like go fuck yourself,' he said.

We laughed.

'It's good to hear that,' he said.

'To finally hear you laugh the way you used to.'

I smiled.

'Do you remember what her father's job was?' he asked.

'Perhaps a Public Works Department employee,' I said.

'Big shot?'

'I think so,' I said.

'Let's go to the PWD office tomorrow and find out. Sometimes, the sidekick's ideas are no ideas at all.'

'What do you want?' The *babu* in the PWD office who was poking his ear with a matchstick and collecting the treasure on the back of his hand, snarled with all the irritation of an artist disturbed while in pursuit of a grand creation.

'We just told you,' Jai said with equal irritation. 'We need to find Wardesaheb. W-A-R-D-E.'

I elbowed Jai. There was no point in getting antsy when your life was at stake.

'Saheb,' I jumped in, 'We really need to find Wardesaheb. It is a matter of life and death.'

'Whose life and death?' the babu asked, his eyes lighting up with morbid interest.

'How the hell does it matter to you?' Jai snapped.

'It's his brother-in-law, saheb. He was estranged from his sister decades ago. I am his sister's son. My father is dying and I need to inform my uncle,' I said.

'Hm . . . let me ask around. Why don't you come tomorrow and I will see what I can do? Now get out of here,' he said, putting the matchstick inside his ear and resuming his ear-orgasm expression. The next day we found the babu (his name was

Bhende), outside the office. He was putting an impossibly large paan into his mouth.

'Bhende saheb, namaskar. Your help could save a life,' I said, meaning every word..

'I don't believe your stupid story. Do you think I am a fool?' he said, while chewing the paan. His words came out all muffled.

'Saheb. Please look at me. I mean every single word of what I told you. We are not scammers. I am like your son, saheb. Please help me,' I said.

He looked at me for a while and then held out a dirty chit of paper: 'Wardesaheb retired a few years ago. He lives in Worli. This is his phone number and address.'

I thanked him and we left.

Jai started to laugh as we stepped out and said, ' You should've been in Bollywood! What an actor! What dialogues!'

I smiled and said, 'I wasn't acting.'

✧

I dialled the number many times, but nobody answered. The address turned out to be that of a sea-facing apartment complex in Worli. Mr Warde's flat was on the second floor. I pressed the doorbell, hearing it echo loudly inside the house. We waited. Nobody opened the door for a long time. I pressed the button again.

I recognised the man who opened the door. It was Anjali's father, the pipe-smoking, goggle-wearing man who used to drop Anjali to school every day in a white Ambassador bearing the official emblem of the Government of India.

His right hand was hidden behind his back.

'What do you want?' he asked in the kind of tone generally reserved in Mumbai for aggressive beggars.

'Good evening Mr Warde. How are you, sir?' I said.

He didn't answer.

'I need to meet your daughter. I am . . .' the rest of my sentence died in my throat because there was a revolver pointing right between my eyes.

'Get out of here,' the man hissed, 'and don't dare to come back. Next time I won't talk. I will just shoot.'

I was frozen. Jai tugged at my shirt. We walked backwards with our arms raised and when we reached the staircase, we ran like never before.

'Hell! What did you say to him?' Jai shouted at me.

'Shut up! Just let's get out of here,' I shouted back.

We bent over to catch our breaths after we had run at full speed for five whole minutes. My left leg was throbbing as if I had flogged it.

'That guy is crazy!' Jai said between loud huffs.

I raised my hand to tell him to keep quiet till I had shushed my hammering heart.

✧

'This doesn't make any sense at all,' I said as we sat on the wall at the Worli seaface. 'I think I asked him a perfectly normal question.'

'Perhaps we knocked at the wrong house.'

'No, it was Anjali's father. I recognised him.'

'Now what?'

'I have no bloody clue,' I said.

'Why don't we find the phone number of the neighbours? Just call them and ask them what's wrong with papa Warde.'

'How are we going to find the neighbour's number? I'm not going back within a kilometre of that apartment complex.'

'I remember the name of the neighbour. I have this habit of reading nameplates. The name of the neighbour is Mansukhlal Tahilramani.'

I looked at him, awestruck.

'Remember how you used to chide me for reading the nameplates aloud when we were kids?' he asked, wiggling his eyebrows. I laughed.

Jai dialled Directory Inquiry and got the number for Mr Tahilramani.

'Hello Mr Tahilramani. I am calling from the Worli Seaface house owner's association,' I rushed through the fake spiel.

'Who? What?'

'We have heard a lot of complaints of your neighbour's behaviour,' I said without giving him a chance to get a word in. 'Can you please tell us what is wrong with Mr Warde?'

'Oh . . . Mr Warde,' he said and started laughing.

I looked at Jai. He shrugged.

I cleared my throat loudly to stop Tahilramani.

'Mr Warde and his family have gone a little mad in the last couple of years,' he said.

'What happened?'

'Don't you know? The whole world seems to know.'

'No. Can you please tell me?' I disliked Tahilramani's high-pitched voice.

'It's their daughter,' he stage-whispered into the phone. 'Since she has become this big porn movie star, Mr Warde thinks every man is looking at him with the thought of screwing his daughter.' Tahilramani was laughing again.

I had been expecting something terrible. I had even been prepared to hear that something had happened to Anjali that had made her father go nuts. Jai gestured 'what?' at me. I couldn't say a word. I disconnected the phone.

'Is Anjali dead?' Jai asked.

I shook my head and told him what Tahilramani had said. It was Jai's turn to be speechless.

'Anjali Warde, porn star,' he said, hesitatingly.

✧

We had all fallen in love with Anjali Warde when she had joined the school midway through our eleventh grade. We were dealing with disgusting things like pimples, cracked voices and frequent erections. This was also the time when we boys were smack in the middle of witnessing a rapid transformation in the other gender. The snotty-nosed, wild-haired, grimy beings who cried at times when we punched, kicked or generally bullied them, were transforming into something alien. Not the 'Aliens' alien but 'Supergirl' alien. They walked differently, talked differently. Heck, some of them were not even recognisable from their one-day-before selves, having just discovered the magic of make-up.

Anjali Warde couldn't have come into our lives at a worse time. It was as if God had decided to test our hormone outbreak to the limit by sending down His most beautiful creation. She had the face of an angel, large blue eyes, lips like lotus petals. This sounds rather hokey, but she made us think those genuinely true hokey thoughts. She could quiet a straining-at-the-tether bunch of boys. She could quiet an openly jealous bunch of girls. When she wore a see-through school shirt over her red bra, she could quiet the teachers.

Once a teacher, an old man who wore thick glasses, had narrowed his eyes at her, and asked her if she was really sixteen years old. The class had burst out laughing. Any other girl in the same situation would have been extremely embarrassed. Not Anjali. After the laughter had died down, she coolly asked the teacher what he thought. Did she look twenty-five to him?

The class had been stunned into silence. The teacher had gone quiet. Finally, he had shaken his head, which I believed meant he kind of thought she looked twenty-five and continued to drone through the history lesson.

There were five hundred boys in the school, thirty in our class, and she had chosen one perennially bruised boy called Sameer Sathe as her best friend. She spoke to *me* first on her seventh day in the school (yes, I counted the days). When you grow up in the same school, you build up a disgustingly long list of embarrassing memories. The worst thing about those memories is that they are shared – every single boy and girl remembers that you had peed in Class Two when the teacher 'Gonsalves, the Monster' had twisted your ear a little too savagely. These memories also morph. So what could have been a tear or two becomes a full-blown bawling. And what could have been a potentially ear-damaging twist becomes a little feathery touch. There were a few more such memories about me than about the average kid. Okay, far more. The reason was simple – my accidents. You're an easy target if at least one of your limbs is useless for a large part of the year. The result? I was a loner. Jai kind of stuck around with me, but since each of us treated the other like an extension of our bodies, he didn't really count.

And so, it was a massive shock when Anjali Warde spoke to me.

'What's wrong with your leg?' she said to me one evening. (Jai was absent, otherwise he wouldn't have let Anjali speak to me, would have risen from dead to prevent it.) It was the day when the school football team had been chosen and three guys from my class were on the team. It had struck me in the last ten minutes of the school day that there was a whole bunch of happy moments I would never have, moments like getting selected for the stupid school team for any sport. So I was just sitting there on my bench, oblivious to the fact that the school day had ended and everyone had left the classroom. Everyone except Anjali.

'Uh . . . it broke. For the fifth time,' I said.

'Fifth time?'

'Jai says it wasn't my fault,' I murmured.

And then it hit me with all its force that the person talking to me was the object of everyone's affection.

She tilted her head. When I thought about it later, what struck me was the obvious lack of sympathy or pity in her eyes. Everyone who heard the sorry tales of my mishaps either clucked their tongue or made a 'tch tch' sound or said something 'compassionate'. Anjali did none of that. What I saw in her eyes was a strange curiousity, as if she had discovered something unique.

'And what were you looking at so intently on the blank blackboard?'

'Nothing,' I said. I felt like a fool. Which Class Eleven kid stared at a blank blackboard? Especially after school?

'You go home by bus don't you? I can drop you home in my father's car,' she said.

I followed her out.

It became a routine for us. Her father didn't come to pick her up in the evenings so we had the back seat of the car entirely to ourselves. And all we did was talk. Sometimes our hands brushed. Many times I had to summon every ounce of my hormonally challenged willpower to not shift towards her by a lousy inch. The most striking memory of our times together in the back seat was the way she used to sit: her head in the nook of the door and the headrest, one leg carelessly flung out, almost touching my feet, another leg resting on the seat and her skirt barely hiding her thighs. The curiosity never left her eyes.

She rarely spoke to any other boy in school and she never spoke to any girls. The fact that she had chosen me made my already-miserable life even more so, but I didn't care. If someone said you could go on an exotic holiday with Angelina Jolie for three months and after that your life would be hell for nine months, you would still take up the offer, wouldn't you? It was something like that, just the teen-league version of it.

'So how do we find her? Is she worth it, Sam?' Jai asked me. It snapped me out of a strange mix of beautiful and terrible memories.

'She is right up there, Jai. We have to find her,' I said.

'The best way could be getting hold of the porn video. We can get her contact details through that,' he said.

'The makers of smut advertise their contact details in the movies?'

'You'd be surprised. Let's go find this video on the internet,' he said.

'Internet?'

'Yes, internet, my dear Watson. There are clones of Youtube that run exclusively for porn movies. I am willing to bet my pathetic accountant's salary that one of the videos has Ms Warde in it.'

Despite my protests, Jai insisted we find that video in the confines of the bookshop. 'We won't be able to discuss it freely in a cybercafé' was his argument. I didn't know what we were going to discuss. Not the storyline or the cinematic merits of Anjali Warde's porn movie for sure.

It was already close to nine when we reached the Sathe and Sons Bookshop. I pushed Baki and Pinky out, telling them we needed to do something very urgent and private. Later, I regretted saying 'private'. I should've known the extent of Pinky's curiosity and how determined she can be when she wants something. She gave me a strange look when I waved goodnight.

'How do we go about finding the video now?' I asked Jai.

He typed Anjali Warde and porn in the search window. We weren't lucky.

'Oh, for heaven's sake, Jai. She won't be starring in those movies as herself.'

'You have a point,' he said.

We searched Indian porn websites for the next fifteen minutes, but Anjali's video was not to be found.

'The way I remember her, she would have won the Oscars for porn. How could her movie not be famous?' Jai said, scratching his head.

Just then, I heard a little giggle. I turned back and to my everlasting embarrassment and horror, found Pinky standing a few feet behind us with her hand on her mouth. Jai frantically closed all the windows on the computer.

'What are you doing here?' I shouted.

'I should be asking that, boss. What are *you* doing?'

I looked at Jai for some help, but he shrugged.

'Who is Anjali? And why were you trying to find her on porn sites? She's the latest star?' Pinky said taking a seat.

'Look, Pinky. I'm sorry. This is not what you think,' I said.

'And what is it?'

'Yeah, what is it?' Jai joined in.

I looked at Jai, grinding my teeth. I had been caught surfing porn by my employee and he was finding it amusing. As far as embarrassing situations go, this would feature in the top three of my life.

'Anjali Warde is an old school friend of mine. I need to find her desperately. Someone told us she has become a porn star. So we were trying to search for that video,' I said and hated my guilty tone. Leaning forward she said, 'This sounds interesting.'

'To me too,' Jai said.

'You just shut up, Jai, and find her. Pinky, I assure you we weren't being a couple of horny men trying to . . .' I said.

She laughed until she doubled over. Jai joined her.

I leaned on the bookshelf and smiled. Then, I told her everything. She listened, the levity in her eyes turning to deep concern when I told her about my recurring accidents. And finally when I told her about Babaji and the curse, her jaw dropped. I had almost perfected this little tale by then. I wondered how many more tellings were in store.

'My god, boss. I am sorry,' she said.

'It's okay. Now will you go home? Your father must be worried already,' I said pointing at the back door through which she had crept in.

One evening, she had stayed back until after ten. A couple of rough-looking men had swooped onto the bookshop. They had asked me about her and I had had a strange feeling that my well-being depended on my answer. She had coolly walked up to them and slapped one of them. She had called up her father and screamed at him for five whole minutes. Since then, I had made it a point to see that she leave the bookshop at sharp nine.

'You should've told me earlier, boss,' she said shaking her head as though I had made a mistake by not telling the wierdest girl I knew the biggest problem of my life.

She fished out her mobile phone and dialled a number.

'Santo, hey! How are you, man? Hm . . . hm . . . behave! Santo!'

I looked at Jai, dumbfounded.

'Hey baby, need some help,' she laughed at what the person on the other side said. 'Sure, baby. Sure . . . I know you would do anything for me. Need to find someone in your line of work.'

Jai raised an eyebrow with admiration written large on his face.

'Her name is Anjali Warde . . . Oh! You know her. You are my prince, baby! Gimme her contact . . . oh, it's a long story. I'll tell you some time,' she said winking at me. She said some more sweet nothings and switched off the phone.

'This is her number. She works out of a hotel in Colaba,' she said giving me what she had noted down. It was a telephone number.

'She is Number One with the best escort service in this city.'

After I found my voice I said, 'I think as your boss, I have nothing to do with your personal life, but this is going to be an exception. Who was that guy and how do you know such characters?'

'I joined this wonderful bookshop just a year back. I had a life before that,' Pinky said, and left for home.

The only sound for a few moments after she left was the hum of my PC's fan.

'Well, that was quite simply . . . amazing,' Jai said.

I nodded.

'So are you going to call her?'

'Tomorrow morning,' I said.

'Yeah, she could be working right now,' Jai said with a kind of awe in his voice.

The next day, I dialled her number and someone picked up at the third ring. It was an automatic recording which said 'press one if you are a new client, press two if you are an existing client.' I pressed two. The voice told me to dial my unique identification number. I shook my head and disconnected. It was like dialling my bank.

I redialled and pressed one. A woman with a seductive, husky voice told me she was Ms Anamika's assistant and I would have to go through a background verification process before I became a client. *Anamika? Background verification?* I wondered if Pinky had given me the right number.

'Just tell her, Sameer Sathe called. He needs to talk to her urgently. Matter of life and death,' I said and disconnected, praying she would deliver my bizarre message to Anjali. I was getting tired of saying *life and death*.

I sweated the whole of the morning and afternoon waiting for her call. Pinky didn't even look at me that day. She morosely handled the customers, and had her daily dose of quarrels with Baki, but pointedly avoided me. By afternoon I was debating telling her that her information was incorrect. It made my stomach churn every time I thought about her 'life before the bookshop' sentence. What kind of life involved getting to know, presumably intimately, the likes of Santo, the mysterious source of Anjali's number? I was about to talk to her when my cellphone rang. It was Anjali.

'Sameer Sathe?'

It was her voice, without any shred of doubt. It would sound clichéd if I said she had had a husky voice even in eighth grade, but she really did. She had been the complete package, perhaps one of a kind that the Almighty had made.

'Anjali,' I said hoping to sound like the boy she had once shown her red bra to.

'What the hell do you want?'

This wasn't the question I was hoping for. I had imagined that some of the smouldering embers of our torrid love would have lasted.

'I . . . uh . . . I need to meet you. Something very important,' I blurted. I was tired of blurting too.

'I charge thirty-five thousand rupees a night. The night starts at nine and ends at one. Usually my assistant conveys all this information, but you left that strange message without letting her complete,' she said, her voice business-like, as though we were acquaintances who were discussing how much it would cost me to repaint my house.

I had no clue what to say and like so many times during those months we were together, I ended up saying yes to her.

'My assistant will call you to fix a date based on my calendar,' she said.

Near panic, I said, 'No Anjali . . .'

'Call me Anamika,' she said brusquely.

'Sorry, Anamika. I need to meet you soon. It *is* a matter of life and death.'

'Whose?'

'Mine,' I said, hoping she would make an exception for me in her busy calendar.

There was silence for a while. My left leg was throbbing away.

'Okay, I will meet you tomorrow afternoon. Only for a couple of hours, full charge,' she said, 'Call me on this number at three and I will tell you where to meet.'

She disconnected. I realised I was sweating the Mumbai sweat.

✧

The place of her choice turned out to be a pub in Versova. I had hastily withdrawn thirty-five thousand of my hard-earned money. I was sure she wouldn't accept a credit card or a cheque.

I sat at the table she had told me to, which was on the first floor of the pub, directly facing the staircase. I hoped I would recognise her when she stepped in. I didn't. All I saw was the most beautiful woman I had ever seen reach the top of the staircase and look towards me. She wore huge sunglasses covering thirty per cent of her face, but she would have beaten the hell out of any Bollywood beauty with her visible seventy per cent. She glided across to me and sat down, an intoxicating fragrance wafting in my direction. She gently removed her sunglasses revealing her blue eyes, the colour of a calm sea. *Hokey, hokey, hokey!*

She said, 'Have you got the cash?'

It was as though I had been raised high on a bed of feathers and then let fall painfully on my ass.

'Yes, sure. I have,' I said and fished out the thirty-five thousand rupees from my bag. She put it in her purse that seemed too small to hold the money, but she made the currency disappear into it like a magician.

'Tell me,' she said and lit a cigarette. Just then the pub's band started playing *Moondance* by Van Morrison.

I gathered my thoughts, a strange confidence flowing through my body. Perhaps it was the thirty-five thousand I had paid for her time. She was mine for the next two hours.

'I need your help. Please listen to me carefully. I'm in deep trouble. Do you remember the time when I told you about my accidents? That I believed there was some sinister force behind it? Well, there really is,' I said hoping she wouldn't run away with my thirty-five thousand.

She nodded, impassive apart from her intent eyes. Taking a long drag of the cigarette she gestured to me to continue. I repeated my sorry tale. I had by now added many dramatic details to the story. She lit one cigarette after another while I told her about Madhuri Joshi and my two weeks with her. I asked her if she wanted Madhuri to vouch for me. She shook her head. After twenty minutes of this monologue I shut up and gulped down a glass of water, all the while looking at her, trying to gauge her reaction. Nothing had changed, she was still inscrutable.

'What makes you think I give a damn about your life?' she said.

'I think we shared something fifteen years back. Also, there is such a thing as basic humanity,' I said, almost regretting my aggressive tone.

'Order a drink for me,' she said.

I called the waiter.

'A vodka on ice,' she said. I nodded at the waiter who noted it down, his eyes on Anjali.

We didn't speak till her drink arrived. She didn't stop smoking either.

'Do you know how to use a gun?' she asked.

'Uh . . . no,' I replied.

'Pity. How will you be my bodyguard then?' she said with a hint of a smile. I let out a very audible sigh of relief.

'Thank you, Anj . . . Anamika,' I said. 'Thank you so much.'

'One lakh,' she said. 'The cost of my help.'

My heart did a massive doubletake, but I nodded. At this rate, I would have to sell a kidney or two to save the rest of my body.

'You want a fuck now?'

My already jumpy heart leaped.

'No,' I said, almost regretting it.

'You've paid for it,' she said. 'Don't tell me you are one of those talkers.'

She smiled a little. It seemed like an inside joke. I smiled back.

'Tomorrow, two. Don't be late. My nights start a little early,' she said, and got up. The vodka on ice was untouched.

◇

She was the sexiest sleepy woman I had ever seen in my life when she opened her door at two the next afternoon.

'You are too punctual,' she said, her already throaty voice made coarser by her sleep.

Her flat in Colaba was done up with great care and class. It was spotless and peaceful. There was a faint smell of alcohol in the air, perhaps a remnant of what might have happened there in the night.

'Make yourself comfortable in the spare bedroom over there,' she pointed in the direction of what would be my territory for the next two weeks.

'Thanks,' I said.

'I have a couple of back-to-back appointments, so get ready,' she said and walked into the bedroom.

An hour later, an obese old man wearing gaudy jewellery and a white, starched *kurta* stood at her door. He looked at me as though I were a gnat on a wedding cake.

'Who's this?' he asked Anjali.

'He is my new bodyguard,' she said offhandedly as though it was a stupid question.

I was a big misfit in the role of a bodyguard. Like Stephen King writing romance. Or Katrina Kaif cast as a village belle.

'Since when do you need a bodyguard?'

'Since today,' she said. 'Now are you going to play *dus sawaal* or do you want to get your money's worth?'

The old man shrugged and walked in.

It was the first act of prostitution I had seen in my thirty-year-old life. You don't get to see that too often if you are a small-time bookseller. Fifteen years back, I would have stopped her, asked her what the hell she was thinking. You could've made me walk on shards of glass, but I wouldn't have let the slimy bastard touch her. Now? I just sat on the sofa, trying to convince my fifteen-year-old self that we were grown-ups and could make whatever choices we wanted to. After a couple of hours, the man walked out with a Cheshire cat grin on his face. Anjali walked behind him. They kissed at the doorstep, the man put on his sun glasses and stepped out. Like a patient waiting at the doctor's, the next man walked in. He was quite suave, dressed in an Armani suit and flashing a sleek smile. I thought I vaguely recognised him. He ignored me, lifted Anjali in his arms and they disappeared inside. I thought Anjali seemed somewhat happy to see him, unlike the fat man.

I sat on the sofa, feeling like a fool, battling Sameer Sathe, age sixteen.

✧

Later that evening, she asked me if I would like to have some dinner. I nodded and she called a maid who appeared in no time, cooked a wonderful meal and disappeared. I sat on the couch where I had been sitting most of the afternoon, feeling completely hollow inside. Anjali was giving instructions to the maid like any suburban housewife – 'You put too much salt nowadays, Shantabai. Make smaller pieces of the bhindi. Add less water.'

'So, are you done judging me?' she asked as we ate in silence.

'What are you saying?' I asked, avoiding her eyes.

'You know, this is the first time someone has stayed in my house for this long. This must be the first time in many years that I am actually having dinner with someone.' She sounded genuinely surprised.

I felt a sudden warmth inside me, a reminder of what I used to feel all those years ago when we fooled around in her palatial house. Her earlier question was forgotten. It was an old habit of hers. She always twisted the conversation, jumping from one thing to another, always keeping me guessing.

'It's true for me too,' I said. 'Since my fiancée and I broke up, I haven't had dinner with anyone at home, if you don't count the hospital food my mom used to feed me in the first month after the latest accident.'

'So speak up, Mr Sathe,' she said, 'have you judged me already?'

'Yes I have,' I said quietly.

'And the verdict is?'

'The jury takes some time to debate before the verdict is out,' I said.

She stopped eating and smiled at me. A smile that was so pure and dazzling, it could blind anyone. It was the first time she had smiled since we met.

'So the little boy has developed fangs in the last fifteen years,' she said.

'The little boy is long gone. And so is the little girl.'

'There never was a little girl, was there?'

'Yes there was, even though she tried her best to hide herself,' I said.

She stopped smiling, got up from the table and almost smashed her plate in the sink. I wondered if my little nugget of truth merited such a violent reaction.

The next day, when Mr Suave walked in and took her in his arms, she had a smile on her face. I remembered that smile very vividly. It was the same smile she had smiled when she had asked me to sit on her bed fifteen years ago, and proceeded to take off her school blouse. The red bra, the most cherished object for the entire male population of the school, was in its full glory. She had quickly put her blouse back on, but the smile had remained for a long time. Many years later, I had understood that smile in a blinding flash. It was the smile of conquest. Mr Suave was in big trouble.

◇

The next three days were a routine. I mean, as routine as living with someone like Anjali can be. People came and people went. Their reactions towards me ranged from indifference to open hostility, but I slugged through it all. We had dinner together on all three days, without speaking a word to each other.

On the fourth day, Mr Suave made his grand entry, with his sweeping-Ms Warde-off-her-feet act. After he left, I thought I heard Anjali humming. Some human feelings obviously still resided in her.

'You don't have to look at me like that,' she said.

'Like what?'

'With damnation in your eyes. Pity, even.'

'Who am I to pity you?' I said.

'Someone who saw me in my childhood.'

'Whatever you chose to show me.'

'Don't tell me you still jerkoff remembering that red bra.'

'No I don't. I didn't then either.'

'Stop bullshitting.'

'Look, I am nobody to you. Just a memory from your past, nothing more. I'm here because I need to save my ass. What I think or thought doesn't matter at all,' I said. She was quiet for a few moments.

'He wants to marry me,' she said. 'The man you look at green-eyed.'

Were my feelings so naked? And could she still read me like a sky-obliterating billboard?

'Do you want to marry him?' I asked.

'Should I?'

'You could do worse.'

'What? Like prostitution?' she said and laughed without humour.

'Yeah, there is that,' I said.

She nodded her head and disappeared into her room. I hoped I would be able to see the 'inside' once. What was in there apart from a large double bed? Did she have all those toys I had read about? All those costumes? *What was her specialty?* I knew it was a terrible thought. The lowest of the low. Sometimes, your most shameful moment has no audience. We used to be friends, she and me, and I had cared about her like I had cared about no one else.

Over the next few days, she was on 'visits'. An Audi came to pick us up. Every day the car took us to a palatial house near King's circle. I waited for her in the car, feeling like a dog waiting for its master. The first day, the driver gave me a hard stare. The next day, there was a new driver and he made it a point not to even look at me. I felt overwhelmed by what she was willing to do for me.

She would emerge promptly after two hours. All that time, I thought of ways of stopping her from doing this. But everything I thought of saying to her could've been condensed to – '*Anjali, and you are Anjali, not this hideous Anamika, you have to stop it. This is wrong.*' But I could never say it.

A week later, Mr Suave returned. He skipped the sweeping-her-off-her-feet routine before disappearing with her into the bedroom. She seemed a little flustered by his lack of enthusiasm. This time, Mr Suave emerged from the bedroom a lot sooner and left in a mighty huff.

'He's given me an ultimatum,' she said when we were eating that night.

'What are you going to do?' I said.

'All my clients,' she said the word 'clients' as though they were naughty children, 'are absolute pussycats. They are pleased by the sight of me, by just being with me for a while. They know their ownership over me is fleeting and it awes them.'

I nodded as though I understood her warped logic and where she was going with it.

'*This* bastard thinks of me as a whore with a heart of gold, pining for true love. The *idea* of marrying a damned woman and giving her salvation gives him a hard-on. He fancies himself as the Saviour with a capital s.'

There was a bitter smile on her face that made me shudder. It made her look truly ugly.

Every lesson I had learnt since childhood screamed in my ears. There were some unalterable truths. Some things were always wrong and no matter how much you defended them they would still be wrong. There was a slanging match in my head between every single person I had ever considered worth listening to, and Anjali. And those people were losing.

There was a pause and then she continued: 'The way you looked at me back then, when I showed you my red bra . . . I just wanted to know if you would ever look into my eyes again after looking at it. I was hoping you would be different. But you weren't. You failed my little test too.'

I couldn't move for a long time. It was as if someone had plunged a hand inside my chest and squeezed my heart.

'Did you miss the fact that I was sixteen years old? You concluded that I belonged with the rest of the mortal world because I didn't look up at your face?' I finally said.

'You thought about that bra every single moment we were together. Six months, wasn't it? And those few minutes of staring were all you were going to get. So why look somewhere else, right?'

I was speechless. It was true. She smiled and got up. 'And nothing much has changed since. You and the rest of the "mortal world" are still stuck in that juvenile fantasy. So I thought, why not make all of you pay for it?'

There have been very few moments in my life when I have felt truly crushed. Some memories are not meant to be trampled upon. Those fleeting months with Anjali were the few golden moments in the most miserable time of my childhood.

Two days later she surprised me again. Mohini walked into our lives.

✧

I had been waiting for her 'appointment' to get over when the bell rang. For the last twelve days her appointments had happened like clockwork and nobody had ever knocked on the door. The bell rang a few more times with increasing impatience. Warily, I opened the door.

A little girl, not more than five, stood there. I was too stunned to say anything. She walked past me, entered the house and sat on the sofa like a cheerful little wind-up doll.

'Hello!' she said.

'Hello,' I replied.

'Where is my Mommy?' she said.

I felt a little dizzy. It couldn't be.

'She . . . she isn't here,' I said.

The little girl sat back on the sofa with her chubby hand on her cheek, as though thinking deeply about what I had said. I was wondering who had dropped her at the doorstep when Anjali stepped out from her den. The girl let out a happy cry and jumped off the sofa.

'Oh my baby,' Anjali exclaimed and swooped on her. They did a cute routine of rubbing noses, making cuddly sounds and giggling. Anjali tickled the little girl and she laughed with her eyes squeezed shut.

I felt like a voyeur spying on someone's happiness. I cursed my curse for making me an intruder in Anjali's most beautiful moment.

'This is my daughter,' Anjali said holding the girl in a tight hug. 'Mohini.'

Mohini smiled at me shyly.

'We met,' I said.

I was dreading the though that Anjali's client would come out of her den and spoil everything. I looked at the door but nobody came out.

'Don't worry, I have another door at the back,' Anjali said.

Now the only encroacher remaining was me.

'I'll be back in a while,' I said and headed for the door.

'Sameer, wait. You don't have to leave. We're going to have a lot of fun today, aren't we baby?' she said rubbing noses with Mohini.

And we did. We spent the rest of the day going to Mohini's favourite places – the zoo, the aquarium, the Gateway of India – where we ate her favorite candy floss, and finally Juhu beach. I'm terrible with kids but I think I did okay with Mohini. Anybody would do okay with Mohini.

After the little girl had gone to bed that night, we sat at the dinner table eating our customary meal, silently.

'Thank you for being with us the whole day,' Anjali said.

'Anj . . . Anamika . . .'

'Anjali is fine,' she said.

'I never thought you could be so tender with someone,' I said as a way of accepting her gratitude.

'Wonderful, isn't she? I know you are dying to know who the father is. But that doesn't matter.'

'No, I am not dying to know who the father is. I am dying to know where her mother hides herself when she is this . . . someone . . . she shouldn't be.'

'Choices aren't that straightforward. They weren't for me.'

She had this gift for being disarmingly vague. She was at her beautiful best when she said something that made me question my preconceptions.

That night, while lying in bed, I thought I had had one of the best days of my life. And of course like so many times in the past, everything got messed up the next day.

✧

A couple of accidents in my life have given me a notion as to what death could possibly feel like. None of those accidents however came close to the terror I felt when Mr Suave swung a hockey stick at me with all his strength. The day had started as usual. I had woken up feeling like a leech in Anjali's house. I could hear the chatter between mother and the daughter and couldn't help smiling. Anjali had 'cancelled' all her appointments for the day. Mohini was to leave in the evening, to be back with her grandparents. Apparently, old man Warde wasn't such an asshole after all. He had promised to keep his granddaughter away from the evils of his daughter's life. In return, Anjali got a two-day-a-month peep into Mohini's life – an arrangement Anjali had gladly accepted. Every time I thought about it, it felt all wrong. How could a mother, so obviously in love with her child, agree to live away from her? Her words echoed in my head: 'Choices aren't that straightforward. They weren't for me.'

Then, somebody had banged loudly on the door. Anjali had walked up to it, irritated. She had looked through the peephole and sprang back as though hit. Then she had run inside.

'You okay?' I shouted after her. I had to shout – the banging on the door was unrelenting.

She had emerged holding a small revolver, a terrible feral look on her face, the kind I had seen on a lioness protecting her cub from a predator.

'Sujit, you get the hell out of here! And don't you dare come back,' she had screamed.

'I am going to tear you apart, you bitch!'

Perhaps the gun and the blinding anger she was feeling had made her do what she did next – open the door.

Later, the only thing I remembered for many days was how red Mr Suave's eyes had been. There was a hockey stick in his hand. He had tapped it on the ground twice.

'Get out of here,' Anjali had said, pointing the gun at him.

He had laughed. And without warning, he charged at her.

Anjali had overestimated the power of that little revolver and she had underestimated the rage consuming Mr Suave. When she fired, the bullet hit him on his shoulder blade, but he had been close enough to swing the stick with all his might and hit her on her head. She had gone down like a deflated doll.

'Mommy!'

It was the shriek from Anjali's daughter that had galvanised me. I threw myself at Mr Suave. We grappled and fell on the floor. He kicked me hard on my chest and stood up unsteadily. I grabbed his legs, all the while aware of the five-year-old running towards Anjali.

The crazed bastard swung the hockey stick at me. I managed to parry the blow and yanked his legs with all the power I had. He collapsed on the ground. I hurled myself at him. Just a few feet away, Mohini was sobbing and trying to wake up Anjali.

I would have lost the battle very soon. What saved Mohini was not me, but the arrival of a couple of security guards from the building. These two angels had heard the ruckus Mr Suave had created, walked up to Anjali's flat, swooped down on the bastard and restrained him before he could do anything more than hit me once on my face.

◇

I didn't need much patching up this time. I sat next to Anjali who had a turban-like bandage on her head. She looked sexy in it. She held my hand and cried for a while. I said nothing. Baki, Pinky and Jai stood a few feet behind me. The hospital staff were staring at Pinky as though she needed to be loaded onto a stretcher and wheeled into the operating room. She was, as always indifferent, to the reactions she caused in people.

'Thank you,' Anjali whispered.

'Don't speak,' I said.

'Mohini?'

'She is with your father outside. Safe.'

She closed her eyes. She seemed to be dismissing me, as if she wanted me to go away and never remind her of what her choices had come to. Her hand went limp in my palm.

'You told me you would come when I was in trouble,' I said to Jai as we stepped out of the hospital. My left leg was aching and I thought the limp was increasing with every passing day.

'Sorry, Batman. You forgot to flash the Robin signal,' he snapped.

'Boss, that must've been exciting!' Baki said, as though I had taken a particularly fascinating roller-coaster ride.

'Pretty much all of it. Except the part where he was trying to kill me.'

'Is she the one?' Jai stopped and looked back at Anjali's hospital room.

I shrugged. 'I have no clue. I hope she is there on D-day.'

The only thing going through my mind while we were packed like sardines in the Mumbai local on the way back to the bookshop, was the thought of how Anjali's life would pan out. She was one of those unearthly characters in my life. She had been a myth of my history and seeing her display human emotions had been a myth-buster. I wondered what would have happened if I had not let her down all those years ago. Maybe we would have stayed in touch, writing corny letters to each other. Maybe we would have professed our undying love to each other and got married one day. Marry Anjali Warde? Was *that* my childhood fantasy? Of course, I did wonder what the true motives of this thought process were. Was I, like Mr Suave, imagining myself to be her saviour? That our *undying love* would prevent Anjali from taking the path she had chosen for herself?

A few days later, I received a cheque for ₹1,35,000/. It was accompanied by a small note: *Thank you. You are the only friend I ever had.*

But I still couldn't shrug off the feeling that I too had let her down.

✧

Chapter 4

'I'VE WRITTEN THE FIRST CHAPTER OF MY NOVEL, BOSS. AND I want you to critique it,' Baki said to me the next day.

This was going to be the year of surprises. I was going to die after experiencing a series of bizarre incidents. But nothing could beat this.

'You are writing a novel?' I asked.

Baki shyly nodded his elfin head.

'Don't tell Pinky though,' he whispered fiercely, as though Pinky could hear him even when she wasn't at work. 'She won't understand.'

'Don't worry. Your secret is safe with me,' I said. 'And what is your novel about?'

'It's about this hobbit from Middle Earth who embarks on a great journey,' he said, licking his lips, as though revealing the greatest story ever told. I realised I had asked a redundant question.

'I think I have heard and read that premise before,' I said.

'Not in the way I present it,' he said, smacking the shop counter with his palm. This was the most excited I had ever seen him.

'So how *are* you going to present it differently?' I asked.

'By making the hobbit blind,' he said.

'Blind?'

'Yes. Blind. You'll enjoy it, Boss. He'll be carrying an amulet that has to be submerged in a great river. When he wears that amulet, he can see everything. So our hero is torn between his duty and his desire. Get it?'

'Yeah. Kind of.'

'Read the first chapter, Boss! I am telling you, it will be the best first chapter you have ever read,' he pleaded with the look of a puppy who wants a little bone.

I nodded my head ever so briefly. He shrieked in joy and ran to his velvet duffle bag, pulled out a bunch of papers and kept them in front of me. They were neatly held together with a binder. The title page said '*A Wondrous Journey*' in bold letters. Baki's full name was printed below it.

'*A Wondrous Journey*?' I said.

'That's the working title. I might change it eventually.'

'Hmm . . . I kind of like the title,' I said.

His chest puffed up.

'Thanks boss, thanks! You've made my day. Will you give me the critique tomorrow?'

'Let's go slow on that. I need to be very thorough, don't I?' I said.

'Yes of course. Please take your time,' he said, trying hard to hide his disappointment.

I was putting the pages in my drawer when Pinky ambled in. She looked at Baki's excited face and then at me.

'What are you guys talking about behind my back?' she said.

'We weren't,' Baki said.

'You have the look of the cat that ate the cream,' she said.

'You've got to look at the thrillers section today, haven't you? You haven't dusted those books for weeks,' Baki said pointing at the 'Thrillers' bookshelf.

'Did you miss something very obvious? They haven't been dusted because nobody has bought anything.'

I wondered glumly if there was any other bookshop that had unsold thrillers. 'Books are like your parents, Sameer. You should have them around you, because when they are gone you will miss them terribly.' My Uncle's soft voice echoed in my ears. He was a good man who thought about nothing else in his life apart from books. I wondered if that was enough of an achievement. If a year later my epitaph said (I needed Jai to promise me an epitaph) 'Sameer Sathe was a good man who loved books,' would that make me proud?

'Did you hear what I said boss?' Pinky asked.

'Huh? No. Sorry.'

'I asked if you have zeroed down on the next woman on your list.'

'Yes.'

'Who is she?'

'You don't have to worry,' I said.

She looked at me for a few moments with a mix of contempt and sadness in her eyes. I shrugged.

'What makes you think I was worried?' she said and stormed off.

✧

'Maya called me last night,' Jai said, 'She asked why you are behaving weirdly of late, and why you are not reachable.'

I shrugged.

'Yeah, that shrug tells me everything. Like you want her to come to you begging for forgiveness for the big mistake she made by walking out on you.'

'She didn't walk out on me. We both did,' I said defensively.

'And I am the best accountant ever.'

'I think she is with someone,' I said.

'That was fast. You were expecting ten years of solitude for her, weren't you?'

'Not that long,' I said, 'But a while at least.'

'Did she tell you about it?'

'No – there was . . . a glow on her face. The kind of glow she had when *we* were together.'

He looked at me for a moment and then started laughing.

'You moron, when you saw the glow, you guys *were* together!'

I hadn't seen it like that.

After doing the scared-after-not-finding-her-in-bed routine that night, I had stepped out of the house at two-thirty. Everyone says Mumbai never sleeps and it is true, but there's a time in the night when it dozes off for a while and it seemed to be that rare time when I had walked out onto the deserted streets.

After the autorickshaw dropped me in front of Maya's apartment building, I had waited at the gate for several minutes. Maya's flat was visible from a distance and to my surprise, the light in her bedroom was on. The security guard, who wore a uniform with strangely-shaped pendants stuck all over it, reminding me of President Zia ul Haq, stared at me as though I was dog shit.

'What do you want?' he said in a voice that would have shaken a battalion.

'Nothing,' I said.

'Then get the hell out of here.'

'That is your gate,' I said pointing at the giant metal structure, 'And this is the road, which believe it or not, doesn't belong to you. So I can do whatever I want to do as long as I am outside the gate.'

He raised his thick black baton menacingly and said, 'You look like you need some spanking.'

Spanking? I laughed. It had been at least twenty-five years since anyone had wanted to spank me, not counting a few games me and Maya used to play, sometimes.

'Take a walk, asshole,' he said, coming out of the little booth.

'Thanks for the health tip. But I prefer the gymnasium,' I said, wishing Jai was there to hear me – he would have been so proud. 'Now will you shut up?'

Just then I saw the movement in her bedroom. I thought I saw two silhouettes. A buzzing began in my ears. My body went numb, except for the intense shooting pain in my left leg. I felt dizzy and closed my eyes. When I opened them after a few moments I was staring into the nostrils of Zia.

Tapping my chest twice with his baton, he said quietly: 'Get lost.'

I was startled and took an involuntary step back, which gave him the impression that I was scared. He gave me a nasty, pleased smile. I recovered quickly.

'Listen to me. There are two options. I can make a huge ruckus here and wake up the people living in the nearest building. When somebody comes down I am going to tell them I caught you reading porn magazines. Although I am dressed like this. (I was dressed in my torn pajamas). I know many people here. Who do you think they will believe?'

He was stunned and couldn't utter a word.

'I know you are thinking they would never believe me, but they would be *awake* and it would be all your fault. Instead, just tell me who went into flat 12-B, Ms Maya Saxena's flat, and I will be on my way,' I waded in.

I heard the gears turning in his head. For a few agonising moments, I saw him battle with the dilemma. He clenched his teeth and took a step at me, and I thought he had called my bluff. But then his shoulders drooped and he let out his breath loudly.

'Okay, but you will have to leave the moment I tell you,' he said.

'You have my word,' I said.

'Look, I can't tell you who went in because we don't keep a record of visitors who come in expensive cars like a Mercedes and are accompanied by the people living in the complex. All I can tell you is it was a man who seemed a little drunk. Ms Saxena told me to open the gate and I did,' he said and pointed at the road. 'Now be on your way.'

The dizziness from a while ago assaulted me again. I was shaking and almost lost my balance. Incredibly, Zia steadied me.

'You all right?' he asked.

'I am fine. Just a little betrayed,' I said.

'What?'

'Never mind. Thanks,' I said and started walking.

I must've walked aimlessly for hours, because when I hailed an autorickshaw to go back home, there was bright sunshine and Mumbai was awake.

✧

That night, I had a nightmare in which I was on an icy land. There was no horizon, the sky and the land seemed to be made up of white ice. A black speck appeared far away. As it came closer, I realised a huge black vehicle was hurtling towards me. I realised that my legs had turned into ice too. Screaming, I tried to move, but couldn't. The vehicle was getting closer every moment. I stared at it with morbid fascination. Incredibly, it had a front resembling Babaji's face. A laughing face.

'Five women more!' the face said.

Anjali and Madhuri were standing atop the vehicle and looking at me with pity, as though they had tried their best to stop the vehicle and had given up. Just then someone whispered in my ear.

'Don't look at it. Look at me.' It was Maya.

I woke up gasping her name and couldn't sleep for the rest of the night. For the millionth time, I wondered if I should tell her about Babaji's prophesy. I knew she would laugh at me, call me a *despo idiot* (her favourite derogatory term) and think it was just a bizarre pretext I had thought up under which to call her.

'To hell with you, Maya! If you can't be with me when I need you the most, you weren't supposed to be my soulmate,' I snarled. A dog started barking somewhere far away.

The next woman on my list was Devi Mathur. She was the first and the only woman to slap me.

◇

'Devi Mathur?' Jai said incredulously. 'You fell for *her*?'

'It was a bit of a rebound thing. After Anjali left the city, you might remember I wasn't myself,' I said. There were very few facts about my life that Jai didn't know. I had my reasons for never telling Jai about me falling for Devi Mathur.

'Yeah, I remember. You weren't yourself especially when you had drunk almost three quarters of the rum bottle from your father's closet and puked and cried the whole night,' he said.

'Thanks for reminding me of things that it took me years to forget,' I said.

'You remember how your father had refused to buy you a bike after that? You practically fell at his feet . . .'

'Jai, I know you have chronicled all of my proud moments, and one day you can write my biography, but can we focus on Devi Mathur?'

'I bet it won't be too difficult to find Ms Mathur,' he said, scratching his stubble.

'You're right. I know where she is,' I said.

'Then why are you sounding like Rajesh Khanna of the melancholic Seventies?'

'She's in a small town called Khasanpada.'

'Khas . . . what?'

'Khasanpada. It's a small village a few hundred kilometres from here,' I said.

'And what's she doing there?'

'She's a doctor.'

'And how do you know all this?' asked Jai, genuinely puzzled.

'We've been in touch,' I said quietly.

'In touch with *chalni*?' He used the name we had given Devi in school after a terrible bout of chickenpox had left her face pockmarked. It meant sieve.

'Let's never use that word again, okay? It was fifteen years ago and we've all moved on.'

'Whoa! Holy chivalry, Batman!'

'Cut it.'

'Okay. So are we going to meet her now?'

'I am not sure I want to,' I said.

He stared at me for a few moments.

'A sense of déjà vu?'

'Something like that,' I agreed.

'But you have your ass to save this time.'

'Yeah. That's the only reason I'm even considering it.'

'Good. So let's head out to Khasan . . . whatever, today.'

Before meeting Madhuri and Anjali, I had felt frozen with anxiety. But somewhere deep inside, I had believed they would help me, even after hearing my seemingly crazy story. With Devi, I felt a deep dread. I was sure she wouldn't even want to be anywhere near me, let alone allow me to stay with her for two whole weeks. After all, I had broken her heart. No, not broken it, I had stomped on it, crushed it under my boots, and walked away from it. I was scared. She was the only woman in the world apart from my mother who had hit me.

'You remember everything Babaji said, right?'

I nodded.

'We've come quite far. Don't throw it away now,' Jai said patting me on my shoulder.

✧

I got my bag and stuffed it with clothes for two weeks, wondering all the while if it was futile. There was no way Devi was going to even listen to me. I had lied to Jai when I told him I was in touch with her. *She* was not in touch with me, *I* had kept tabs on her. This might sound very creepy, but every few months, I always found out what she was doing. Maya would have called this 'Sam's Legendary Guilty Conscience'. A few years after messing up Devi's life, I had conjured up enough courage to apologise. I was eighteen or nineteen and under the delusion that the magical word 'sorry' meant your slate was clean. I had found out where Devi was. She had been in the first year of her medical degree. I had walked up to her college gate and without even pausing walked right back. Since then, it had been a vicious circle – I found her, couldn't apologise and so had to find her again a few months later when my guilt-metre overheated.

Jai got an SUV and off we went on our quest.

'The Batmobile!' he screamed when we hit the highway.

'I think the Batman joke has gone on for far too long,' I said.

'You started it.'

✧

'Where is the hospital?' Jai screamed in the face of a villager who regarded him with curious bemusement. He gave us the directions in a dialect of Marathi that sounded like a foreign language to me.

'You needn't talk to them as though they're deaf,' I said to Jai.'Or daft.'

'Are you suggesting I am being condescending?'

'No. I am suggesting that you show some patience.'

It had been a long journey and we both felt tired. The summer sun was right above our heads at five in the afternoon.

The villager stood as though he wasn't quite sure whether we had understood his directions or not.

'Mama,' I said, using the term for maternal uncle, 'Do you mind coming with us to the hospital?'

He nodded and hopped into the jeep.

There was nothing remarkable about the village. Like most villages, it had the same depressing poverty on open display. Little children, who used the scourged roads like an extension of their shanty homes, stared at us curiously. The grown-ups ignored us.

My mother was born and raised in a town that had barely escaped being called a village. My maternal grandfather, who was the only lawyer in town, had owned a huge house. And he was perhaps the only lawyer in the whole world who never asked his clients for money. So, the *wada*, as the house was called, was always full of people. Many people I know have fond memories of their grandparents' homes. Not me. I used to be miserable there. So many people around – that suffocated the hell out of me. My animated mother achieved her most hyper-animated state in that house. And when her four sisters and six brothers congregated too, it used to be almost cosmic chaos – eleven siblings, their spouses, their children, their bawling, fights. I was reminded of those times as Jai drove through the cratered pathways of the village.

The man told us to stop in front of a ramshackle structure that had a board hanging askew on one nail with 'General Hospital' painted on it.

Switching off the ignition Jai said, 'Welcome to hell.'

'Bringing you over here was a bad idea,' I said.

'Couldn't agree more,' he said almost cheerfully.

We got out of the vehicle and stood in front of the 'Hospital.' There were a few wooden benches sagging with the weight of the people crowding on them, everyone in various state of distress: sneezing, coughing, crying, whimpering, screaming.

A litter of piglets led by a big fat mamma pig crossed the entrance to the hospital.

Jai and I waited outside for a while. I tried to muster up enough courage to face the woman I had scorned many years ago.

'Well, what are you waiting for? The receptionist to call you in?' Jai said.

Taking a deep breath, I walked towards the entrance.

'You can't go in.' A man who was at least twice my size stood in my way. 'We have been waiting for a long time.'

'I just want to meet the doctor,' I said.

'You, and everyone else.'

I looked back at Jai who gave me an indifferent shrug.

'Wait for your turn. Unless you are about to give birth – which I think you are at least nine months away from,' he said.

A few people took a break from their coughing, sneezing and whimpering to chuckle along with him.

'Look, you don't understand. I am not unwell. The doctor . . . she knows me,' I said. 'I just need to tell her that I am here and I will be waiting outside.'

'You city people think that we are all fools, don't you? You take one step towards that door and I will smash your teeth.'

Suddenly, everyone was quiet. I had the same feeling I used to have as a kid when I unknowingly made an enemy of some bully because of my big mouth.

I raised my hand in a gesture of surrender and retreated to the safe environs of our jeep. We waited for over two hours, watching a succession of people go in and out. All the while the XXXL man kept looking at me as though I was a naughty dog about to pee on his feet.

'Wrestlerman is pissed,' Jai said.

'I am glad you found your voice inspite of your fear,' I said.

'I am not scared! You backed out too soon. Now I can't go and pick up the fight where you left it.'

I said nothing.

I finally spotted Devi. She was helping a very old woman walk out. She held her head down and was helping the seemingly arthritic woman negotiate the stairs, when as though on a cue, she looked up.

I raised my hand and waved. She was saying something to the old woman. Her mouth dropped open in surprise. The old woman almost tripped. Devi tore her gaze away from me and after apologising profusely, she handed the woman over to an equally old man.

The last time I had seen Devi, her pockmarked face had been streaked with tears. She had looked so forlorn that her face had haunted me, forcing me to realise the full extent of my meanness towards her. The face of the woman looking back at me now was flawless. There was a glow on it, the kind that you see on the face of a tired but immensely satisfied dancer after a bravura performance. She waved back at me, with something close to a pleasantly surprised smile, gesturing at me to come closer.

I walked past the XXXL man who had a morose look on his face. I wanted to give him the finger, but considering his size, I desisted.

'You haven't changed one bit,' she said, looking at my face. The oaf who had stopped us from entering the hospital grunted loudly, as though he found it ridiculous. She looked at the man and I thought I saw her flinch, thought her smile dimmed a little. The oaf walked away, slouching.

'And you are unrecognisable,' I said.

'From what? The chalni?' she said and laughed. She seemed relieved at the XXXL man's sulky exit.

'Is that the crab?' she said to Jai.

In fourth grade, Jai had lost all the teeth between his two canines in rapid succession. Whenever he had laughed, it had reminded us of a crab. Somehow the name had stuck right through school.

'Yes it is,' Jai said. Since leaving school, I had never called him that.

They shook hands, a little awkwardly. They had been at each other's throats two decades back.

'What makes you come here all the way?'

'It's a long story,' I said.

She looked at me for a moment, perhaps surprised by the graveness of my voice.

'Why don't you wait? I have some more patients to attend to,' she said.

'Sure. We'll wait in the jeep. Take your time,' I said.

✧

'I hope you didn't miss the smile on her face when she saw you,' Jai said as we were heading back to the jeep.

'It surprised the hell out of me,' I said.

'She isn't a chalni now. Shocking!'

'I don't think that's the right word,' I said.

'What?'

'Stunning, not shocking,' I said.

'Will you ever stop correcting people? What the hell, I am shocked. Shocked as though I saw a bloody ghost! Do you have a problem with that?'

'It's as though you were expecting her to be worse looking,' I said.

'And you weren't?'

I was. So I said nothing.

'Just because we are twenty years older doesn't mean we ought to forget everything that happened in the past,' he said. After a few minutes of silence, Jai said, 'Have you ever wondered why Maya left you?'

'More than I care to admit,' I said.

'Are you wondering right now?'

'Yes I am,' I acknowledged.

'Hmmm . . . ,' he said.

We said nothing for a long time.

'What's bothering you?' Jai finally said.

'I didn't like the big guy.'

'Barring his mother, I think the rest of the world probably shares your sentiment.'

'Devi seemed scared of him,' I said.

'I hate to admit it, but so am I.'

After what seemed like forever, Devi stepped out of the hospital. It was dusk, and the streets were suddenly very quiet. A solitary bulb hung at the entrance of the hospital, making the evening even more melancholy.

Devi scanned the area and smiled when she saw us. Then she looked around some more, as though she were trying to make sure that it was safe to proceed.

When she didn't see whatever it was she was checking for, she walked up to us and said, 'You waited.'

'This time, I did,' I said.

'So why are you here?' she repeated the question. 'And I have all the time in the world to listen to your long story.'

'Where do you live?' I asked.

'There is a small two-room house I've got, thanks to our government.'

'Good! You can share one room,' Jai said.

I clenched my teeth. Devi narrowed her eyes and looked at me and Jai.

'Did I just hear him correctly?' she said.

'Can we go to your place?'

'You are worrying me now.'

Standing in that filthy hospital yard, in the unsettling quiet of the evening, I told her the story. I was afraid that she would laugh it off and walk away from us. She stood there, looking into the distance, as though she was thinking very deeply about what I had said.

'I am having a tough time convincing myself that what you have told me makes any kind of sense,' she finally said.

'Well, you are perhaps the millionth person to think so,' I said.

'It's true, chalni. I mean, Devi.' Jai said her name as though he was surprised he could utter it.

'You call me that again and I will pluck your eyes out,' she said.

'Don't use your surgeon's knife, the one you use to pluck off balls,' he said.

'What do you know about balls? I mean, considering you don't seem to have them,' she snapped.

'Hey! Guys, can we keep the focus on the problem at hand please?'

In school, there had been a legendary rivalry between them. I hadn't guessed that the silly race to the first rank in the fourth grade would be so strong as to carry their feelings across the decades. Bringing Jai along was beginning to look like one of my worse ideas.

Surprisingly, they smiled at each other.

'Okay, this is getting weirder by the minute,' I said.

'Come on, let me offer you two tired men a cup of tea,' she said.

'I have issues here, Sameer,' she said handing me the cup. We were in her tiny house. 'I don't think the people in this village understand the concept of a man staying with a woman unless the two are related.'

'I could be your cousin from the city,' I said.

'Do you think these people are fools?' she said.

It was the second time this question had been asked of me. I didn't think anyone was a fool, least of all the villagers.

'I have a lot of respect for the intellect of these people. The biggest man in the village made sure that I always remember it,' I said.

She avoided my eyes. I watched her, sipping my tea.

'Who is that guy, Devi?' I asked.

She said nothing. I waited.

'None of your business,' she said, still refusing to look at me.

'Does he do that to everyone who wants to meet you?'

She closed her eyes, took a deep breath and nodded as though she was done talking about it. 'I am sorry, Sameer. I can't do it. You need to go.'

I had a sudden upsurge of panic. Bile rose up my throat. I gulped the hot tea to push it down, to block its way out. My biggest hope had been that every woman I would make this bizarre request to, would be compelled to acquiesce out of guilt. Perhaps I had hurt Devi so much years ago that she had forgotten but not forgiven me. This was her way of getting even.

'I know what you are thinking, Sameer Sathe. You're thinking that I am this psychotic woman who has waited years for vengeance. But it's not true. I really care for the people in this little village and I want them to care for me. I am not doing this internship because I need to get the hell out of here after my obligatory two years are over. I won't leave this place for a long time. These people need me. And I won't let them down,' she said.

'I could be dead very soon,' I said.

'There is very little chance of that happening. I am surprised you of all people could believe such drivel,' she said. 'Babaji indeed!'

'He knows about the canoe, Devi,' I said quietly.

She dropped her cup.

✧

We had finished the eleventh grade and were all destined to go through the hell of surviving the twelfth, which determined what our middle-class lives would turn out to be. There was a movie which was popular at that time, about a boy and a girl who fall in love, anger their families, elope, and finally get killed. It had been

Amir Khan's debut movie, in which he had sung a memorable song '*Papa kehte hain . .*' – (*Papa says I am going to be a big guy soon*). That song did put a lot of pressure on all of us. All our Papas, Mamas, uncles, aunts, neighbours told us every minute of our waking lives that our collective moments of reckoning were just a year away. So, when the most enthusiastic kids in the class organised a day trip to a nearby hill station, every single one of us got on the bus.

We quickly separated into groups having the same agendas: Boys who believed their sole reason of existence was to impress girls. Boys who clowned around. Boys who were relentlessly picked upon. Boys who were outcastes. The last 'group' had just one member in it. Me. I was the pariah who had dared to spend the last five months with the object of everyone's desire – Anjali Warde. Jai had started his journey back through the valley of jealousy to resume his best friend role, but he was still fighting for his survival in the group of 'impressers'. The impressers had guitars and banjos and mouth organs. Most of them could play a maximum of two songs, and that too, terribly. Bollywood was the source of our dubious understanding of what women wanted. If Shahrukh Khan used the little mandolin, the guitars were replaced. The impressers were a desperate set of people, although I must admit, I had wanted to be one for most of my childhood. The girls must've had similar groupings.

On that day, I was sitting in the back of the bus, observing each group do their thing. All of us knew this was going to be the last getaway where we could just forget about the impending long hours pouring over physics and chemistry books, shuttling between tuition classes for each and every subject, and keeping up the act of assuring our parents that we were going to achieve all that they hadn't. There were a couple of teachers accompanying us, but they too were largely indulgent about what was going on.

◆

When we reached the hill station, everyone wanted the bus to go straight to a small waterfall where the impressers could take off their shirts and show the girls their recently acquired muscles. We alighted from the bus and walked to the top of the falls. It had rained just a day ago, a very unusual thing to happen in the month of March, and the waterfall was in its full glory.

The leader of the impressers was a boy called Tej who at the age of fifteen had the IQ of a five year old, the body of a twenty-five year old, and a hormonal imbalance of the worst kind. He had been a class bully till we were in fifth grade and many of us had memories of the bruises he had given us. Little, mousy Devi Mathur used to be his prime target. All the other girls he had considered as his audience, but not Devi. And he hadn't missed a single opportunity to make her life miserable.

The scene at the waterfall was played out like a series of set-pieces. The impressers quickly got rid of their clothes and strutted around like puffed-up roosters in front of the best-looking girls. The girls giggled, their hands covering their mouths, as though they were looking at male bodies for the first time. The losers got busy with stupid games like a contest to see who could spew water the farthest. The two teachers started gulping what looked suspiciously like spiked cola. I sat on one of the rocks observing Tej and feeling seriously envious.

Then Tej got into his act.

'It really is fresh here. I almost gagged on the stink coming from *chalni* in the bus,' he said and laughed hysterically. Some of his brethren joined in.

'Shut up!' Devi screamed.

The girls giggled. Better Devi than them.

'We should've left you back with your books. They must be missing you,' he said and did a lousy imitation of Devi's stammering while she read in class, 'The f-f-f-irst Ma-ma-ma-ratha king was Sh-sh-sh-shivaji.'

'Tej, we're all getting tired of this nonsense,' I said.

For a few seconds, everyone was silent. Nobody had ever dared to talk to him like that. I was as surprised as everyone else.

'Oh! The lover boy can speak. I thought she had taken your tongue with her when she left town,' he said.

I had been very quiet since Anjali had left, but I hadn't realised it was so obvious as to not even escape the low attention span of the biggest moron I knew.

'Why don't you take your brain and put it in your bicep? I think it will be better used there,' I said and regretted it immediately.

Tej's face turned red. For a guy who was relentless in the pursuit of making everyone around him miserable, Tej was pretty sensitive when someone picked on him. I knew I had something terrible going on with all those accidents, but none of them were caused because of my big mouth. This was going to be the first.

'What's going on?' the teacher intervened.

'Nothing, sir,' Tej said.

'You two stay away from each other,' the teacher said, 'If I see the two of you within five feet, we will leave you behind when we head back.'

'Okay, sir,' Tej said with a nasty smile. I shuddered a little. The teacher walked away from us, and resumed his drinking session with his buddy, the Sanskrit teacher.

'Hey, Tej. Look, there is a little canoe over here,' one of his cohorts shouted, pointing at a little boat. It was an old, bust-up discarded canoe which could seat two people.

'I know boating. My father taught me when I was five ,' Tej said and looked at the girls. The girls did the giggling routine. There wasn't a thing in the world that Tej's father hadn't taught him when he was just five – painting, singing, boxing, driving (a car and a motorcycle), shooting, hunting and some exotic ones like converting iron into gold and invoking rain.

'I have a challenge for you,' Devi said.

Everyone looked at her, stunned.

'I'll go back to the bus if you can pull that canoe to the top of the fall and come down in it,' she said.

'Ha! What kind of silly challenge is that? I've been doing that for most of my life,' Tej said and started laughing.

I had a strange feeling that he was scared. Nobody had asked him till then to prove his wild claims.

'Then show us. I will do a salaam to you every time I see you,' I joined in.

Tej was caught. The trap was set. I almost saw a heavenly spotlight coming down from the sky and Tej desperately trying to get out of it.

'I don't have time for this,' he said.

'Do it Tej! They are doubting you!' the cohorts helped our cause. I saw him looking at the girls who looked back at him in anticipation. There was no way he could back out now. I had expected him to act as though we were asking him to do something way below his dignity. I had hoped to forever remind him that he had chickened out. But what he did surprised me, and perhaps it surprised Devi too. He nodded his head and looked at us.

'You promise you will salute me every time you see me?'

'Yes,' I said in a hollow voice.

'And you promise you will go back to the bus?'

Devi nodded.

'Okay. Guys, help me pull out this canoe,' he said to his fellow impressers.

I remember thinking of calling it off. Telling Mr Adrenaline to cool it and forget this little prank he had fallen for. But a large part of me wanted him to do it. I looked at Devi; there was a fascinated expression on her face. I had a feeling she too wanted to call it off. It wouldn't have helped. Tej was too far gone to listen to any sane voice.

'Tej, I think that's too dangerous,' one of his cohorts dared to utter what was fast becoming the unspoken consensus.

'Shut up! Not a single word from you, you wimp,' Tej said as he dragged the canoe up the little hill.

The hill had seemed small, but it was tall enough to kill a man. The teachers, who were later rusticated for negligence, suddenly came alive from their drunken ignorance and screamed at Tej after he had already dragged the little canoe up the hill. His brethren, who had helped him drag the boat up, scurried away.

I thought Tej looked really lonely up there. For the first time I saw something close to fear in the eyes of the boy whom everyone feared. He looked down at his classmates who were foolishly egging him on, while the instigators, me and Devi, wanted him to stop. Tej raised his hand high in the air and that's the way I forever remembered him. A boy, all of sixteen, an asshole perhaps but certainly not one who deserved to die. He was dead five minutes later.

We watched helplessly as Tejinder Singh Malhotra, class 11B, stepped inside the rickety canoe and pushed it into the waterfall.

I knew he was going to be in trouble the moment he started his descent. His mouth dropped open once gravity worked its deadly magic on him. He descended at a speed none of us had expected. There were admiring ooh and aahs from the girls and his brothers in arms, but these soon transformed into screams. Tej's head, the one I had proclaimed to be devoid of a functional brain, collided with a protruding rock. He went into freefall.

Tej battled for his life for two days in the hospital before he died.

We were hounded for the rest of the year. Sameer and Devi – the murderous duo. Nobody spoke to me for months. Jai never left my side, and so he too became a pariah. I never told him, but I think I would've done something terrible to myself had he, too, deserted me.

There was a place near the school, right next to a small lake, where Devi and I used to hide, hold hands, and cry. She didn't have a Jai to stand by her. I was the only hope she had of crawling back to a life that had been miserable even before Tej's death, and was now pure hell. She clung to me with all her force.

I think I clawed my way back to some kind of sanity a lot sooner than her, perhaps because of Jai's unflinching friendship. And I couldn't carry her back with me. It was a matter of my own survival – I needed to let go; either that, or drown with her.

She had cried bitterly when I had told her that I didn't want to go to the lake anymore. Cried, and then slapped me hard, calling me a selfish bastard. She had never spoken to me again.

◇

'It was a terrible accident. An accident!' Devi whispered.

'I never said otherwise,' I said, 'All I want to say is that Babaji knew about it.'

She trembled with anger for a while.

'I had forgotten about it,' she said with tears in her eyes.

'Me too. I guess some memories are destined to haunt you forever,' I said.

'Not unless someone wants you to,' she said.

'I am so sorry, Devi,' I said.

'Do you think our shared crime is enough to make me help you?'

'There was no crime. We didn't know what we were doing.'

'Did anyone ever tell you that you're a selfish bastard?'

'Many,' I said.

She held her head down for several minutes and cried.

'Look, if it's any consolation, then I am also part of the crime,' Jai said.

'Shut your mouth! Not a word from you!' Devi screamed.

'Okay, okay. I was just trying to spread the guilt around.'

'Get out of my house,' she said dully, without looking at us.

'Devi, look . . .' I said.

She pointed at the door.

✧

'That went very well,' Jai said as we sat in the jeep.

'Will you be quiet for some time?'

'I have been quiet for a long time,' he said and resumed swatting mosquitoes.

It was almost midnight. The quiet was interrupted sporadically by barking dogs,whining mosquitoes and Jai's grunts as he killed them.

'Are we going to sit in this jeep for the rest of the night?' Jai said.

I had no answer to that.

'You shouldn't have brought that up,' he said smacking a mosquito on his forearm. 'Look at the size of this bastard!'

'I . . . just wanted her to understand the situation,' I said.

'By bringing up the most terrible incident of her life?'

I looked at him and nodded, 'I messed up, didn't I?'

'Yes, you did,' he said.

'Aren't you going to suggest that we head back?'

'Ding! Assumption alert! What do you think I am – a quitter? There's no way back till we do it. And I am right here beside you,' he said.

I smiled at him.

A knock on the jeep window woke me up after we had dozed off. I rolled down the window.

'What the hell are you still doing here?' Devi hissed.

'Devi, I am extremely sorry. I know I messed up again,' I said.

Jai woke up with a start, 'Chalni, please. You will discover two dead bodies in the morning. These bloodsuckers are killing us.'

She made a face and said, 'Come back inside.'

'Yes! I knew there was a kind soul behind that tough exterior,' Jai said.

I elbowed him, fearing she would change her mind.

'This is the second time you have called me that. Third time I *will* pluck your eyes out,' she said.

'Yup. Deal.' Jai said.

'You will live in this room for the next two weeks. And you,' she said looking at Jai, 'I want you to be gone first thing in the morning.'

'Never to be seen again,' Jai said with his fist on his heart.

✧

When I woke up the next day, my body was covered in mosquito bites the size of ulcers. I had not been able to sleep for most of the night wondering how to undo the damage I had done the day before. So I was a little surprised when I heard laughter from the little makeshift kitchen Devi had made in the government quarters. I got up and walked in silently. Devi was laughing at something Jai had said. I could never imagine her laughing like that. She had barely smiled when we were kids, and not only because all the kids used to make her life outright miserable.

'Did I miss something between last night and this morning?'

'I think you missed all the bloodsuckers who left their mark on you,' Jai said.

Devi said, 'I have to go to the hospital.'

'Give me a minute,' I said and rushed to the bathroom.

When we reached the hospital, it was already swarming with people. The oaf was sitting in what seemed to me his customary position, at the entrance of the doctor's room. He seemed shocked to see me at the hospital with Devi.

She asked me to wait for her and walked up to the man. I couldn't hear what she was saying, but I thought she was pleading with him. The man looked at me and narrowed his eyes, as though he didn't believe what she had said. He stared at me for a few frightening moments and said something to Devi. She let out an exasperated sigh. The man said something and walked away. She just shook her head as though trying to get rid of a bad feeling and gestured at me.

'At least tell me what his name is,' I said, walking up to her.

Her lips quivered. She said nothing.

When I entered the hospital, the sight was not what I had expected. I was dreading being assaulted by the squalor, the lack of basic equipment and the chaos. But the place was clean, smelling faintly of disinfectant. The equipment was basic, but functional. After being in hospitals countless times, I had a sense of what a good one looked and felt like. This *was* a good one.

'Don't be surprised,' Devi said with a smile.

'I was expecting far worse,' I said.

'When I took over this hospital, it was a terrible mess. The guy who was running it before me was an intern and he must've come to the hospital for not more than a day or two in the entire two years. The first thing I did when I landed here was to clean up the place. It took me more than a week to get rid of the accumulated grime,' she said.

I remembered the little girl who used to be praised by the teachers for the condition of her books through the school year. For us, school books were hateful things that were supposed to be trampled upon and abused.

I saw her work like a maniac through the day – there wasn't an ailment she didn't treat, from old men with leprosy to newborns with a cold. She interspersed this with a childbirth, during which I had to step out.

The XXXL man gestured at me to come closer. I shrugged. His mouth hardened. If I could now replay those few moments, perhaps I would have, instead, walked up to him with my head bowed meekly. He stood up and walked towards me. He could decapitate me with a blow, I was sure of that. Suddenly, I regretted not taking those karate lessons my mother had wanted me take when I was twelve.

He stopped very close to me. I could smell the tobacco in his mouth and the sweat on his body. The throbbing in my left leg matched my thudding heart.

'Ganpat Patil. That's my name. Remember it,' he said.

'Not as memorable as Gabbar Singh, but catchy,' I said.

He breathed in and out, warming my neck. He stood there for some time. Perhaps he hadn't understood what I said, because he took a step back and walked away. I felt the air rushing back into my lungs.

That night when we were walking back to her house, Devi said, 'So what have you been doing all these years, Sameer?'

'Reading books and selling them,' I said. I told her about my uncle and the bookshop I had inherited from him.

'But you got your degree from one of the best engineering colleges, right?'

'Yes. Guilty as charged. Chemical engineering.'

'So?'

'So? So why am I selling books when I could be creating a soap with a high TFM content?' I said.

'Maybe,' she said and shrugged.

'I love books,' I said.

'Nothing wrong with that. I remember you used to bury your head in those stupid novels when you were ten years old,' she said.

'They weren't stupid,' I said defensively.

'It's all fiction, Sameer. And it was good when we were kids. But you have to let things go.'

'Now you are sounding like my fiancée. I'll ask you the same question I asked her: *Why* do you have to grow out of things?'

'Because we need to experience new things in life,' she said.

'Like you? Trying to save Tejinder for the last four years?' I said and stopped in my tracks.

She looked at me and I saw a kind of sadness I had never seen before in her eyes. And anger too.

'How dare you?' she breathed. And then shouted: 'How *dare* you?'

'How dare *I*? You are the one who was asking me to grow out of things,' I shouted back. 'And you think I can't see what is so obvious? You never wanted to be a doctor, Devi. It was your mother who never stopped pushing you to do it. And I remember you telling me how much you hated her for that!'

Both her parents were doctors.

'This is what I always wanted to do!'

'You are lying. You wanted to be a dancer,' I said.

We hadn't realised it but we were screaming at each other in public with the villagers staring at us in amazement. She became aware of them and started walking away quickly. I followed her.

We didn't speak for the next two days.

✧

On the fourth day, Jai arrived.

'Say, were you guys missing me?' he said when Devi opened the door.

'No,' she said.

'Your eyes tell me a different story,' he said. Jai was nothing if not persistent.

'Go back,' she said.

'Not without having a cup of tea.' And he walked past her into the house.

After a while, sipping a cup of tea, he said to me, 'Looks like you've messed up again.'

'None of your business,' I said.

'Looks like you've messed up big time!'

Devi came into the room.

'Why did you guys come back into my life?' she said.

'I had no intention of doing it. Just the small matter of my life came up, which obviously you don't give a damn about.'

'What I don't give a damn about is what you think about my life,' she said.

'I accept that. Now are we going to move ahead from here?' I said, 'because to tell you the truth, I just need you to bear with me for ten more days.'

From the next day on, Jai came to the hospital with us. Whenever Devi found time, she only spoke to Jai, and ignored me. She was a fanatic about work and seemed to have endless patience to listen to the woes of the villagers. We also tagged along with her whenever she made her house rounds, when she usually tended to babies and old people. These home trips were a frenzied succession of activities – weighing babies in the sling she always carried, scolding careless mothers, teaching them how to make nutritious porridge, goading them to never miss vaccinations. I overheard her telling Jai that she had never lost an infant and she had delivered close to a hundred in the last six months. For a village with a population of roughly fifteen thousand, I thought the number was astronomical.

◇

'You're causing her a lot of discomfort,' Ganpat said to me on the tenth day.

'Excuse me?'

'Are you really her cousin? And who is the other man? How exactly are you related to her?'

My patience with the oaf was fast running out. I turned to walk away but he grabbed my shoulder and turned me around like a revolving chair.

'Answer me, you city moron!'

Just then Devi arrived and pleaded, 'Ganpat! Is this the way you treat visitors?'

'This man was insulting me,' he growled.

'He didn't mean to. I apologise on his behalf,' she said.

'I am not going to protect you anymore,' he said.

The oaf kicked the ground and walked away.

'Protect you? From what?' I asked.

'Don't meddle,' she said turning to the pregnant woman she was examining.

I cornered Jai in the evening.

'Has she told you anything?'

'If you are asking about what the big man said today, forget about it,' he said.

'What does she need protection from?' I insisted.

'You promise me you won't do anything silly about it?'

'Go ahead,' I said.

'She hasn't told me directly, but I believe she gets forty thousand rupees a month from the government as part of a medical budget for this village,' he said.

'Okay.'

'When she got here, the money was being deposited with a local politician, who also happens to own most of the village.'

I felt a deep dread. This big guy is the politician's son. She told me that since his son fancies her, the politician doesn't take the money. She gets to spend the entire budget on what it is supposed to be spent on. But she has to pretend to like the bastard.'

'And now I have managed to anger the oaf,' I said in a whisper.

'Possibly,' he said. 'Let's hope this is a momentary sulk. Hopefully tomorrow we will see the man at her doorstep again.'

None of my greatest hopes had materialised in the last few months. And all my worst fears had come true. The way it turned out, the trend continued.

✧

I would've loved to say that I knew something terrible was going to happen because the day started with a heavy downpour, or the sun shone too brightly, or because a crow sat on the windowsill and cawed for a long time. But none of those things had happened. It was just an ordinary day.

'Last day,' Devi said handing me a cup of tea. She was a good tea-maker – rivalling my mother.

'Yeah, it seems like ages,' I said and realised that it sounded stupid. 'I don't mean that I didn't enjoy it . . . Okay, I wish I had the whistle I used to keep in my pocket when we were in Class Five.'

Jai had given me that whistle. I blew it every time I thought I was talking too much.

She smiled and shook her head, like the way you do when a dog refuses to learn a trick.

'I never wanted to see you again. But I think I am glad I did.'

I thought of telling her about the numerous times I had tried to contact her, but said nothing.

'I've been thinking about what you said the other day. Dancing was special. You know, I still do it. I close all the doors and windows of the house, and I dance. But it doesn't make me feel alive anymore.'

She looked at her lap for a few moments as though making a decision. 'And I'm sorry for what I said about books. They were your life. They still are.'

I said nothing.

She would've been a great dancer.

Jai and I were helping her move a bed in the hospital when I heard her name being called. She froze.

'Doctorin Bai! O Doctorin Bai!'

When we stepped out of the hospital, I saw Ganpat. He was surrounded by four men who were, if it were possible, even broader and taller than him. Ganpat looked at one of the giants and pointed at me. The man chuckled, nodding at the other men. They were carrying the biggest sticks I had ever seen.

The destruction began.

The men first smashed the window.

They entered the hospital and slapped an old man sitting on a makeshift bed.

'You bastard!' Devi screamed and lunged at the goon. He shoved her aside. Her head banged against the wall and she collapsed on the floor.

Jai raised his fist and hit the man who had assaulted Devi. The man didn't even flinch. He grabbed Jai by his hair and punched him in the stomach. Jai's face contorted in intense pain. He doubled over.

The old man walked in and said to me, 'Don't try to be a hero.'

It was too late.

I had already lowered my head and rammed it into the chest of one of the men. I thought I did hurt him, because he let out a soft, muffled cry.

The old man raised his stick and hit me on my thigh. The pain was intense, but I didn't scream. Which was a mistake because the old man raised his stick again and hit me again, incredibly, on the same spot. This time, I screamed.

'The third blow would've broken it,' he said a little disappointedly.

The men grabbed me and Jai and shoved us out of the hospital. Devi had managed to get back on her feet.

'One man isn't enough for you?' the old man spat the words at Devi.

She recoiled as though he had hit her.

Ganpat looked at me and Jai, shook his head and said, 'Cousins! Lying bitch.'

The old man chuckled indulgently, as though his son had cracked the greatest joke ever. I realised that he was Ganpat's father.

'I'm happy that you are no longer fascinated with her,' the old man said.

'Please let them go,' Devi said. It was the voice of the bullied little girl, the one I thought she had buried long ago.

'My men are itching to do something. Either these two get it or the hospital does. You choose,' Patil, the father, said.

Devi walked to us with unsteady steps. She was crying.

'Leave them alone,' she said to Patil.

In the next five minutes, the men systematically smashed everything in the hospital. Nobody said a word.

'Thirty-five thousand every month,' Patil said in a a bored tone after the men had stopped.

She nodded with her eyes closed.

I knew I would never forget the name Patil. The nonchalance with which the old man had destroyed four years of Devi's life was numbing. The men walked away as if nothing had happened.

'I am so sorry, Devi,' I said after we got back to her house.

'None of it is your fault,' she said applying some kind of lotion on the black and blue bruise on my hip. 'I guess that's that, isn't it?'

My impotent rage made me want to shoot myself.

'What are you going to do?'

'Pay him the money, what else? Can't run away from what I always wanted to do,' she said, 'Anyway, this was supposed to happen one day. How long would I have carried on with the charade of tolerating Ganpat?'

'You are rationalising all this,' Jai said.

She sighed deeply and said, 'I promise I won't be saving Tejinder Singh Malhotra anymore.'

'And I promise I will undo this damage one day,' I said.

✧

Chapter 5

'WILL YOU SNAP OUT OF IT?'

'What?'

'Being this bloody Devdas!'

'I'm not,' I said.

'Okay. Let me think. You've averaged close to six pegs and five beers a day for the last three weeks. We need a lawnmower to remove your beard. Everything needs to be told to you at least twice to break through some kind of sound barrier. You sit in the bookshop ignoring your regular customers. You haven't read a book in . . .'

'You have to grow out of certain things in life.'

'Who says so?'

'Your new best friend, Devi Mathur.'

'Look, what happened was terrible. We screwed up. There isn't a thing in the world that we can do about it. And this . . . this onslaught of horrible things that you are doing isn't going to change it one bit,' he said.

'We *screwed up*? Jai, I destroyed that woman's life. Again. In some ways, I have damaged the lives of Madhuri and Anjali too.

And you call that screwing up? Let me give you some perspective. Missing a train *is* screwing up. The courier service guys losing my consignment of books *is* screwing up. What I have done isn't in the same league, is it?'

'So, there's a question of degree. But what you're doing right now is messing up your life. Or at least your liver. You have a responsibility towards your life.'

'Life? There isn't a bone in my body which has escaped being hurt. Look at the way I walk with this limp! I hate my birthdays. Because it means another year and another accident. Someone who knows every single thing about my past says I am going to die in a few months. I am on a crazed journey of destroying the lives of women I have loved and who were living quite happily without me. The one woman, who I thought loved me, has found someone else. And that's the life you want me to have a responsibility towards?'

'What about your parents? You are responsible for their happiness,' he said softly.

As if on cue, my mobile phone rang. It was my mother. I had been disconnecting calls from my parents for a few weeks. What Jai said made me pick up the phone.

'Sameer? Thank god! Are you all right? Where are you? And why haven't you called or picked up the phone even once? I keep calling Bakthavar and Jai. They say you're not around! Where are you?'

There are only two things that my father very openly gave feedback to my mother about: 1) Put less sugar in the tea and 2) Give people a chance to answer your first question before you go for the the follow-up. Both these criticisms were royally ignored by her.

'*Aai,* I'm at home,' I said. My father and I had learnt to answer only the last question in her tirades.

'Catch the next train or bus and come home,' she ordered.

'*Aai*, I've got some work here. I'm calling an author for a booksigning next week.'

'Do you remember the time when you had typhoid? In your first year of engineering? Do you remember calling me from the hostel? Do you remember how you had sounded?'

'Yes.'

'You sound like that now. Your father had rushed to pick you up then, but his back has hurting again. So you will have to catch the bus yourself. I want you here tomorrow morning and I am not going to listen to anything,' she said and hung up.

I looked up at Jai who was dialling a number.

'Two tickets for Akola. Volvo,' he said into the phone.

◇

'Did you have typhoid again?' my mother asked me as we entered the house.

'No,' I said.

'Something really wrong between you and Maya?'

'*Aai*, can we have some water before the interrogation, please?'

'You don't have to be sarcastic with your mother,' she said.

'Okay. So can we please have some water?'

'Remove your shoes. Shantabai has just mopped the floor.'

Shantabai, who had been the maid in the house since before I was born, looked at Jai shyly with her cataract-infested eyes.

'Sameer dada has really grown up,' she said.

'Yes. I've even changed my colour,' Jai said.

I shook my head at Jai.

My father walked in gingerly. He wore a huge lumber belt around his waist that covered most of his torso and hips. Over the years, the belt had grown in size. In the last decade or so, my mental image of my father came with that damned belt.

'Hey Baba,' I said.

'Your mother worries too much nowadays, doesn't she?'

It was his way of telling me what he, (not my mother), felt.

'I'm sorry. Been busy of late,' I said.

'Dadu used to be busy during these days of the year,' he said referring to his brother, my uncle, the late owner of Sathe and Sons, Booksellers.

I said nothing.

'How are you, Uncle?' Jai said.

'Jai, you've forgotten us,' my father said.

'Can't. You caught me peeing on your neighbour's flowers. It's an unforgettable event,' he said.

They laughed at some memory which I wasn't part of. I had asked Jai several times about it before. But he had refused to divulge anything. My father laughed whenever I asked him anything about it.

'It's the refrigerator water,' my mother said walking in with a tray with two glasses.

'Look, I'm sorry. I should have called or answered your calls. But you two don't have to behave as though the sky has fallen,' I said.

'You heard him,' my father said to my mother.

'Yes. And that makes me even more worried,' she said.

'Here we go again,' I sighed.

'I have been talking to Maya and she seemed to be in perfect shape! Wonder what will happen after their marriage? How can she sound so happy when you look so miserable? How can she tell me . . .'

'Wait, wait,' I said and (for the first time in my life), asked her to go back to the start of her volley of questions. 'What did you say first?'

'How can she sound so happy?'

'You've been talking to Maya?'

'Everyday!'

✧

We were sitting on reclining chairs on the terrace of the ancient Sathe family house, overlooking the breathtaking sight of the terrace of another ancient house hung with clothes like flapping cadavers, chillies spread to dry at their feet.

'She talks to my mother every day,' I said.

'Apparently.' answered Jai. 'But your mother, I am sorry to say, can exaggerate at times.'

I raised an eyebrow.

'Her talking to your mother doesn't mean they chat like long-lost sisters. For all you know, she might be cutting off your mother's call after a few sentences.'

'Are you suggesting that she is rebuffing my mother?'

'Not exactly, but something like that, yes,' he said with a shrug.

'I'll wring her neck for that!'

'What would *you* do if you were in her position and your ex-boyfriend's mother called you everyday?'

'Ex-fiancé,' I said.

'Okay. A matter of degree, again.'

'On second thoughts, I will wring *your* neck.'

'I'm just saying your thoughts aloud. I know you are scared to even think them,' he said.

'If she can talk to my mother, why can't she talk to me?'

'Beats me! The fact that she dumped you five months back might have something to do with it,' he said.

'That, and her total dislike for my best friend,' I said.

'Oh, we got along like a house on fire.'

'Not even a brick on fire,' I said.

'Focus, Sam, focus. It was never about me. It was always about you,' he said.

'You think I should call her and ask her why she has been rebuffing my mother?'

'You might end up grovelling,' he said. 'And I think you should focus on finishing your list.'

'I'm done with that nonsense, Jai. Some hack told me to do idiotic things. I didn't even pause to think it through,' I said.

'He isn't a hack! Have you forgotten the gory details he knew?'

'No, I haven't. But it's turning out to be something else now. These women . . . they have lives which are just fine without my intrusion. Many of them never liked me. And I'm messing up their perfectly normal lives.'

'From what I have seen, their lives weren't exactly the stuff of Mills and Boon romances,' he said.

'Just forget it, Jai. I am resigned to what might happen some months from now. *If* that's going to happen.'

'Resigned? This isn't some bloody job that you decide to *resign* from day one. You could be resigning from your life,' he said, his eyes bulging to twice their size behind the glasses.

'Nothing you say can make me sway,' I said.

'I know that rhymes, but it's still stupid,' he retorted.

'Let's assume for a minute that what Babaji said was true. That I am really going to die a few months down the line. What should I rather be doing? I don't think anything can stop death. So why not spend the last few months of my life with Maya? Even if that involves a little grovelling, who cares? Maybe spend time with my parents, my best friend, my bookshop, my weird assistants. Why should I go on spreading my misfortune to all those women?'

'Because one of them is going to save you,' he said.

The very next day, Babaji came back into my life.

✧

'Sameer . . . Sameer!' I heard my mother's voice the next morning.

'Aai, go away,' I mumbled.

'There's a man at the door. He says he has to meet you. He is strange . . . in a divine sort of way.'

'What?'

'Says you call him Babaji,' she said.

'Are you joking, Aai? Did Jai tell you something?'

'What? No. What's going on? What is Jai hiding?'

'Okay, okay, Aai. Just stop,' I said, getting out of bed. I had had a surprisingly peaceful sleep in my old bed.

I dressed quickly and rushed downstairs to the living room. Babaji was sitting in my living room with a beatific smile on his face.

'Here he is,' he said.

My father turned towards me. There was a stunned expression on his face. I dreaded what Babaji had told him. As though reading my mind, Babaji shook his head.

'Sameer, you never told me you have turned to prayer! This friend of yours tells me you have started believing in god. You are following his advice,' my father said.

'Well, I wouldn't put it that way, but yes, I have prayed more in the last few months than in my entire life,' I said and hoped Babaji wouldn't utter a word.

'Would you care to come to my room, Babaji,' I said. I knew it sounded ridiculous to address a man of my age as Babaji, but I didn't know what else to call him.

'It's upstairs, on the right, isn't it?' Babaji said following me out.

'I believe you're having second thoughts about what I had told you to do,' he said as he sat on my ancient, study chair.

'Who . . . who told you?'

'Nobody has to tell me anything,' he said with a smile.

Right. I had forgotten *that.*

'I am rethinking the entire thing,' I said, evading his brilliant eyes.

'You will not repent not doing it,' he said. 'There won't be any time. You'll have to say goodbye to you parents and friends before that, though. Are you willing to do that?'

'I don't believe you,' I said, desperately.

'I'm no one in this entire quest. I am like the boatman who carries people to the shore but that's generally not their final destination. You will have to choose between life and death, my son.'

My son? There was no denying the magnetic power he had over people around him. It was as though he was the only one speaking, the rest of us were just reacting to what he had to say.

'I know you've gone through terrible pain in the last four months. And I won't promise that there is none in the future. But you will have to take the journey.'

'Why are you so keen on that?'

'Because I want that terrible thing beaten,' he said.

'What terrible thing?'

'Death,' he said.

I thought over everything Babaji had said long after he had left. Two questions were jumping around in my head like crazed monkeys in a cage: How had the man travelled all the way to where my parents' home? Why had I promised him that I would resume my quest?

✧

'Boss, did you read the manuscript?' Baki asked me the moment I entered the bookshop.

'What manuscript?' I asked distractedly. I recalled the sheaf of pages he had given me a fraction of a second after I said that.

'*The Wondrous Journey*?' he said with hurt clouding his eyes.

'Oh yes, I am sorry, Baki. Really sorry. I couldn't find the time.'

'Okay, boss, no problem,' he said and walked away, his shoulders drooping.

'He's been waiting to pounce on you all these days,' Pinky said, blowing an impossibly large bubble.

'He told you about his novel?'

'I've read it.'

'And?'

'I'll leave it to you to decide,' she said.

'Look, Pinky, I appreciate what you and Baki are doing for me at this tough time. I couldn't have expected even my siblings, if I had any, to do that for me,' I said.

'You're welcome, but I don't exactly know what you mean there,' she said. 'I'm going to write the greatest bestseller the world has ever seen and what better place to keep my writing cells active than working in a bookshop?'

'I don't recall seeing you write anything, ever,' I said.

'That's because you don't see many things, boss,' she said. Everybody seemed to have decided what I was, or wasn't, capable of.

'By the way, Maya dropped in a couple of times. She asked me what was going on.'

I actually wanted to hear that she had told Maya everything. Better her than me. I looked at her expectantly.

'I told her nothing, if you are wondering. I told her she should ask you herself. She said she had and that you refused to answer her. Why?'

I shrugged. Pinky looked at me as if she was looking at someone who had a foul smell. She walked away.

◇

The first time I had seen Maya was when she had walked into the bookshop with a strange request. It had been a busy day, as in, as busy a day can be at Sathe and Sons. People make plans to shop for dresses or shoes, but not books. They step into a cozy bookshop if they happen to pass by. And many pass by on the weekends. Saturdays were the best days for sales. Pinky and Baki loved books and that helped, especially when someone asked Baki for any fantasy novels, or asked Pinky for some vampire books. They came into their own on Saturdays.

Despite it being a Saturday, my ears pricked up when I heard a woman say, 'Do you have the '52 edition of *The Old Man And The Sea*?'

She had her back towards me. I was attending to a customer, but I looked at her. She had lovely hair. Quite tall, even without her high heels. Baki was attending her and from the look on his face which I could see, I knew she was stunning. Baki made that face whenever he spoke to beautiful women. He whispered something to her and pointed at me. She turned and walked up to me. I was wrong. She wasn't simply stunning, she was the most stunning woman ever to walk into my bookshop. Period.

'He says you are the owner and I should talk to you,' she said with a smile.

'Well, the owner is no longer in this world, but I can certainly help you,' I said.

Her eyes narrowed but the smile didn't leave her face.

'A friend told me you can get some First Edition Books here,' she said.

'Amongst other things,' I said.

'What are the other things?'

'You'll have to discover that,' I said.

We smiled at each other.

My Uncle had been a collector of first edition books. There were few such people in the city and from time to time, I met some customers who wanted such books. Mostly old men. So it was a surprise to see her ask for an old book. I got her the fifty-two edition.

'This is for my father,' she said. I loved the sudden twinkle in her eyes. 'You've made my day.'

There weren't many people in the world whose days I could make.

'Don't you read?' I asked.

'Oh, all the time.'

'Well, you're most welcome here,' I said and thought it sounded totally offkilter.

'What I meant is, you can come any time, like many others, to read books,' I said.

She laughed a little and said, 'My friend told me about you too.'

'And your verdict is?'

'In time,' she said.

I liked that answer.

She walked into the bookshop the very next day and placed *Middlesex* by Jeffrey Eugenides, *The Glass Palace* by Amitav Ghosh and *Atonement* by Ian McEwan on the counter. This was the first time someone had picked up a combination of three of my favourite authors.

'This is incredible,' I said, 'For the first time a customer has chosen my number two, three and four authors together.'

'Who is the first?' she said leaning on the counter.

'Stephen King. So to complete the order, I will throw in one of these,' I said pulling out a copy of '*It*'. 'For free. Coffee?'

I had no clue where that last word came from. There was no correlation with the sentence preceding it. I knew it seemed desperate and dreaded her answer.

'Yes,' she said.

We ended up having coffee every day for the next two weeks.

I wasn't very good with women. Some of my loser classmates in the engineering college used the beneath-me attitude to hide their 'loser-ness'. If asked why no woman ever expressed even a remote interest in them, they would put on that attitude. They would come up with gems like – 'You know I really don't care to talk to women. All they want to talk about is silly things like what the milkman told them in the morning, what they did with their mothers, what clothes they bought and some such drivel.' I knew for a fact that these guys would gladly give up their lives if any half-decent-looking girl even hinted at talking to them about the milkman or their clothes.

I had no delusion about where I belonged. I was a loser. The limp in my left leg added to the overall effect. And like any other self-respecting loser, I believed girls didn't talk to me because *I* wasn't ready to compromise my conversational values. It took us band of losers' years to understand that there was basically no difference in what we talked about and what women talked about. If girls talked about milkmen and shopping and what they did with their mothers, all we talked about was how many beers we could guzzle without stop and tell tall tales about our childhood escapades (beating up ten guys single-handedly). After growing up we had nowhere to hide, so nobody mentioned the real reasons why girls never showed an interest in us. At least the girls that mattered.

So, with that kind of baggage, I had no idea why someone like Maya Saxena would like me. She was this uber-cool woman who followed the latest fashion trends. She had an MBA from the Indian Institute of Management, worked with the biggest, meanest, richest, highest-paying investment banking firm, drove a high-end sedan, lived in one of the classiest apartment complexes in Mumbai. I could count many more reasons to conclude that she was way out of my league. Sameer Sathe and Maya Saxena couldn't, shouldn't, ought not to be together. But we *were* together.

I don't exactly remember when I felt that I more than liked her. When I asked her, she told me she had liked me when we met the first time. It would've been fair to say we glided into love rather than fell into it. After the couple of weeks of coffees later she called me and told me it was her birthday and she was going to throw a little party and it would be great if I came over to her place.

Every single loser cell in my body told me not to go to her house. I knew Maya would say hello to me, ask me to feel comfortable after introducing me to a couple of guys (maybe some fellow recovering losers) and off she would go. I would meet her again only when I was saying goodbye and thank you.

I was wrong.

I picked up a little bouquet of flowers on the way to her house, which I found very funny. What was the point of giving someone flowers on birthdays? The poor flowers were chucked into the bin the very next day. It was as if your wishes were disposed off too. I would much rather leave the flowers where they belonged – on the plants. But I didn't want to look like the only moron in a crowd who didn't bring flowers.

I reached her apartment a good forty five minutes after the party was supposed to start. I knew she wouldn't be waiting for me with baited breath. I told the security guard where I wanted to go and to my surprise, there was no buzz outside her apartment. For a moment I thought she had whisked away the entire crowd to some place and I was too late. But since I was standing in front of her apartment, I decided to go ahead and ring the bell. I knew she wouldn't miss me if she had shifted the party.

To my great surprise, she opened the door.

'Are those for me?' she said, probably wondering why I was looking so stunned.

'Oh yes, they didn't want to come along, but I dragged them,' I said.

She laughed, took the bouquet and invited me in. A middle-aged man was sitting on the expensive couch. He stood up when I walked in.

'Sameer, meet my father,' she said. 'Dad, this is the man I was telling you about.'

There was a little buzz in my head. *This is the man I was talking to you about?* What was she telling her dad (!) about me? 'There is this man who manages a bookshop and . . .' Even I would've trailed off telling a story about myself.

I shook hands with her father.

'Maya tells me you own a bookshop,' he said with a warm smile. Yup, that's the thing about me. And then the trailing off.

'Actually, my Uncle bequeathed it to me,' I said.

'Have a seat,' he said and we sat on the couch.

'Maya, this might sound a bit weird, but did I get your invitation right? Or rather, did I get the date right? Don't tell me your birthday isn't today?' I said.

She laughed and said, 'No, no. Today is my birthday. My father and I have a rule. On my actual birthday we don't invite anybody. I generally have the party a day before. The party goes on into the wee hours and so technically, it still is on my birthday.'

I felt a sudden upsurge of emotion. It was as though I was the luckiest, most blessed man in the whole world.

Her father knew a great deal about books. I had bragged to many people that I was yet to meet someone more wellread than me, but I thought between Maya and her father, they could prove me wrong. It was the best evening I had had in years.

Later that night, I said goodbye to her father. She walked me out to the foyer. And walked with me to the lift. When the lift arrived, she stepped inside with me.

'Thanks for coming,' she said.

'Thanks for the loveliest evening,' I said.

'None of the guys I know would have liked to have my father around.'

'You were around too,' I said.

She smiled a little. When we reached the ground floor I stepped out of the lift. Before the lift door could close she held out her hand. There are many ways in which girls hold out their hands. One of them is the most beautiful and she held it out that way. Our fingers touched for the briefest of moments. It sent shivers all over my body. We smiled. The lift door closed. I stood there for a long moment before walking away.

'You were around too?' I thought I had blown it away with that line. But something in her smile before the lift door closed told me that perhaps I had not.

She was an incredible woman. I meant it in the way I would if I came to know that Aishwarya Rai owned the collected works of Dickens, Hemingway and Faulkner and loved them too. Maybe Aishwarya Rai does. It would make her the most incredible woman, wouldn't it? When I told Jai about this analogy, he said what I meant was beauty with brains. I agreed, though it sounded a lot cruder to say it that way. That line of thinking – she likes me! Oh my God, she likes me! – made me terribly nervous.

It was perhaps more than a year later (Maya would remember the exact date) when it happened. It started off as any other highly looked forward to, exciting meeting with her. We were having dinner at one of her favourite restaurants. And we ended up ordering a lot of wine. Maya was plain pathetic at drinking.

'Do you like this?' she said.

'It's an excellent place,' I said looking around the restaurant.

'I am not talking about this dump, you fool. I mean this . . . this thing we are going through,' she said. Her voice was delightfully slurry, as if I was listening to the porn star version of her.

'Yes, I am just loving it,' I said looking into her dreamy eyes.

'I've never met anyone like you ever, Sam,' she said.

There weren't many people who called me Sam. It was just Jai before her. And it sounded fantastic when she said it.

'You're someone who can make me laugh,' she said. 'Promise me you'll do it forever.'

I looked at her and sensed a sudden realisation in her eyes that perhaps she had asked for something far bigger than what the words literally meant.

'I promise you, Maya. Till the time you have all your teeth and your laugh is as beautiful as it is today, I will make you laugh,' I said. She giggled. I had a strange feeling this was the way she had laughed when she was a teenager.

'And you can rest assured because no one else has ever laughed at my jokes,' I added.

'That's what makes this so special, isn't it?' she said.

I looked at her as if it was the first time I had seen her – the way you look at someone who could be a significant part of your life. She had lovely brown eyes. The most beautiful, even teeth I had ever seen. She was exceptionally tall, almost my height. And yes, I couldn't not notice, a great body behind those clothes.

There were non-physical things about her that I loved too. For the last three years, she had travelled on weekends with a bunch of people in *khadi* clothes to the villages surrounding Mumbai and volunteered to teach kids English and mathematics. I had accompanied her team once. It was the most uplifting experience of my life watching those kids surround Maya as though she was their fairy godmother. What I liked was that she never made a big deal out of it.

Things moved pretty fast after that. We officially became a couple. As in, my parents knew, her father knew, our friends knew, some of my regular customers knew, Baki knew. She had lost her mother when she was a little girl. This might sounded outright mean but she didn't make a big deal out of that either.

My parents weren't typical people. At least I didn't think so. By typical I mean, I didn't think they were the kind of people who would nag me about an engagement and marriage and subsequent procreative responsibilities.

So when my mother spoke about me and Maya becoming a single entity, I couldn't understand the violent reaction it caused in me.

'The other day I was thinking March would be a good month. Even your father agrees,' my mother said.

I knew what she was indicating and the shock made me go quiet.

'Did you hear?'

'I wish I hadn't,' I said.

'What? Anyway, do you want to do it here in Akola or in Mumbai? Many of our relatives are in Mumbai itself. So we would prefer to have it in Mumbai,' she said.

'Aai, I think you and baba should come here more often. But don't even think about engagement or marriage or some such nonsense,' I said.

'Nonsense? What in the name of God are you talking about? You think what me and your father did was nonsense?'

She had gone on and on about it. I had listened with as much patience as I could muster and I had hung up after throwing an angry tantrum. Of course, I had called her back and listened to the same stuff once again. I had told her that I would think about it. I even promised to talk to Maya about it. When she still wouldn't stop, I had disconnected the call.

So when Maya brought it up herself, I was flummoxed.

'When do you intend to ask me about it?' she said.

We had stepped out in the interval of a movie and were in the popcorn and coffee queue. When I thought about it later, I realised there was a reason she had asked me about it then. She must have been absolutely frustrated because I hadn't picked up any of the signals she had sent my way at places much better than the queue for popcorn. We were sandwiched between a middle-aged woman who was in a big hurry and was pushing me with her huge bosom, and a teenager who was more interested in staring at Maya's.

'Yup, large or medium popcorn for you?' I said.

'It's not funny anymore, Sam,' she said.

'Okay, hit me with it,' I said.

'When are you going to ask me the big question?' she said.

'Do you want to remember me asking you while this pimple-face stares at your breasts and the human bulldozer behind me wants to crush me with hers?'

'I would take it here rather than not have it at all,' she said.

I was quiet for a few moments.

'The queue's moving, Sam,' she said. 'We don't have much time before we reach the coffee counter.'

It put a lot of pressure on me. She looked at me as though she would cry if I didn't. I wanted to ask the kid to divert his horny gaze to some other woman's breasts and I wanted to snap at the woman to stop pushing me. But I couldn't imagine doing these things before I asked her the question. So I did, ignoring the ache in my left leg.

'Would you like to spend the rest of your life with me?' I said.

'I'll have to think about it,' she answered primly.

I looked at her in shock. There was a faint smile hovering at the corners of her mouth. But she couldn't hold it back and burst out laughing.

'Yes, you moron. I would!' she said.

I held her hand and kissed her on the forehead.

'Would you two lovebirds mind taking your nest somewhere else?' the woman behind me said.

'Don't you think you're going to burst if you put any more food in that body?' I said.

Then I turned to the kid.

'I will pull your ear in front of this entire crowd, like your mother used to do just a few years back, if you don't stop that ogling,' I said.

The kid was so scared he actually stepped out of the queue and disappeared.

'That's my man. One of the things I fell for you is your valour in the battle against little boys and pushy women,' Maya laughed.

'You forgot old men,' I said.

I generally didn't understand Pinky's reactions, but I got her expression completely when she looked at me as though I had said something foul when I told her I couldn't tell Maya what I was going through. Maya and I had shared something beautiful once.

That night, I didn't sleep at all. I imagined me and Maya five years into our marriage. She had lost all her wonderful muscle tone. There were crow's feet at the corners of her eyes. She had developed worry lines (she would say they were laugh lines, but I would disagree), the last time we had had sex was on our anniversary eight months ago. I had put on a six-month-pregnant paunch. My hair was receding at the temples. My accident-prone body was taking bigger blows every year. And then I saw something that made me sit up in bed and switch on the light. There were two kids who were squealing and crying, fighting, breaking things.

I did have a feeling that something was more than wrong with me and all those accidents. I was yet to meet someone who had more accidents than I did and although I seemed to heal except for the scars and the limp, on average I had spent at least two weeks every year in the hospital. There were no comebacks for me though. I had already popped the question. The lady had said yes, and that was it.

✧

Babaji's visit to my house kind of galvanised me back into action. For once, I wanted to finish something I had started.

The next woman on my list was responsible for saving my life.

'So where would she be now?' Jai said.

'I was kind of hoping that she is still part of the faculty,' I said.

I called my four years in the Engineering College the missing years. For the first seven months of our first year, we were ragged non-stop by the seniors. It was a vicious circle. The seniors were ragged when they were in first year, and it was considered perfectly normal to mete out the same terrible treatment to the new batch. We were in a meat grinder, getting butchered, both physically and emotionally. Some of the kids, we were still seventeen or eighteen, couldn't bear it. Some ran away. Some lost their sanity.

On the first day of our initiation in the meat grinder a senior told us about the suicide. Every year, one of first-year students tried to commit suicide. The bastard said six out of the last eight attempts were 'successful' and laughed. . He said it was the safety valve, because after the suicide, the pressure was let off and the ragging eased. He asked us to have a look at each other very carefully, as one of us was the safety valve for our batch. The sadistic bastard had laughed after that. The only wonderful thing I remembered from my first year was Professor Angela Jacobs.

'Why don't you call her?' Jai said.

'Is this going to be the norm? Every time you ask me the same question, *"why don't you call her?"* Call her and tell her what?'

'Okay, won't ask you again. So do you have any other bright ideas?'

'I'll meet her in the college,' I said.

'Boss, will she remember you?' Pinky asked.

'I doubt it. It's been nine years since I graduated. And I wasn't a memorable student.'

'Why don't you take a picture of yourself with all these women after you are through with them? Also, you can ask them to write just below the picture that what you are saying is totally true. So when you go to the next woman on the list, you will have solid credentials,' Pinky said with a smile.

'Thanks for that. Why didn't I think of it before?'

'You're just too close to the problem,' she said.

✧

When I entered the hallowed grounds of the best Engineering College in western India, I was reminded of the countless nostalgia-inducing novels about the protagonist's escapades during his or her college years. Those novels are loaded with stupid, downright inane, everyday antics that some guys are engaged in, like sipping vodka or smoking dope or bunking classes. I find them very amusing, because the life I had, and I am sure the life most people had within those walls couldn't be less dramatic and forgettable. I enjoyed the antics, we all did, but there was nothing worth celebrating about it.

I had an overwhelming feeling of being in cliché-land. The first thought that came to my mind was 'nothing has changed'. I paused for a few moments, gathering the courage to walk up to Mrs Jacobs' cabin. I believed she was one of those freaks of nature who look more beautiful with age. She could be the mother of two and wear her motherhood with exceptional grace. She would still be the most wonderful thing in the life of a first-year student.

I entered the alley that housed the staff cabins. This was a path less trodden for me. I had visited a professor's cabin only a handful of times in my four years. Half of the professors during my time were demented and you wouldn't want to be alone in a closed place with a sadistic nutcase. Some of the professors were standing outside. Students were talking to them deferentially. I recognised many of them. But they didn't remember me. Which was just fine. This wasn't a bloody trip down memory lane.

I stopped in front of Mrs Jacobs' cabin. After knocking a couple of times and getting no response, I pushed the door and entered the cabin with my heart thudding. It was empty. I decided to wait for her and sat down on a chair. Her desk was as neat and clean as I remembered, but the cabin was austere. I had a strange feeling that something beautiful, something that once made this drab eighty-year-old staff cabin almost alive, had deserted it. That was when the door opened and a woman stepped in.

Standing up, I said, 'I am waiting for Professor Jaco . . .'

I couldn't complete the sentence.

The woman who stood in front of me *was* Professor Jacobs. In the worst possible way. She wore thick glasses, which coupled with the layers of fat she had acquired, made her look like a giant bug. There were dark circles under her eyes that were magnified by her glasses.

'Sameer Sathe?' she said.

I was speechless. It couldn't be. This caricature couldn't be the most beautiful thing I had ever seen in the most violent year of my life.

'Yes Ma'am, how are you?' I said in a voice I had trouble recognising as my own.

'This is a surprise, and I am fine, thank you very much,' she said coming around the desk.

'I'm sorry Ma'am. I didn't . . .' I trailed off.

'You didn't recognise me, right?' she said with a smile. When Maya had said she couldn't meet me anymore while I was in hospital she had smiled the saddest smile I had ever seen. I was reminded of that smile now.

'I am a bit surprised you remember me,' I said.

'Why?'

'There wasn't a more forgettable guy than me.'

'That's something you can't decide, can you?' she said leaning back in her chair, 'And you haven't changed at all. Or rather grown up at all, I must say.'

I was glad her biting sarcasm was still intact.

Smiling, I said, 'You are officially the millionth person to say so.'

'Person? I doubt there are too many men out there who would say this to you. So I must be the millionth woman. I am impressed,' she said, and laughed. I thought there was a terrible bitterness in her laugh.

My instinct was to walk away. She was like the faded, distorted copy of a beautiful painting. But Babaji's face flashed in front of my eyes.

'Ma'am, I am in a desperate situation and need your help,' I said. She listened to my story without betraying her surprise. When I finished, she said:

'Oh, you're most welcome to my house!'

I looked at her in disbelief.

'Surprised?'

'Very much. I had thought I would be sitting here, pleading all day,' I said sheepishly.

'Ah, but there is something I need from you too,' she said.

I made a quizzical face.

'All in due course of time. So, come over this evening.'

◇

'She just said yes?' Jai said.

'Yup.'

'Makes me a little uncomfortable.'

'A welcome change in my luck makes you uncomfortable?'

'This seems a little too easy, Sam. Have you investigated her a little bit?'

'Investigated? Do you have the number of Sherlock Holmes?'

'I am an accountant and anomalies distress me. We are expecting a lot of resistance from these women for your bizarre request. Someone saying yes, with a "most welcome" thrown in the mix, is an anomaly I find most unsettling,' he said.

I shook my head, 'I think she is basically a good human being who wants to help a former student.'

'Just close your eyes.'

'Oh come on.'

'Do it!'

I did.

'Now recall the faces of Madhuri, Anjali and Devi when you told them what you wanted them to do. Done?'

I nodded.

'Now recall the face of the teacher,' he said.

The excited face of Mrs Jacobs' *did* seem a little strange, I had to admit.

I opened my eyes and said, 'You have to learn to be positive, Jai.'

'Learn to be positive from you? You got to be joking,' he said. 'And remember what Maya told you once about your waves?'

I did. Maya called my sudden outbursts of enthusiasm and subsequent lows of melancholy, waves. I had told her I could be bipolar with extreme mood swings. She had told me not to confuse stupidity with a disease.

'To hell with the waves. Maya is gone from my life and she's taken the waves with her,' I said.

'I think you need to let go of your delusion. Maya is right here,' he said.

'What?'

'She is always the second person with you when you think you are alone. And she is always the third person when we're together,' he said.

'You sound as though you and I are married,' I said.

'Focus, Sam, focus!' he said.

'Focus my ass.'

'When I look at you, I feel as though I am reaching you through a transparent Maya. She is wrapped around you all the time.'

'You are completely losing me,' I said, fully knowing what he was saying: I *was* wrapped up in Maya. I still felt her presence, woke up at nights wondering if she had fallen off the bed. I smelt her perfume – the one I had hated when we were together.

'By the way, have you called her and grovelled?' he said.

'No.'

'I thought you were most eager to do it.'

'I thought better of it,' I said.

'Now *that* is a wave,' he said.

Calling up Maya and telling her about the hell I had gone through in the last few months was an overpowering thought I had fought hard against. I often wondered if she ever felt like talking to me. Was it once daily? More? Less? Did she pick up her cellphone, twist her lips in the severely cute way she had when she was going through a dilemma, dial my number and then disconnect?

Mrs Jacobs, not Maya. I corrected my mental image.

'Mrs Jacobs has invited me over this evening and I am going. Nothing can change that,' I said.

'Yeah. Just be careful, okay?' he said.

I felt overwhelmed by his concern.

'Okay, okay . . . don't start a new wave,' he said.

The way it all panned out, I wanted to kick myself for not listening to him.

✧

I reached the address given to me by Mrs Jacobs. It was an apartment complex and her house was on the eighth floor. The lift wasn't working, so I had to climb all the way up. The dislocated hip still gave me trouble and I was sweating and puffing by the time I reached her flat. Perhaps the pain blinded me to the very obvious darkness on the floor. There were four doors almost touching each other like any typical, cramped, Mumbai apartment complex. It was so dark that I couldn't read the numbers on the four doors. I waited to give my eyes an opportunity to get used to the gloom, feeling the silence, not the kind you feel in an empty temple, but the deserted graveyard kind.

After a while I could see the number she had given me on one of the doors and I rang the bell. It didn't ring. I pressed a few more times and then knocked on the door, first softly and then a little loudly. I had to wait for five whole minutes and ten knocks before the door opened, just a crack. I waited for a few moments more and then pushed it open. I saw someone, most certainly Mrs Jacobs, walking away from the door down the narrow hallway. There was no light inside the house. I felt a little queasy when a fetid smell assaulted my senses.

'Mrs Jacobs?' I said. My voice echoed in the house. When she didn't stop, I walked in and closed the door behind me, although some deep-seated instinct warned me to keep the door open.

Trying to shake off the unsettling vibes I was getting, I followed her receding form. The foyer led to a living room where a solitary candle added to the murkiness.

'Sit,' she said.

She was sitting in a reclining chair. The light of the flickering candle cast a long, wavy shadow of her on the wall. I sat down.

'You have already lived with three other women,' she said.

'Yes,' I whispered. Strangely, her voice didn't echo at all, while mine bounded off the walls like a banshee.

'Why is it so dark? Is the power off?'

I thought I had seen lights on the lower floors.

'I still have power, just of a different kind,' she said. This was quite unbelievable.

'How was it?' she said.

'How was what?'

'Living with them?'

'Well . . .' I had no clue where this was going. 'It was distressing.'

'Here, it won't be so,' she said.

'Okay,' I said, trying to suppress the overwhelming desire to bolt.

She didn't speak a word for a long time. The only sound I could hear was the rhythmic drip of water emanating from the bowels of the house.

'Mrs Jacobs, I am thankful for what you are doing. I know this is very inconvenient, downright bizarre. But there is a very good reason why I am doing it . . .'

'Do you still apologise non-stop?'

'Sorry?'

'There you go again!'

'Well . . . what surprised me was the "still" part,' I said.

'The enduring memory I have of you is of a backbencher who stared vacantly at me, and said sorry too many times,' she said.

The first time I had seen her, I had been on the verge of crying. The so-called ragging had degenerated into something far more vicious. I had been slapped ten times on the first day of my stay in the hostel. For me, getting slapped was right up there in the humiliating things. The twisted, grinning face of the senior who had slapped me haunted me for months. Many seniors had slapped me after that and the number of slaps increased, but I could never forget the face of the first guy. The second night of my life in the meat-grinder, a senior had asked me to sit on the windowsill of my room and told me not get up till he was back. I hadn't dared to budge. The senior had returned the next morning and slapped me because I had slipped from the windowsill after dozing off some time in the night.

There were a lot of stories about the brutality, but I could never forget what happened to my room-mate who was a quiet Hyderabadi with a stammer. The seniors asked him to recite Sanskrit hymns. If he stammered, they slapped him. When they were tired of slapping, they had got a fly swatter and hit him on his balls every time he faltered. He had cried and they had beaten him mercilessly. It had gone on for a large part of the night. My room-mate didn't speak a word for the next month; his father had one day arrived, helped him pack his bags and had taken him away. I had got the room all to myself, but I could never forget him.

It was the day after my mute room-mate had left that I had seen Mrs Jacobs for the first time. I had been sitting on the back bench, feeling lonelier than before, about to hide my face in my palms to cry when she had entered the class.

I hadn't been able to take my eyes off her for the next forty-five minutes.

She was angelic, just like her name – Angela. There was a strange glow on her skin. When she smiled, one couldn't help but forget the most terrible pain and smile with her. Her voice had a mesmerising quality that could transport you to a trance-like state. She was breathtaking. But like any other seventeen-year old, acne-scarred kid, all I could see were her magnificent breasts.

I had looked around to see every single boy, and incredibly, every single girl, looking at her with their mouths open. What she taught us was immaterial; it was as if she was this messiah sent by God to balance the onslaught of misery we were going through. Her class was the forty-five minute oasis we were granted in exchange for the suffering.

The woman who was sitting in front of me in the darkness of her house couldn't be the same Angela Jacobs who had once saved me from committing suicide.

✧

I didn't realise it, but she hadn't spoken for a long time while I had been revisiting some of my most terrifying memories.

'I knew I would meet you again one day,' she said finally.

It struck me that I didn't know a thing about her current life. Fifteen years back, she had been married to a man who was a genius. He was a professor too, but we never saw him much. He used to closet himself in the laboratories of the institute. The few times we did see him, he had been in the library. We only saw his big curly hair, like steel-wool coils, bobbing up and down behind a pile of books. The students used to call him a *langoor* – an ape. Mrs Jacobs was the *hoor* – an angel. The hoor and the langoor. Although, I was sure, every single guy in the whole college would have gladly become an ape to be with Mrs Jacobs.

'I hope I am not a burden on you, or anybody else in your house, Mrs Jacobs,' I said.

She laughed.

'Didn't you see? There isn't anybody here apart from me and you,' she said. 'But don't you worry. Very soon we will have company,' she said.

I had stopped trying to make sense of what she was saying. I rationalised that perhaps Mr and Mrs Jacobs were in the middle of a massive quarrel, which had led to her losing her bearings for a while. All those years back, they had seemed like such a made-for-each-other couple.

'My husband will return soon,' she said.

I wondered if he was still with the college. Perhaps he had become the assistant principal.

'Now that you are here, there is very little those demonic forces can do,' she murmured and rose from the chair.

This was more than I could take.

'Mrs Jacobs, I am sorry to say this, but I just don't get half the things you are saying,' I said.

'This is the second thing I remember about you. Honesty,' she smiled.

I have been called an escapist, a fantasist, hopeless, immature, juvenile. Even meek. But being called 'honest' was a humbling experience. I had a set reaction to all the invectives. Many of those came from long hours of practice with Maya. I had no idea how to react to being called honest.

'My husband is stuck between this world and the next. There is a rope that ties my heart to him. I am holding on. Soon, I will pull him back,' she said, as if explaining the most mundane thing. 'There is very little time left before his soul is lost forever.'

✧

I couldn't move for a very long time. Everything made sense then. The darkness, the deterioration of Mrs Jacobs, the strange, high-pitched voice.

'I am so sorry, Ma'am,' I said in a whisper.

'You don't have to be,' she said.

'When did it happen?'

'When did what happen?' she snapped.

I was generally very clumsy around grieving people. More often than not, I ended up saying things I regretted. What do you really say to someone who has lost a loved one? Especially, if they are not very close to you and you're supposed to spend a significant time with them in that state?

'When did he . . . transition from this world?'

'It's been seven years,' she said. 'The longest years of my life.'

We sat quietly for a while, with me having a vigourous battle with my better sense about whether I should pick up my bag and make a run for the door. My left leg was aching like it had never done before.

'Let me show you your room,' she said getting up. I followed her, banging my knee into unseen furniture.

She opened a bedroom and for the first time there was light.

'There,' she said.

The bedroom was a shrine to her husband. All the walls were covered with his photographs. One wall had a series of pictures showing the growth of Isaac Jacobs from a toddler to a full-fledged professor. The room was full of things used by him in his lifetime. His shoes, his clothes, his watches, his worn wallet. Even some of his laboratory equipment.

I shuddered a little when I saw what was on the neatly-made bed: a pair of navy blue trousers with the legs spread-eagled; a white shirt with the sleeves spread; a knotted tie neatly placed on the shirt; and Mr Jacobs'old cap resting above the shirt collar.

'Isaac, meet Sameer Sathe,' she said.

I felt something run down my spine. My breathing seemed to have ceased.

'Oh no,' she said laughing, 'Did I scare you? I know Isaac isn't here!'

'Thank God for small favours,' I thought.

'But he will be very soon.'

◆

'Next time you want me to investigate the women we have on our list, do so with a gun pointed at my head,' I hissed to Jai on the phone.

Mrs Jacobs had picked up the items on the bed as though she was helping Mr Jacobs get up. She had pointed at the bed and told me she wanted me to take Isaac's study room for the next two weeks. Then, looking at her watch, she had told me to come for dinner at sharp nine, and disappeared into the darkness of the house.

'Sometimes you've got to listen to your friends. We are good people and have your best interest at heart. We have the experience and the necessary . . .'

'Jai,' I whispered as loudly as I could, 'Stop rubbing it in!'

'I haven't even started,' he said and laughed.

'I am going to kill you,' I said.

'So are you going to flee from the nuthouse?'

I thought about it for a few moments and said, 'Let me see how it goes for the next day or two.'

'Okay. I'm totally scared of spooky places. Every little sound in such places makes me jump. You never know what or *who* is making those cling-clangs.'

'Thanks for making this easier for me.'

'You call me whenever you want,' he said magnanimously.

'I dread that the most,' I said and disconnected.

The room enveloped me in a cold embrace. I thought my breath was coming out in jets of steam, like it happens in sub-zero temperatures. But my body was sweating. I looked all around the room. Mr Jacobs grinned down at me from the walls. I wondered how he had died and what had driven Mrs Jacobs to the state she was in. Should I alert the authorities about it? But what would I tell them? That there is a woman who is still grieving, in the weirdest possible way, seven years after the death of her husband? I was sure they would think *I* needed help.

✧

Thirteen years back, after my room-mate had deserted me, the loneliness in the hostel room had been was my biggest enemy. The ragging had reached a crescendo and one of the diktats from the seniors was that we weren't supposed to be in any other room apart from the one allocated to us. The bastards watched us round the clock and the guys who dared to enter another room were thrashed for a long time by the psychos. I used to stay awake the whole night, expecting the seniors to barge in and start their torture.

One day, after I had had my quota of slapping, the senior looked at me and said, 'This guy is not going to take it anymore.'

His cohorts had asked me to sit on the bed and to look at them.

'I see rebellion in his angry eyes,' one of them said. 'What are you going to do? Complain to the professors?'

'No, sir,' I said.

'You know what happens to such guys,' the bastard said giving me a rotting teeth grin.

'Yes, sir.' I knew it very well. A guy who had committed that transgression had been paraded naked the whole night in the hostel, a black slate hanging around his neck with 'Responsible for more pain' written on it. It meant the torture of the entire batch was going to be ratcheted up a notch because of him.

After they had all walked out of the room, the overpowering thought in my head was to commit suicide. Killing myself would at least stop the pain in the bloody left leg.

'Sameer Sathe,' Mrs Jacobs said after the heat transfer class had ended the next day. It took me a while to process the highly unlikely event of her calling out my name.

'I will see you after the class in my cabin,' she said. Then she had gathered her papers and walked out of the classroom.

There was an uncomfortable silence in the class after she left. The guys were looking at me with a mix of amazement and anger. The girls just looked with suspicion. I wondered what I had done to add more misfortune into my already overflowing cup of woes. I walked out with a hundred eyes boring holes in my back.

'Please come in,' she said when I knocked on her cabin door.

I went in and sat in front of her. This was the closest I had ever been to her and she was simply stunning. She had the pinkest lips I had ever laid my eyes on. Her teeth were like pearls and when she smiled, the smile lit up the drab cabin.

'What is going on in your head?' she said.

I had expected her to quiz me on my listlessness in the class. About never raising my hand to answer her questions. About staring at her with glazed eyes.

'Did I do anything wrong, Ma'am?' I asked.

'Yes. You have been sitting in the classroom like you don't belong there. Was engineering forced on you by your parents?'

The last thing I remember my parents 'forcing' me to do was when my mother pushed the cereal spoon down my throat.

'No Ma'am. It was all my fault,' I said.

She looked at me for a few moments as though not believing what I had just said.

'Is the ragging terrible?'

I sat there frozen with fear, remembering the terrible teeth and bad smell of the seniors who never missed an opportunity to pummel me. What was I supposed to say to her? The bastards always *knew* who had ratted them out.

'No Ma'am,' I said.

'You're a bad liar,' she said with a smile.

I said nothing.

'I see many of you covered in bruises every day. There are things I want to do to stop this atrocity, but I know it is you people who will suffer more if I step in,' she said.

I didn't realise but I was nodding in agreement. There was a pained helplessness in her voice.

'Will you do one thing every day till the ragging officially ends?' she said.

'Yes, Ma'am,' I said, a cold sweat breaking out all over my body. I believed she was going to ask me to bring some kind of proof to nail the bastards.

'Come and see me every day after the class. Okay?' she said.

I said yes.

✧

At nine in the night I found my way through the dark house to the kitchen. I tried to find the light switch but couldn't.

'I don't need light anywhere apart from Isaac's room,' she said.

'Okay,' I said feeling totally foolish.

'Your dinner is on the table. Wash the dishes after,' she said and walked away.

'Yes Ma'am,' I said to her receding form. I ate alone.

A loud scream woke me up later that night. I hadn't been able to sleep for a long time and had just dozed off. I got up with a start and banged my hand on Isaac Joseph's collection of trophies.

Like dominoes, the trophies fell over each other. Ignoring them, I ran out of the room hoping to locate Mrs Jacobs. There was a different quality to the darkness of the house in the night – it was a solid, black mass.

'Mrs Jacobs?' I said, standing outside a door, which I believed was her bedroom. I heard another scream behind my back. Feeling my way with my hands I tried to reach whoever was screaming. I shouted her name again. After several minutes of banging my accident-ravaged body all over the place, I still hadn't found her. I tried to listen to the sounds. There was no sound in the house. The stink I had smelt in the evening was now replaced by a strange fruity aroma.

I wondered if I was still in a nightmare. However, all my dreams in the last few months had prominently starred Babaji.

'Mrs Jacobs, are you in pain?' I shouted. There was no response.

Somehow I found my way back to the shrine of Isaac Jacobs. I was puffing as though I had travelled miles. I switched on the lights and sat on the bed trying to catch my breath. I looked at the photograph of the dead professor and thought he was mocking me. I could have sworn his face had changed. Gone was the genial, benign smile. It was replaced by this sinister grin, the kind I had seen on the faces of those seniors in the college years ago. I searched frantically for my cellphone and dialled Jai's number.

'This better be good,' he said in a groggy voice.

'I am out of here! There is something terrible in this house!'

'Hey, slow down,' he said, more alert now.

'I will die here if I don't make a run,' I said bringing down my voice to a whisper, afraid that the Late Professor might get offended by my shouting. I told Jai about the screams and how

I had tried to find out who it was and how it took me forever to go all over the house and return to my room.

'What time did you first hear the scream?' he said.

'It must've been half past one,' I said.

'You sure?'

'Yes!' I said.

'Because my watch tells me it is now thirty-five minutes past one,' he said.

✧

I couldn't sleep for the rest of the night. Jai had told me to grab my stuff and get the hell out once the sun came up. He thought we could tell Babaji that this had to be treated as an exceptional scenario where my life was under threat even before the deadline he had given. I kept the lights on the whole night and didn't even look at the 'Darwin's Theory of Evolution' series of photographs of the professor.

'Breakfast time!' Mrs Jacobs stood at the door.

I recoiled as though I had seen a ghost.

'What's the matter?' she said.

'I heard someone scream in the night,' I said standing up, ready to sprint. 'I thought it was you.'

'Of course it wasn't me. I am right here, standing in front of you, all in one piece, am I not?' she said with an offended expression.

'But . . .'

'Breakfast is on the table,' she said, 'Get ready. I don't want to miss my first lecture.'

Against my better judgment and to avoid another visit from Babaji, I decided to give it one more day.

In the college, she was her usual self. There were remnants of the woman she once was. She cared for the students the way she had when I was in college. Although the guys weren't staring at her the way we used to, they were still more alert during her classes than in the moribund spells of other professors.

'You remember the long chats we used to have after the classes all those years back?' she asked.

'Yes I do,' I said. 'And I can never thank you enough for what you did then.'

Thirteen years back, the first time I had gone to her cabin, even the professors had stared at me as though I was entering a forbidden sanctum. I had wanted to scream at everybody to mind their own bloody business. What was all the fuss about? What made her someone who couldn't be approached in a normal way? What was the big deal about her calling me to her cabin?

'How many times were you slapped today?' she had asked the moment I sat down.

'A few times,' I said avoiding her eyes.

'You are honest even when you are lying,' she said.

I hadn't exactly understood what she meant, but I smiled nevertheless.

'So what do you want to do in your life?'

'Not yet decided,' I said with a shrug.

'It has to be something related to engineering.'

'Don't know,' I said.

'You're paying a heavy price here, aren't you?'

I said nothing.

'You are getting bruised and battered in a place where you never wanted to be,' she said with a deep sigh.

It made a lot of sense. Just then Professor Isaac Jacobs entered the cabin.

'I told my husband about you,' she said.

I wished Professor Jacobs good morning and in his endearingly shy manner, he accepted it with a thank you and wished it back to me.

'There is a suicide or an attempted suicide every year,' she said as her husband pulled up a chair next to her.

'I know,' I said.

'You boys are all away from your families and it can be distressing,' Isaac Jacobs said.

'This is what I want you to do every day. Come and spend some time telling us about yourself. Okay?' she said with a smile.

I was overcome with such gratitude that I started to cry. Mr Jacobs stood up and patted my back for a while.

It became a routine after that. For the next three months. while the ragging went on unabated, I visited her cabin every day and we talked. Sometimes Mr Jacobs was there, sometimes he wasn't. She was always there. We talked about everything under the sun during those fifteen minutes. When I told her I loved books, she suggested I do something about it and maybe join the publishing industry.

Saving a life is not only about rescuing people from terrible tragedies like earthquakes or tsunamis. It could very well happen in the drab environment of the heat transfer laboratory.

Nobody committed or tried to commit suicide that year.

✧

'This isn't some kind of payback time,' she said.

I said nothing.

'Just don't leave me, yet. Okay?'

I nodded.

That night the whole drama was repeated – the screams, me trying to find out who it was, not succeeding, sleeping fitfully. By the fourth night, I was used to it. But on the fifth, there was a big deviation from the routine.

I woke up hearing some kind of chanting. First it was a low hum and after a while, it became quite loud. It was interspersed with screams, the kinds I had been hearing for the last three nights. I clutched the pillow so tightly that my fingers hurt. And then I heard something which sent a paralysing chill down my spine. I heard my name, and there was no doubt about it, because I heard it chanted like a mantra. Many times over.

I got up from the bed and screamed, 'Shut up!'

The chanting stopped for a few moments and then resumed with renewed intensity. It was as if something wanted to tell me it would do whatever it wanted to no matter how loudly I screamed.

I had had enough of whatever was going on in the house. I wasn't in a horror movie where the protagonist stupidly carries on believing everything will be fine if he hides under the bed.

I opened the door and screamed, 'Okay, you bastard! Whoever you are, I'm ready. Come out!'

I had come prepared too. I pulled out the big torch I had got that morning and flashed it around the house. Suddenly, the flat seemed like just any ordinary flat, with cream-coloured walls and tiled flooring. I saw a door and knew Mrs Jacobs was on the other side. I walked to the door and banged on it. The chanting stopped abruptly.

'Mrs Jacobs, you need to give up this stupidity,' I shouted.

There was no reply. I waited for a few moments and banged the door again.

'Ma'am, if you don't open this door, I swear to God I will break it down. Even if it means I will hurt myself.'

The door opened.

◇

Somehow I had imagined Mrs Jacobs would be standing there with wild eyes, wearing her torn, blood-stained, wedding dress. It wasn't like that at all.

She was sitting on the floor in the centre of what I thought were pictures of her husband. The pictures of Isaac Jacob had my name written on them in red. What scared the hell out of me was that she was chanting my name.

'Ma'am, if you're listening to me, please stop chanting,' I pleaded.

'Isaac, my love, have you finally found me through the worlds?' she said with a heartbreaking smile.

'Yes I have,' I said, following my intuition.

'I knew it! I knew it would happen!'

'Angela, will you come out of the room please?' I said in a voice barely recognisable as my own.

'You will take me away with you?' she said in a smile so painfully like the one in my memories.

'Yes I will,' I said and held out my hand to her.

She grabbed it with all her strength. I almost cried out.

'Honeycheeks, you have to promise me one thing,' I said.

Sitting in front of her all those years ago, I had heard her husband call her some things. I would never forget the happiness on her face when he called her 'honeycheeks'. Now, she glowed at the mention of that word.

'What is it?' she said eagerly.

'You have to let me go. You have such a big responsibility, don't you? There are so many things we wanted to do. We had dreams of creating great lives out of these students. Are you going to let that dream die?'

She began to cry.

'You have to promise me you will fulfil our dream. You will never turn your back on it,' I said.

She nodded her head: 'It meant so much to you.'

'It still does. Now, hand me the photograph,' I said and raised my hand. She put the picture on my palm.

'You need to sleep, Honeycheeks,' I said and gently pulled her towards me. I picked up the torch and walked her towards the living room.

I made her lie down on the divan.

'You sleep now,' I said. She closed her eyes.

I patted her head. When I was sure sleep had taken over her exhausted body, I tiptoed to her room. The sight inside was saddening and scary. Figurines of demons lay all around the board. The floor was covered with scary, indecipherable markings. I understood what she was trying to do.

I extinguished all the candles, but left the markings and statues the way I had found them. I went back to the living room and sat on the couch. Her sleep was fitful. I didn't move from the couch.

✧

For the next four days, it became the new routine. I interrupted her chanting, trying to bring back her dead husband back to life. In my body. I called up Jai and told him I had decided to stick around with Mrs Jacobs. I told him about what had happened three nights back and how it had become a routine.

'What do you think you are? A fricking psychiatrist? You tell a doctor about her, or tell her folks. I thought she was the only one delusional here,' he said.

'Look, thirteen years back, she was no more a psychiatrist than I am today. She just did what she felt was right,' I said.

'You were so scared of what was going on just a few days back!'

'Yes I was. But I am not now. And I guess I will see how it goes.'

'I think you are trying to repay some kind of ancient debt to her. She did something great for you all those years ago. But what you're doing, though well-intentioned, can be disastrous.'

'You should see her at night, Jai. There can be nothing more disastrous than what she is already going through. I am just trying to remind her of what she was damn good at. She was a great teacher and someone who changed lives,' I said.

'Okay. But watch yourself,' he said.

On the tenth night, I didn't hear the chanting. I waited outside her room for a long time. I peered through the gap between the door's hinges, but I couldn't see the light of the candles. I feared she had done something terrible to herself. Maybe she was sprawled on the floor, bleeding, on the verge of dying. I stopped myself from banging on the door. Perhaps she needed to fight this battle herself.

The next morning, she didn't call me for the customary breakfast. I ran to her room, fearing she had hurt herself. I was about to knock on the door when she opened it and was startled.

'Sameer, where are your manners?' she said and smiled. It was the first time I had seen her smile the way I remembered her.

'I am so sorry Ma'am,' I said. I wanted to laugh.

'Always apologising,' she said.

On the thirteenth morning, I told her that I would be moving out of her house in a day and finally she would be getting rid of the uninvited guest. She said I was most welcome to stay as long as I wanted.

'There's only one thing I want your help with,' she said.

'Anything Ma'am.'

'Can you get some cardboard boxes? There are a few things I need to pack.'

I felt like crying.

✧

Chapter 6

'SO, FOR THE FIRST TIME IN YOUR QUEST, YOU THINK YOU haven't devastated someone's life,' Pinky said as I told my team what had happened.

I didn't react.

'What? Are you waiting for a certificate from Professor Jacobs which says you saved her life?' she said.

'I didn't save her life.'

'Like she didn't save yours?'

'She did.'

'So what's the harm in admitting that you've done something special? Boss, even you are capable of doing something extraordinary,' she said.

'Even me?'

'Yeah, even you,' she said.

'Are you reading some inspirational literature?' I asked.

'No I'm not.'

'She is, boss, she is!' Baki said laughing. 'All the *Chicken Soup for the Soul* copies have dog-eared pages!'

'Were you a rat in your last life, Baki?' Pinky snapped.

'This is the latest thing, Boss. The other day, she told a customer to keep *Ulysses* free of charge because he didn't have any money. She says what goes around, comes around and some act of kindness will happen to her too!' Baki was all excited now.

'What? You gave her which book?' I said, very quietly.

'*Ulysses*, Boss,' Baki said, cowering.

I ran to the shelf where I had kept a copy of the 1916 edition of *Ulysses*. It was probably the only copy which had James Joyce's initials. It was missing. I shouted. 'Pinky! Are you out of your bloody mind? That copy wasn't even for sale, let alone for giving away to someone!'

'How am I supposed to know?' she shouted back at me. 'And if it was so special, why have you kept it on the shelf?'

'Who buys James Joyce anymore?'

There wasn't a safer place in the whole world than the 'J' shelf of Sathe and Sons, Booksellers. I had liked the idea of walking down the aisle and looking at the book that would be on the shelf forever, like an old, kind, neighbour who never forgets to wave at you.

'You're just a complete disaster, Pinky. I don't know why I've bothered to even have you here for so long,' I said with a sigh.

Pinky looked at me as though I had slapped her hard.

'No. Wait . . . that sounded terrible,' I said and tried to approach her.

She raised her hand to stop me from coming any closer.

'That's enough. For your information, the man was about seventy and he told me he had been looking for it for a long time. He had tears in his eyes when I told him the price of the book. An atrocious figure you had pasted on it, calling it a "collector's edition" or some shit like that. I told him he could have it for as long as he wanted and he could return it after he was done reading it. He promised me he would,' she said.

I was speechless.

'Okay, listen . . . I was wrong,' I said.

She waved dismissively and walked out of the shop.

Running after her, Baki turned back and said to me, 'Boss it's my fault. I shouldn't have made it sound the way it did. I will get her back.'

Jai walked into the shop.

'Did I just see our Miracle Lady go out crying?' he grinned

✧

I sat there feeling like a total asshole. My mother's words echoed in my head like a mantra – Sameer, you value trivial things a little too much. Maya used to say something similar too. It was just a bloody book. A damn good book, perhaps the best ever written, but still – a book. Was it worth hurting someone for?

'So Mrs Jacobs is back on her feet, eh?' Jai said.

'She was always on her feet,' I said dully.

'You're snippy today. Were you responsible for the Miracle Lady's walkout?'

'No, the book,' I said.

'Which book?'

'The Book,' I said with an eyebrow raised.

'My god! That stupid bitch sold the Joyce?'

'She isn't a stupid bitch. And she didn't sell it. She gave it away,' I said.

'Hell! That's bad. How dare she do that?'

'It's just a book,' I said.

He looked at me as though I had said something insane.

'Are you sure you're all right? Has your mental imbalance been further disturbed because of the two weeks in the nuthouse?'

'It's still a book, whether I am imbalanced or not,' I said.

A few months back, I would have run out of the bookshop to find the man who had taken my Joyce. I would've fired Pinky, berated Baki forever and snapped at Maya. Now? *It is just a book* – a sentence I never thought I would ever utter. It was something Maya used to say a lot, especially during the last few weeks we were together.

Jai sat down behind the billing counter. There were only a few customers in the bookshop and one of them came up to the counter.

'What do you want?' Jai barked at him.

The customer was a middle-aged man with a long beard – a regular at the bookshop. I mean, as regular as one can be at Sathe and Sons, Booksellers. He came in roughly four times a year.

The man, a little flustered by Jai's tone, placed the book on the counter.

'That's ₹2000,' Jai said without looking at him.

'What? But the price says 250,' he said.

I looked at the book. It was the *Chicken Soup*.

'Today, this is for 2000. You don't like it, go to the next shop,' Jai said.

'This is outrageous!'

'Yes it is. It's my shop and I can sell at whatever price I want,' Jai said.

The man looked at me for help. I just shrugged. He made a big show of being angry and walked out.

'Did you just ask one of my regular customers to take a hike?'

'He was buying this,' Jai said and lifted the book as though it was some dirty porn.

'It's a great book,' I said.

'Great book?'

'At this rate you're going to throw me out of work very soon,' I said.

'Were you ever *in* the business?'

That sounded familiar. I thought about the last time I had had a conversation along these lines . . .

Things had moved pretty fast after me and Maya thought we should spend our lives together. It was as if I was on this bullet train that was carrying me forward with an amazing momentum. In motion, everything was a blur to me. When the train stopped, I stumbled out, breathless, and realised it had been four months since our engagement and Maya and me were virtually living together – mostly in her flat because it was nicer and because, as the owner of my own business empire (collapsing all around me) I could come and go any time, but she couldn't.

One day, she had called me from the office and told me she had a surprise for me. For the rest of the day, I had dreamt of the things she could do with herself and chocolate sauce. Every single scenario was outright corny, and I had loved imagining them. When she had told me she was waiting for me at home, I had practically run up the stairs of her apartment because the lift was too slow.

I had opened the door, believing as usual that she would have left cute notes on the floor, telling me what I had to do ('Just remove your shirt, the rest I will take care of,' etc.). But I saw her sitting on the sofa with a stranger.

'Here he is,' she said in a tone that I heard her use for the first time, a 'trying-too-hard-to-please' tone.

The man was sitting with his back to me. I desperately tried to wipe the disappointed expression off my face before he took a look at me.

'Ah,' the man said rising. 'Maya has told me a lot about her fiancé.'

I tried hard to smile and shook hands with him.

'Sameer, this is Rajesh Bajaj, my friend and colleague. One of the areas he specialises in is publishing.'

I looked at her, a little incredulous. She had told me a few days ago that there was a guy who worked with her who specialised in managing funding for the big players in the publishing industry. She had said that maybe we should invite him over and have a word with him on how to grow the bookshop business. I had laughed at it, thinking she was kidding. Apparently, she wasn't.

'So why don't you tell me a little bit about the business, Sameer?' he said as we all sat on the sofa.

'What would you like to know?'

'What's your turnover? Your profits? What are your growth plans? How much do you intend to make over the next three years?'

'Look, Rajesh, I don't think you really need to do this. You are my fiancée's friend and I appreciate what you are trying, but I don't think this is necessary,' I said, walking out of the flat.

She didn't follow me. She didn't call me either.

We never spoke about it again. I knew she must have felt insulted. She would've had to explain it to her friend, who, in my opinion, seemed like a total schmuck.

Weeks later, she had asked me, 'What do you really want to be?'

'A bookseller,' I had said.

'You already are one. What kind of bookseller?'

'The kind I am,' I said.

'Your Uncle had his reasons to be one. What are yours?'

'Same as his.'

'But then you aren't doing half of what he had done,' she said.

'Well, I admit, he was a better bookseller,' I said.

'You don't have to get angry.'

'I'm not. You have every right to know what kind of guy you are going to spend your rest of life with. But this is who I am. An average bookseller. I am never going to be even close to the guys you spend most of your day with. I will never have a big car or a big house. No fancy designation.'

'You have a business and the least you can do is do justice to it,' she said.

'I don't think so. I think Sathe and Sons, Booksellers is thriving.'

She had shaken her head, let out a sigh and said, 'Why are you so afraid of dreaming?'

Seemed like that conversation had happened a lifetime ago.

Since the time my Uncle had bequeathed me his 'empire of knowledge,' as he used to call it, sales had deteriorated alarmingly every year. We were selling half the number of books he used to sell. Jai repeated his question:

'Well? Were you ever in the business?'

'You're the accountant, you tell me,' I said.

'Maybe we should do something to promote your bookshop. Maybe we can start a discount week. Sell all books at thirty per cent of the cost.'

'That would be a clearance sale,' I said.

'Or maybe we should hire a couple of very good-looking girls as assistants rather than the elf-man and the human raccoon,' he said.

'This is a bookshop, not a boutique. Besides I can't afford pretty girls as assistants. And now you're insulting my employees.'

'Forget it. We'll think of something after June next year, once our *Pursuit of the Saviour* is over,' he said.

'*Pursuit of the Saviour*? That's a catchier title than *Saving Bookseller Sam*.'

'So, who is next on the list?' Jai asked.

I had read countless books and watched numerous movies in which a boy and a girl meet at a place which is as exotic as it can be. Vienna, Prague, Edinburgh, Paris. They have a short one-night, torrid affair, and forever reminisce about it. I used to think it was all a big heap of bullshit, just a gimmick to make a quick buck by showing a lot of sentimental claptrap. That belief was shaken when I met Preeti. And to think that it happened in a city not even in the vicinity of the places shown in movies and novels. It happened in Bengaluru.

◇

When I was in the third year of my engineering course, we were subjected to a pointless requirement of joining a company for a summer project. It was a necessary evil, and had to be done if we were keen on graduating. By that time, I had resigned myself to moving along with the herd. I was a living, breathing zombie, attending soul-numbing classes, paying scant attention to what was happening around me. I was not against engineering. I believed what the daunting textbooks said was priceless. It was the reason the world moved. All those scientists had sacrificed their lives to give us the lifestyle we took for granted. But I could never fathom why it had to be so dull. It had a lot to do with the way the professors interpreted the subject. And how they wanted us to interpret it as a series of arcane facts, which needed to be imbibed like a toddler learning the alphabet.

Most of the kids in the college bought into this interpretation. I didn't have the courage or the energy to argue with the professors and my classmates. I had signed up to be part of the herd when I got into the line to buy the form and spent my father's hard-earned money. I couldn't just walk away from it all. The price was too high. The hardest part of it was the prospect of looking at the disappointed faces of my parents, who had assumed their only son was going to have a life they had forsaken. They never mentioned this explicitly, but I knew it all right.

So I did enough to sail through. I did things that I would remember many years later and hate myself for doing them. Things like attending ninety per cent of the classes, learning every single underlined sentence in the books by rote, religiously copying the readings in the laboratory experiments, wishing the professors goodmorning and goodafternoon and staying just below their radar, and worst of all, stopping reading novels. So when the time came for the summer project, I just closed my eyes and put in my resume. And after the examinations were over, I packed my bags to go to Bengaluru for what I assumed would be another couple of wasted months. They were wasted, no surprises, but I could never forget my journey from Mumbai to Benagluru and my first day in the city.

◇

My father had insisted that I book my tickets in the AC compartment of the train.

'You're joining a company! Your father says you should not worry about money so much,' my mother had told me on the phone.

'Aai, I can't. It's too expensive. And I am not joining the company. I am just doing a project for two months,' I had said.

'You heard me, right? He says if you don't book an AC two tier ticket, he will book it himself and send it to you. So don't waste money. Do as he says,' she had insisted.

I booked the tickets one day before my classmates were supposed to travel to avoid being called a 'poor little rich boy'. Later, when I thought about it, it felt like a chain of events had precipitated my meeting with Preeti. As she would say, it was destiny.

I had never boarded an AC two-tier compartment before. I felt totally out of place, as the familiar second-class compartment crowds were missing. Gone were the wailing and quarrelling children, the persistent stream of hawkers, the families sprawled over the compartment as though it were their living room, and the loud noise. I was greeted by a cold burst of air and silence when I entered the train. I found my berth, pushed my bag under it, ignored my mother's suggestion to lock it and settled down with a novel. It was something I was desperate to do, as I had not read one for so long. The book was *Slaughterhouse Five* by Kurt Vonnegut Jr. I was just turning to the first page when I heard a voice.

'I think you are in my seat.'

She wore a blue denim jacket over a white T-Shirt and jeans – a ravishing combination. The one thing that caught my eye was the little mole on her left cheek. There was a faint smile on her face. 'My ticket says I am in seat number fourteen,' she said pointing at the seat. 'And that's fourteen.'

'Well, I'm sorry. Perhaps it shows this is my first time in an AC compartment,' I said, standing up.

I took my rightful place. She bent down to put her bag under the seat only to see mine.

'You can put it under my seat or I can pull mine out,' I said.

'No, it's okay,' she said and pushed her bag under my seat.

Later I thought it was as though we had shared something even before we knew each other.

She got busy trying to start her laptop. I had resumed my reading and tried not to look at her, which was impossible. She seemed totally oblivious of me.

After a few minutes she had given me a surprised look. I had thought my glances were making her uncomfortable and was about to apologise when she said, 'Are you really reading *Slaughterhouse Five*?'

'Yes,' I said.

'This has to be a first. I haven't seen anyone else reading it in my life,' she said.

'It's a first for me too. I've never seen anyone recognise it before,' I said.

We smiled at each other. She had a cleft chin.

'Student?'

'Guilty,' I said.

'Maybe you shouldn't read it yet then. You can't understand the futility of it all unless you've done it.'

'I understand futility. I'm living it.'

She had narrowed her eyes and looked at me as though noticing me for the first time.

'Aren't you too young to be so cynical?'

'There's no age bar for cynicism, I think. And I don't think you're old enough to call me too young,' I said.

She laughed. Her laughter wrapped you up, like a warm blanket in cold December.

'Well, you're right on both counts. I'm just twenty four. And I've seen kids as young as ten who are more cynical,' she said.

'Where have you seen them?'

'I'm a journalist. A year back, I did a story on the children who work in fire cracker factories,' she said. 'You know, they're just eight or nine years old. I haven't seen more haunted and pained eyes on someone so young, ever.'

I had looked at her without saying anything. She had seemed to be from a completely alien world. She had fallen quiet, momentarily transported to the hell she must have witnessed 'It put things in perspective for me,' she said.

'Maybe I should've thought of taking up journalism. So where are you headed?' I said.

'Bangalore,' she said and told me she worked for the biggest newspaper in the country.

'What about you?'

'I'll be wasting the next two months in front of a stupid computer, trying to write a computer code which will make some machine work faster,' I said.

'*Engineering* student,' she said.

'That's me. So what brought you to Mumbai? Family?' I said.

'My father had a heart attack.'

I had hated myself for possessing the knack of asking unintentionally inappropriate questions.. Was the father all right? Dead?

'He is all right now,' she said as though sensing my discomfort.

'Good,' I said.

'But won't be for long. He drinks like a fish and eats like a hog. And listens to no one.' She looked out of the window for a few moments.

'Sometimes you wonder why people forget what the most important thing in life is. I mean, every doctor we've consulted has told him the same thing. Think about your wife, your daughter, the hell they are going through. He listens to them, nods his head as though he is going to change his ways the moment he steps out of the doctor's chambers, but nothing changes. I think somewhere in his heart he has put his entire life in one pan of a weighing scale and put the bottle in another, and the bottle weighs more,' she said.

'My father smoked at least two packets a day when I was a kid. The biggest fights between my mother and my father centred on those damned sticks of poison,' I said. 'So one day, my Uncle did something great. It scared the hell out of my father and since then he has never smoked.'

'What did he do?' she said leaning forward with her fist on her cleft chin.

'I was ten. My Uncle took me aside and told me we were going to do something very interesting. He fished out the cigarette packet and handed me one. I was horrified but couldn't help wondering how it would taste. He asked me to go ahead, not to worry. I put the cigarette between my lips and he lit the match. He then told me he was going to hold it to the tip of the cigarette and I had to inhale with all my force. I did as I was told. And coughed so badly that everyone in the house rushed to see what was going on. When my father saw me holding the lit cigarette, his face actually turned red. He slapped me hard. My uncle started laughing. My father grabbed his collar and screamed in his face if he had gone mad. My Uncle said something which made my father quit smoking. He said, "like father like son".'

She put her forehead on her fist and laughed till her eyes watered.

'What does your great Uncle do?' she asked.

'He died four months back,' I said.

'I know this means nothing, but I'm sorry,' she said, with a sad smile.

'Thanks.'

'Were you very close to him?'

'I was. He was like this fantastic friend who always understands what you're feeling. He had a great sense of humour and treated life like one big adventure. As my father said – a dreamer who could never understand the practical ways of life. He was a genius though. For all of us in the family, it's a big mystery how he established this little bookshop in Andheri. And he managed to grow it large enough to make a good profit. Another reason I loved him, was that he showed me the wonderful world of books. Nobody knows why he named his bookstore 'Sathe and Sons, Booksellers'. He never married and never had any children,' I said.

'I guess he lived life on his terms,' she said.

'Yes he did. Incredibly, he left his bookstore to me,' I said.

We were quiet for a while. The rhythmic clatter of the train was the only sound.

'So are you married?' I asked and wondered how she would take it.

'I will be after a couple of months,' she said and showed me the ring on her finger. I wondered how I had missed it.

'Oh that's nice. Congratulations,' I said.

'Why that surprised tone?' she said.

'Surprised? No not at all! Why would I be?'

'You tell me?'

'Okay, maybe I am a little. I thought you would be someone different,' I said.

'Different as in, a career-obsessed, commitment-hating woman?' she said.

'You make it sound far worse than what I thought,' I said.

'Because that's what everyone said to me from childhood. Learn to make chapattis. Learn to make *sabjis*. Why do you have to go to Dodhitaal for trekking? Girls are not supposed to do that. Journalism? Why can't you take Arts for your graduation?'

I nodded as though I could understand what she had experienced, but I hadn't.

'So tell me, are you seeing someone?' she said.

'No. I am doing chemical engineering. There are approximately four girls in my class and they find a flask of sulphuric acid more interesting than me,' I said. 'The only night-outs I know of are the times when me and my classmates try to decipher the complex theories written in those tome-like books.'

She smiled.

'Well, I had heard the stories of depraved engineers,' she said.

'The truth is far worse,' I said.

The train stopped at a station. A man wearing a safari suit entered our compartment, plonked his bag on the upper-berth, took out a woolen skull cap, spread the white sheet and sprawled on it. The only thing I heard from him for the rest of the journey was his loud snoring.

I looked at her and knew she was thinking the same thing as I. There was something working for us, as if we were walking on a path together and that something was taking the obstructions out of it. Heck, it had *created* the path we were walking on.

'Do you believe in destiny?' she said.

'No, I don't,' I said, 'I think it is fantasy invented by someone who didn't want to work hard. Someone like me, perhaps.'

'So you shy away from hard work?'

'I would put it this way – I haven't yet found out what I have to work hard at.'

'How will you find out unless you work hard at something? I believe we are all in a wilderness, with no sense of direction and no compass in our hands. The only way we can find out where we are headed is by walking in some direction. Maybe after a long walk, we may realise that we were walking in the wrong direction after all. And then we have to choose some other direction.'

'You're telling me you believe firmly in destiny,' I said.

'Yes I do. I believe there is a higher force at work here. It has already made a decision on what direction we will head into, but it wants us to make an effort to understand. It places these little clues along the way. It's upto us to keep looking for the clues,' she said.

'So are you getting clues that you're headed in the right direction?'

'I am. Journalism is something I always wanted to do. What about you? Any broad ideas about what you want to work hard at?'

'Right now, I'm terribly tempted to quit this engineering course and take up running my uncle's shop,' I said.

'Maybe you should do it then.'

'Can't. The reasons are not as complex as I would want them to be. They are quite simple, really. I can't bear the thought of seeing my parents disappointed.'

She looked at me for a few moments and said, 'Why do I get the feeling you are going to do just that in your life? If we meet, say ten years from now, I think you'll be a successful bookseller.'

I shrugged.

The train reached Bangalore early the next morning. It was a Sunday and I had to report to the company guest house. We alighted from the train and stood on the platform as the crowd bustled around us.

'Well, it was great talking to you.'

'Yes it was,' she said, 'See you then.'

At that moment, I did something I would always question for a long time after.

'You believe in destiny, right?'

She was picking up her bag. She stopped and said with a curious smile, 'Yes?'

'Look, I had a great time talking to you. And something in my head is screaming at me to say this. You might think I am this total psycho, but I can't hold it in anymore.'

'Okay,' she said putting the bag down and folding her hands.

'I was wondering if Destiny wants us to be together. Don't worry, not forever. Just for one day. I'm new to this city. I don't know what I'm going to do once I land up in the company guest house. It's a Sunday – even journalists are allowed to have a day off, right? So why don't you show me your city? And we can keep talking.'

She looked into the distance. I am sure it was a trick of the light and the breeze. She was the most breathtaking sight I had ever seen in my life.

After a few moments of agonising silence, she laughed and said, 'That sounds like a good thing to do on a Sunday.'

'By the way, my name is Sameer Sathe,' I said.

'Preeti Mehta.'

We shook hands.

✧

'So what was it?' Jai asked, 'Didn't it mean enough to either of you to take each other's contact numbers?'

'I've thought about it. We both wanted to ask, but didn't. Somehow it didn't feel right. I think I knew we would never be able to recreate the magic of that day. Maybe it was a way to avoid future disappointment,' I said.

Jai looked at me as though there was something foul on my face. He then looked at Baki and said, 'Hey Frodo, did he just speak your language? Because I didn't get it at all. I bet if I ask you to repeat it, you won't be able to. Now, the key question is, will she remember you?'

'I hope so,' I said, 'And I can repeat everything I just said. I'm sure you wouldn't get it even if I said it a hundred times.'

Pinky Patel had not returned to the bookshop. I had tried calling her up many times. All my calls went to her voicemail.

After my seventh call, I got this voicemail message – 'If you are Sameer Sathe, you are the biggest selfish bastard I have ever met and you can go fuck yourself.' I was stunned to hear it. There must be many people calling her and they would all hear that atrocious message. I wondered if those rough-looking men sent to find her by her father would misinterpret it. What would they do if they thought I had somehow hurt her? It was a question I didn't want to answer. Baki apologised to me every five minutes or so. I got so irritated I told him if he didn't stop doing it I would fire his sorry ass too. When I told Jai what Pinky had done, he asked me for her number.

'Shit! It really says that!' he said listening to the damned message on his phone and laughing. 'I've got to record this and put it on Youtube.'

'Yeah, maybe you'll get four hits,' I said.

'I will be one, you will be two, Baki will be three, who will be the fourth?'

'You have a point,' I said.

'Hell hath no fury like a woman scorned,' he said.

I nodded.

'Have you thought of how you will contact Ms One-Day-Stand?'

'No. All I know is a name, and that she was a journalist,' I said. 'And don't say google. There are a million Preeti Mehtas out there.'

✧

For a while, we said very little to each other in the autorickshaw. It was as if both of us were trying to gauge what the other's true intent was. And then, we both spoke at the same time.

'I'm sorry,' Preeti said laughing, 'Go ahead.'

'No, after you,' I said.

'It's just a stupid question, and you don't really have to answer it. Have you ever been this impulsive before?'

'I don't think I was impulsive at all. I had planned to ask you to spend the day with me five minutes after I met you,' I said.

'Now you're lying.'

'No,I'm not.'

'What would you have done if I had said no?'

'I would have been shattered. I would have wondered why I had asked. And to answer your first question, no I haven't done something as impulsive as this.'

'So what are your top three Most Impulsive Things?'

'Well, I'll have to think,' I said pausing for a few moments. 'Number Three has to be when I was riding my bicycle and wondered what would happen if I did the slide-and-get-up routine they show in movies. So I rode my bike up a big slope and let go. I got the biggest shellacking of my life from my mother when she was dressing my wounds. I was on the bed for three weeks. That was my accident number nine.'

'Number nine?'

'Yes, I'll tell you about it in a while,' I said. 'Second was when I mixed the sulphuric . . . okay, there are these two chemicals you should never get anywhere close to each other. One day I thought, what would happen if I mixed them, and not just a little bit, lots. So I got two big jars of these two chemicals and just poured them in the laboratory sink. There is half a laboratory bay which is still black. Some say they still think something is burning there. And number one has to be this.'

She smiled and looked at me.

'I'm flattered to be your most impulsive thing.'

'You are welcome,' I said. 'My turn to ask.'

'Okay, shoot,' she said.

'How many boyfriends have you had?'

She looked at me as though she had been expecting this question.

'I have asked this to many guys and haven't yet got a satisfactory answer, but why are you guys always interested in a woman's sex life?'

'I'm twenty-one. A chemical engineer. Living in a boys hostel. What else did you expect? And you can't be asking a question to a question.'

She smiled and said, 'Okay. I asked you one, you asked me one. The answer is none.'

'None? You've got to be joking,' I said.

'It's true. The choice when I was growing up was simple. Either books or boys. It was a no brainer,' she said. 'If I'm your greatest impulsive thing, then you aren't all that impulsive, are you?'

'If being impulsive means I do things like disappear for days and return with a big beard and orange clothes, or if it means jumping off a cliff with a rope tied to my waist, then no. I am not impulsive.'

'I've never jumped off the cliff with a rope attached only to my waist. It was also attached to my shoulder,' she said.

She was not from the same planet I inhabited.

I had heard about the great weather of Bangalore and it *was* great. There was a constant cool breeze blowing. Dawn was breaking on the horizon.

'To Ulsoor Lake,' she said. 'I love the sunrise there.'

We sat on the little steps at the lake and watched a breathtaking sunrise. I had seen many sunrises in my life, but none with someone like her. She had a dewy early morning glow, the kind that reminds you of beautiful flowers.

'There aren't many people in this city who know about this everyday wonder here,' she said.

There were a few joggers who were sweating it out in the early morning. A few stray dogs, warming up for another day.

There was a beautiful silence, so precious in a place under the constant assault of chaos and traffic.

'Most of the lakes in this city were constructed by people living here five hundred years ago. It must've taken them so long to make these beautiful places. In the last twenty-five years, many lakes have been wiped out. Some time back I read they constructed a golf course by filling up a lake. Fucking old men passing time by swinging clubs. Pardon my French,' she said.

I sighed a little.

'No comments?'

'I think there is a place and time for everything. The old men liked sitting next to a lake in those times. Old men now like swinging clubs,' I said.

'So that gives them the right to destroy?'

'Maybe not.'

'Do you always take things in your stride like this?'

'I am no one to take these things in my stride. They are way too big for my opinion to matter,' I said.

'I wonder what would happen if that's what everyone thought,' she said.

'I guess we would have more golf courses for sure,' I said.

She smiled and gave her head a little exasperated shake. We were quiet for the time it took the sun to bounce above the horizon.

'Were we having our first fight just now?' I said.

'Maybe,' she said getting up.

'Where to now?'

'I'm hungry. Let's get some breakfast,' she said.

We hailed an autorickshaw, she haggled with the driver over the fare and we were off. There was no space behind the rickshaw seat for our bags and we had to sit next to each other to accommodate everything. I had never been this close to a woman, and she sensed it.

'Do you have to squirm like an earthworm? We're just two people enjoying a ride together. Imagine we're in a crowded bus and you are sitting next to an old woman.'

'That would be taking my depravity to the extreme,' I said.

'So relax,' she said.

I couldn't. It turned out to be a long journey. After the better part of an hour, in which I could hardly breathe, let alone talk, we stopped in front of a restaurant that looked like an old sprawling house.

'This, here, happens to be one of the oldest restaurants of the city,' she said paying the autorickshaw driver and insisting he return the change.

We walked in through a glass door. The image of a a curvy woman holding a food tray was etched on the glass.

'I am not very sure, but this place was built back in the 20s,' she said.

I hoped that they didn't have any ingredients from that era.

It was a busy place and we had to wait a while before getting a table.

'The *rava idli* here is the greatest in the world,' she said, 'I have lived in this city for two years now, but I don't know many things about it.'

'I've lived in Mumbai for a long time. I haven't experienced a single thing those novels talk about it,' I said.

'Maybe that's the way big cities are meant to be. Everyone experiences them so differently. If we go to a village, our impressions might be similar,' she said.

'Have you always been a big city girl?'

'Yes. But I was born in a little town in Gujarat. I hate going back there. Not the place, the people. So much crowd in the house, everyone eating as though it's the last day of their lives,' she said and looked at me, 'Does it sound mean? It's said we have an eternal connection to the place we were born in.'

'That would make the two of us mean, because you eerily chose the same words I use about the place I was born in.'

Though the waiter treated us with slight disdain, I ate the most delicious breakfast I'd had in years. I didn't want the rawa idli to disappear from my plate.

'Here is a choice for you. We could now go to the most obvious place one goes to in Bangalore, Brigade Road, or we could go to St Marks's cathedral,' she said.

'I guess it's a given. Let's go to the cathedral,' I said.

When we were inside the most peaceful place I had been to in years, we spoke practically nothing. A few times, our hands brushed and it was as if some kind of static electricity was at play. Those were the most enduring memory of that day for me.

I can recall every place we visited. It was as if my receptor senses were heightened. I could remember what I felt at each place, what we spoke about, how she laughed, how her look changed over the day – from a dewy early morning freshness to almost melancholic late evening tiredness. It was when we were sitting in Lalbagh that evening that we confronted what had been haunting us through the day.

'I haven't told you yet, but my fiancé will be coming over to Bangalore tomorrow,' she said.

I said nothing for a while.

'So this could very well be the only day we ever

right?'

'Could be,' she said. She was sitting on the grass, leaning back on her palms.

'It was an amazing day,' I said, 'maybe it would be apt if we don't meet again. Nothing could ever match this, could it?'

'Has anyone ever told you not to lie?' she said.

'Many times,' I said.

We were quiet for a while. I hadn't realised we were holding hands.

We stood outside the garden without saying a word for a while. She came very close to me. My lips brushed her forehead. She stepped back, hailed an autorickshaw and left. After the vehicle disappeared, I realised I had no way to contact her.

✧

Destiny, as she had said all those years ago, did play its part. She was right, I did end up taking over my Uncle's bookshop. She could never come back to say so. Preeti Mehta died four years before I tried to find her.

The cruelest part of her death was that destiny played its most horrific role ever. Nobody knew for sure, but she died instantly when she was travelling on the Expressway between Mumbai and its neighbouring city, Pune. Her car tyre burst, the car turned turtle and she was gone forever. I met her husband who was holding their five-year-old daughter. He told me they had tried for years to have a baby. It was the little girl's dimples I couldn't shake off for weeks after. I was sure her daughter would be told by many she reminded them of her mother when she smiled. For that most fleeting of the moments, she would *be* her mother.

When I told Jai about it, he was quiet for a long time, the quietest I have ever seen him. Baki had tears in his eyes and told me how sorry he was, and he was still sorry for hurting Pinky too.

✧

Chapter 7

WHEN THE CONCEPT OF MORTALITY SINKS IN, IT CAN leave you paralysed. There is this life form, breathing, smiling, laughing, loving, and maybe ninety per cent of what it does are mundane forgettable things, and roughly nine per cent unpleasant things, but it is doing something truly marvellous with that little one per cent, which makes him or her so memorable. One day someone or something, a higher power or destiny or whatever you want to call it decides it's enough, and they are forever gone. I had decided if I ever met that higher force, and going by my impressively escalating record of twenty-eight accidents and Babaji's prediction, this meeting wasn't too far in the future, I would ask it a question – why create when you always knew you would destroy it?

I couldn't sleep for several days. Each accident I had had felt like a lucky escape. A cat has nine lives, I had had twenty-five. All of a sudden, Babaji's prophecy made so much sense. Heck, I felt there was no need for a high-profile soothsayer to predict my final goodbye some time soon. I was going to die in a few months and there was very little anyone could do about it.

As though on cue, Babaji visited me. I wasn't sure if it was a dream or if I was awake and hallucinating. Since we were sitting atop a snow covered mountain, I believed it was a dream. However there was a third possibility – perhaps Babaji had taken me there.

'You think you know death a little more now,' he said. His lips didn't seem to move. He was wearing his normal starched white shirt and black trousers. I was shivering in the cold and thought my tongue was frozen. I nodded as I was sure I wouldn't be able to speak.

'Speak. You can,' Babaji said.

Incredibly, I could.

'Who the hell are you and why are you doing this horrible thing to me?' I screamed at him, and I hadn't even opened my mouth.

He smiled as though he knew exactly what I meant.

'Did you know she was dead? If you did, you are the biggest asshole I have ever met,' I said.

'Me knowing anything is immaterial, Sameer,' he said, 'but *you* need to know it. And not from anyone else, but by yourself.'

'To hell with you and your vague comments,' I said, 'Just leave me alone now.'

'I have never stopped you from doing anything,' he said, 'If you want to stop now, it wouldn't matter to me at all. But at some point, it will matter to you. Remember what everyone said when you were a kid? He is brilliant at starting things, but pathetic when it comes to finishing them.'

He was gone the next moment. I was all alone atop the snow-covered mountain. That was when I woke up.

✧

The next day I pulled out Baki's pages and started reading them. I saw him enter the bookshop from the corner of my eye after

I had read three pages. He was so stunned that he stood at the door for a long time. His eyes were moist.

'Don't give me that look,' I said without looking up. 'It's creeping me out.'

'What look, boss? I didn't even notice you. Or what you are reading . . . uh, *doing*.'

'Did you really write this?' I picked up the pages and flapped them in the air.

'Uh . . . well . . .'

'For God's sake, Baki. It's a simple question,' I said.

'Yes, boss. I have tried writing it,' he said.

'You have *tried* writing it. Hell,' I said, shaking my head and got back to reading.

'Don't worry, boss. I will take care of all the customers today. You don't have to be disturbed,' he said.

'Yeah, I am a regular Michelangelo at work,' I said.

After the tenth page, I had still not made a decision about it. Baki was fawning all over me with his eyes as though I was some errant little boy who had suddenly learned to behave.

'What the hell are you reading?' I heard Jai's voice. Perhaps for the first time, I hadn't noticed him enter the shop.

'It's Baki's novel,' I said.

'God, the man may be dead in a few months and the only thing he can think of reading is the *Wondrous Journey*. If I were you, I would finish off all the books of that Russian man, who was he?'

'Dostoyevsky. And I finished all his books about ten years back,' I said.

'Was it ten years back you told me you wanted to do that? Time sure flies. Which reminds me, I think we need to hurry and find the next woman on the list,' he said.

'No, the first thing I need to do is find Pinky Patel and apologise,' I said.

It sounded so very simple.

✧

Before we could embark on the mission 'Get Back Pinky', my worst fears came true. We were about to step out after deciding to go to her house for a collective apology session, when a big black car stopped in front of the shop. The two rough men, who had visited the shop with obvious intentions of leaving my broken bones in an advanced state of distress months ago, stepped out of the car. They had to be the two biggest men I had ever seen in my life.

'Don't worry, they will have to step over me before they reach you,' Jai whispered in my ear.

'I think it will take those guys three seconds to step on you, and besides you are standing behind my back, so technically they will have to step on me before they reach you,' I whispered back.

'Which one of you jokers is Sameer Sathe?' one of the men with a nasty cut across his bald pate growled after entering the shop. I was reminded of 'Shetty,' the head goon from the 70s movies.

'Sameer Sathe? Haven't seen him in a while. He could be dead, for all you know. Nobody's missing him, that's for sure,' Jai said.

'Shetty' looked at Jai as though not able to decide if it was worth breaking his jaw.

'You are Sameer Sathe,' the other man, who had long curly locks, pointed his finger at me. 'I think we had visited this *raddi* store some time back.'

I was sure my Uncle would have had a heart attack if he had heard someone calling his shop a waste paper store.

'This isn't a *raddi* store,' Baki said, 'We sell new books here.'

'Shut your mouth, weirdo. No wonder bhai is pissed off. His daughter is spending so much time with these freaks,' he said and beckoned me with his fingers, 'Get in the car. Bhai wants to meet you.'

'Is bhai in the car?' Jai asked.

The men looked at each other before Curly said, 'Bhai told us not to hit anybody, but I am very tempted to do so.'

'Don't fall prey to temptation, boys. Remember this when you grow up,' Jai said.

Curly took a couple of steps forward with his eyes spewing fire at Jai.

'Okay, okay. I'll come with you. There's no need to get violent here,' I said with my hands raised in surrender.

Curly looked as if he was a little disappointed.

'I am coming with you too,' Jai said.

'No. We only need him.'

'Are you guys so dumb? Don't you see you are getting one plus one free?'

The men looked at each other and shrugged.

'Get moving, *chakko*,' he said.

'That's way too lame. With all that size on you, I had thought you would call us something worse than eunuchs,' Jai said.

'Jai, will you just keep your mouth shut?' I muttered under my breath.

'I don't know about you, but I don't like the way all this is developing,' Jai said.

'It could get a lot worse if you keep blabbering away,' I said.

'I am just a little nervous,' he said.

'I am counting till three. If I don't see you two monkeys in the car by then, I will have to just break your legs and burn this pile of paper,' Shetty said with clenched teeth.

I stepped out of the shop and got into the big car, which was a black Toyota Camry with opaque tinted glass. Jai sat next to me. Curly and Shetty sat in the front with Curly driving.

'Are you guys going to kill us?' Jai asked once the car started moving.

'We would have loved to,' Shetty said.

◇

They took us to a sprawling bungalow right next to the beach. The huge iron gate opened and the car glided to a halt in front of the entrance.

'Get out,' Curly said.

We did. The car moved ahead.

There was another bald man standing at the entrance of the bungalow who beckoned us.

'Do you have a twin brother?' Jai asked him.

'What?'

'I think you look exactly like the man in the car,' Jai said.

Baldy 2 scoweld at Jai.

'Never mind,' Jai said dismissively, 'Is bhai free? I think he asked for an appointment with us.'

I elbowed him hard.

'Follow me,' the man said and ushered us into the most lavish bungalow I had ever seen. My feet sank into the carpet. There were huge chandeliers hanging from the roof, illuminating the place like a theatre. The furniture was all shiny black with velvet cushions. There was a big brood of stuffed lions that looked scarily life-like. The man pointed at the sofa and disappeared.

'Can't we just run?' Jai whispered.

'I think that would be very foolish,' I said.

'Those lions are creeping me out,' he said, barely moving his lips.

'Just the lions?'

A man, wearing a flowing khadi kurta entered the hall. He had the look of someone who was recovering from a rather bad spell of illness. We stood up, my heart was hammering away crazily.

'Sit down, sit down,' he said distractedly.

I looked at Jai with my mouth open and a scream at the tip of my tongue. The man in front of us was the dreaded gangster Usmaanbhai Patel. I had seen his photograph countless times in the newspapers and on television.

'I see you two are shell-shocked,' he said sitting in front of us with a deep sigh.

I remembered the stories I had read and seen about him. One in particular, which told the viewer the gory details of how he had wiped out a budding rival gang. The police had found seventeen bodies in a mass grave, without their eyes and testicles.

He coughed a little into his hand. His voice was raspy, like the sound made by fluttering kite paper.

'I said sit down,' he said, 'Don't make me repeat things.'

We sat down. Suddenly, I wanted to kick myself for overruling Jai's running idea. Pinky had lied to me all along. She wasn't the daughter of a stock broker, unless Usmaanbbhai Patel's impressive list of businesses included dodgy activities on the stock market, which was entirely plausible.

'Pinky, my daughter, hasn't told you about me, has she?' he said.

'No sir,' I said, in the softest voice I had ever spoken in.

He sighed. For a fleeting moment I thought I saw sadness in his eyes. He had a salt and paper beard which made him look like a genial, elderly uncle.

'She says she is ashamed of me,' he said with a little chuckle.

I didn't know what to say.

'Well, I'm sorry to hear that, sir,' Jai said in an equally small voice.

I wanted to choke him to death.

'She is my youngest,' he said. 'She was born after many prayers. I had always wanted a daughter.'

I nodded, not knowing where this was going.

'I don't remember being happier than when I held her in my hands. I had four sons before her, but she was special,' he said and was quiet for a few moments.

'Don't worry, you two are safe,' he said finally.

Jai let out a big sigh of relief and said, 'I can't tell you how happy I am to hear those words, sir. The best words I have ever heard in my life! So can we go now?'

'What would you like to have?'

'Nothing, sir,' I said.

'You own that bookshop where my daughter works,' he said.

'Oh, let me tell you this, sir.' gushed Jai. 'She doesn't have to do anything at the bookshop. Sameer doesn't allow her to even *lift* a book.'

Usmanbhai smiled and asked me, 'Is he your friend?'

'Unfortunately, yes,' I replied.

'You are lucky in more ways than I thought you were,' he said.

I had no clue what he meant.

'My daughter hates me, Sameer. And she thinks the world of you,' he said leaning forward. 'She never wanted to be anywhere close to me since the day she understood what I was and what I had done in my life. I have tried to tell her many times that we become what circumstances compel us to be, but she believes otherwise. In the last one year or so, since she has been with you, I have seen her happiest. I don't know what you have done to her, but I would like to thank you.'

I was speechless.

'She wasn't like this always, Sameer. She was an extremely troubled child. Still is. There was a phase, a few years before she found your bookshop, when I feared I would lose her forever. She got involved with some people from my businesses. Someone taught her how to smoke nasty ganja cigarettes and use drugs.'

He lapsed into a pained silence. The only sound was of his raspy breathing. After several minutes, he seemed to get some control over his voice.

'The people who showed her the road to hell, are all rotting there right now,' he said with the kind of viciousness he was known for. I trembled.

'I confronted her, told her not to do those things. She laughed at me, called me all sorts of vile things. I even locked her up. But . . . but she tried to kill herself,' he said.

Pinky's fierce face flashed in front of my eyes. She had tried to kill herself. It made me want to cry.

'When I saw her lying in a pool of blood, it was the worst sight of my life,' he said and coughed hard into a little napkin he was carrying.

'I have never forgiven myself for locking her up. I have done some terrible things in my life, but this is a thing I will carry to my grave,' he said. 'I am not going to live for long. I have lung cancer. One thing I was so glad to see was the happiness on her face in the last one year. I had thanked Allah for giving me that happiness, and I was ready to face His wrath for my sins.'

I nodded, and knew what he was going to say next.

'But in the last few days, I think fate is playing this cruel joke on me. Rukhsana is becoming again what she was a year back. For the first time in my life, I feel helpless.'

Pinky's real name was Rukhsana. It was a lovely name.

'I don't want to die like this,' he said. 'Now, I don't know what happened for her to leave your bookshop, but I want that to be undone. I have never done this in my entire life, but I have no hesitation in begging you to help her. Please.'

I thought his last word was said with a suppressed sob.

'Sir, I will do everything possible to bring her back,' I said.

'Thank you. Thank you very much. My men will tell you where to find her. She'll be in one of those terrible places right now,' he said. 'Sameer Sathe, I will be forever indebted to you if you could bring back the smile on her face. I will be your slave.'

He got up, coughing a little. An elderly woman entered the hall and walked him back inside. I couldn't move. The most powerful man I had ever seen had crumbled in front of me. Fatherhood is probably the greatest responsibility a man can have. It can make all your worldly power inconsequential. The man who sat in front of us wasn't the nastiest man alive. He was just a helpless father.

Curly and Shetty were standing at the door when we came out. The back doors of the car were open.

'I am not getting into that bloody car again,' Jai announced.

'Are you going to throw a tantrum now?' I said, 'We need to find her immediately, Jai.'

'Hell . . . these guys smell bad,' he said.

'I think, as usual, you are missing the point here,' I said.

'Okay, but you owe me one for this,' he said.

We assumed our positions in the car. Curly and Shetty were very quiet as we moved out of the bungalow.

'Where is she?' I asked.

Nobody answered. I tapped Shetty's shoulder.

'Just shut up and sit,' he said.

'What's your name?' Jai asked.

'I said shut up.'

'I need to tell bhai about the way you guys are treating us,' Jai said.

'Tell bhai?'

'Yes, my dear friend. Your bhai has entrusted us with a big responsibility, that of his daughter. And we expect his dogs to treat us with some respect. Now you don't want bhai to know you guys were unnecessarily mean to us, do you?' he said.

They were quiet for a few moments before Shetty said, 'She is in a disco, and from what I just heard, not in very good condition.'

'Attaboy! Now you are behaving like a trained one,' Jai said and leaned back.

'That was quite smooth,' I whispered in Jai's ear, 'Let's just hope we get to live.'

He shrugged.

After an anxious journey through the frustrating traffic of Mumbai, we stopped in front a very popular discotheque in Bandra. It was notorious for being the den of drug peddlers and addicts. I shivered a little when I imagined Pinky somewhere inside.

When I entered the disc, an ear-splitting noise which was posing as music, numbed my senses completely. The place was bathed in coloured lights. A mass of humanity high on drugs was swaying to something incomprehensible. I tried to look at the faces of the people, but everything looked unclear in that light. I thought I heard Jai's voice. I turned around and my head banged into his. He had been screaming into my ear.

'There's a room back there. People are going in and out,' he said.

We waded through the mass of bodies to reach the room. After what felt like a very long time, we managed to reach the door; it led to a room bathed in red fluorescent light. I could make out human forms lying in various stages of consciousness and undress on the floor. I almost bit my lip, fearing one of them was Pinky. The noise was considerably less in this room.

'Do you see her?' Jai asked me. He still had to shout.

I shook my head.

'We won't be able to find her outside. I guess we will have to wait here for her,' I said.

He nodded and walked up to an empty couch.

I thought the room was the worst sort of wreck you could imagine, was as if the most pathetic place in your consciousness had been physically realised. It was a place you never wanted to visit and could never get out of.

I kept looking at the people coming in, dreading the thought of seeing her walk in and collapse on the floor. People came in and did all kinds of horrible things to themselves. Some snorted white powder. Some injected themselves with syringes. Some smoked. Some used a spoon and a lighter.

'Different strokes for different folks,' Jai said.

I was fast losing hope of seeing her, when she entered the room. I knew it was her because of the shiny silver studs she had pierced her eyebrows with. She was leaning on a guy who couldn't have been older than twenty. His hand was buried inside her T-shirt.

I got up, stood in front of the guy and said, 'I'll take it from here.'

'Who the hell are you?' the boy snapped at me.

'You don't want to know,' I said and pulled his hand out of her T-Shirt.

'Don't touch me!' the boy screamed and tried to hit me.

Jai stepped in and pulled the boy away. Pinky stood in front of me, trying to focus through her drug-induced daze.

'Pinky, let's get out of here,' I said.

'Didn't you hear my phone message,' she said in a slurred voice. I was glad she had recognised me. 'Get the hell out of here.'

'Can we please go outside?'

'No, I won't,' she said.

'Even if I got on my knees and begged you?'

'No,' she said shaking her head.

'Even if I begged you?'

She looked at me with narrowed eyes.

'You'd do that?'

'Yes, I would,' I said.

'Do it then,' she said.

I sprawled on the grimy, smelly carpet and said, 'Pinky I beg you. Will you please come away from this place with me?'

I thought I saw a hint of a smile on her face. She nodded. I held her hand and we waded past the mass of people.

When we stepped out of the discotheque, my ears were hurting.

'Hell, why would anyone want to become deaf voluntarily?' Jai said, rubbing his ears.

The air outside was clammy, but a whole lot better than the fetid air of the disco. I thought she had gained a little more control over her senses.

'Why are you here?' she said, her voice still slurred.

'I am here to take you home,' I said.

'Did my father send you?'

'I would have come on my own anyway,' I said.

'You go back and tell my father he will not die peacefully. He doesn't deserve to,' she said. lurching dangerously.

'Look, we both know I am not going away from here without you. Three choices: We can stand here and fight the whole night. Or I will hover around you inside the disco. Or you can come back home,' I said.

She thought about it for a few moments. Her shoulders drooped. I scanned the place and saw Shetty and Curly standing at a distance looking like two bears trying to pretend they were nonchalant even in the company of humans. I signalled at them and they brought the car to the entrance. I saw a strange kind of respect dawn in the eyes of the two men, as though I had pulled off a miracle they had been trying to accomplish for a long time.

'Abbas, you moron. How dare you bring them here?' she said. Shetty looked back at us and shrugged. I liked the name Shetty better.

I helped her out of the car when we reached the bungalow of Usmanbhai Patel.

'You can't come in,' she said.

'Okay, you will have to promise me one thing, though. You'll be back at the bookshop tomorrow morning.'

'Hell, no,' she said shaking her head.

'There is a very high possibility of my life depending on that. You see, your father would have absolutely no hassles in packing me off to heaven a lot sooner than has been predicted. Also, Shetty here has already threatened to burn down my bookshop,' I said.

'They won't do it,' she said.

'You know these people more than I do,' I said. 'What do you think?'

She stood there with her head down, holding the car. Finally she nodded her head and entered the bungalow.

'That was a job well done,' Jai said patting my back as Shetty and Curly were dropping us back.

'I am not going to burn down your *raddi* . . . uh, bookshop,' Shetty said without turning around.

'I know,' I said. 'But let's not let her in on that.'

✧

The next day, I chewed my nails while waiting for Pinky. I kept seeing this frightful image of Shetty and Curly pouring kerosene all over the shop, lighting a matchstick and burning down my Uncle's legacy. There was no sign of her till noon. I was on the verge of going back to Usmanbhai's den, when she stepped into the shop. She wore a white T-shirt with 'FCUK' written on it in red. She had dark circles under her puffy eyes and looked five years older than when she had disappeared from the shop.

She completely ignored me and assumed her usual position behind a desk. Baki was so stunned that he didn't speak for a long time. He approached her as though he was approaching a raging fire.

'Hey, I'm sorry. But I don't think it was such a big thing that you had to disappear for weeks.'

'Are you apologising or bullying me into forgiving you?' she said.

I smiled a little. She wasn't lost yet.

'No one can bully you,' Baki said.

They actually smiled at each other like long-lost friends. Perhaps they were.

Jai, who had gone to grab something to eat, walked in just then and said, 'Oh Miss Miracle! Great, now we are back to being full strength family again. I have got these wonderful greasy, salty, spicy pakoras. Why don't we share a meal and vow never to be angry at each other?'

He put down the newspaper with the oily pakoras on it. They were steaming hot and looked delicious. I caught her staring at me. She looked away when our eyes met. We ate the pakoras in silence.

I approached her after a while and said, 'You never told me your real name was Rukhsana.'

'Would you have cared?' she said.

'You have a point there,' I said.

'You don't have to make too much of it, boss.'

'I am glad to know you still call me boss. And I need to make too much of it when my fragile business and my life are at stake,' I said.

She smiled and said, 'I won't let that happen. Don't worry. I care for this bookshop too much to put it in harm's way.'

'And the owner of the bookshop?'

'Well the owner thinks he isn't the owner,' she said.

'Pinky, I know there are things we need to talk about. But I guess there is time for that. The first thing I want you to do, and please don't say I wouldn't care, is to see you write. You have been claiming you'll write the biggest bestseller for far too long now. So why don't you start acting on it?''

'I don't know, boss. It was just a ruse that went on far too long,' she said putting her head down.

'Okay, fine. But you have to promise me you will be here from ten in the morning till six in the evening every day,' I said.

'I can do that,' she said, smiling her dazzling smile, 'But you have to resume your quest.'

✧

Before I could embark on finding the next woman on my list, I sat and thought about it all. As in, really sat in a place that had always given me peace – on the beach at night. Alone. The intention was to zero down on one thing most important to me. One thing worth staying alive for. Of course, I had great parents, a great friend and enough books remaining in the world to last me a few more lifetimes. But there had to be something more, something which would make me pick up a weapon and fight Yamraj, the God of death before He plucked me with his sword like a chicken tikka and made the choice – heaven or hell for young Sameer Sathe? And like a distant ship, which looks like a tiny speck on the horizon but starts assuming monstrous dimensions the closer it gets, I realised after three hours of sitting on the beach that there was only one such thing in my life – Maya.

The entire mosaic of the beautiful relationship between Sameer Sathe and Maya Saxena began to crack when the doubts in my mind, those little demons I had unconsciously decided not to even acknowledge, came together and formed a monster.

It was like a level in a video game. You kill a lot of bad guys, cross a lot of hurdles and generally sail through. It's only when you reach the end of the level that you realise there is a big boss and he is damn hard to kill. The big boss keeps cutting you down to pieces and you keep reloading the game from the last save. Every time you start it, you think you are going to kill that bastard. But the big boss kicks your ass again. You have to be determined. And you have to keep telling yourself that once you dispatch this bugger, there is a great new level waiting for you. I had reached the big boss in this level and I had no motivation to slay it. The next level for me was marriage, the possibility of dragging Maya to hospital every year, and crow feet and my impending paunch.

In my relationship with Maya, the big boss reared his ugly head on the day when she said she was desperately looking forward to having babies. At first, I was a little surprised because babies had never figured in our earlier discussions about what kind of life Sam and Maya would live. The way she said it, I had a feeling she had thought about it frequently. It was as if there had been an unspoken 'and' clause in everything we had dreamt of. We will buy a house in two years (and have babies). We will buy a car two months after the marriage (and have babies). We will go for our honeymoon to the Mauritius (and have babies). I was the fool who had never heard the unspoken 'and'. It had frightened me.

'Let's just think about this, okay?' I said to her. We were heading home from a restaurant after dinner and she was driving.

'Think about what?'

'About what you just said . . . babies,' I said.

'What's there to think about? It will be absolutely all right,' she said and honked at the driver in front. She was a borderline maniac behind the wheel. Billie Holiday was singing *Don't Explain* on the car stereo.

'Have you even considered taking me into this grand plan of yours?'

'Grand plan? What the hell are you talking about?' she said looking at me.

'Look ahead, will you? It seems to me you have already made all the plans on this little aspect of our life,' I said.

'How will I do it without you?' she said.

There was a frown on her face. I knew she was very close to exploding. I had a feeling she had always anticipated some kind of extreme reaction from me on this matter and had visualised this conversation many times over. And now when it was actually happening, she had no patience for the preamble and wanted to get straight to the core of it.

'As usual, you are going to postpone thinking about it,' she said.

'Maya, I have no clue what you are talking about. All I am saying is this is a big decision in our lives and we should discuss it with calm heads,' I said.

'Just like all the decisions you have made about your life? By avoiding them?' she said.

'Here we go again,' I said raising my hand and looking out of the car window.

'I know you have "avoided" talking to me about it. And as a result I have avoided talking to you about it. But since it has come up now, let me give you some news. You have avoided every single big decision in your life, Sameer. Your Uncle bequeathed his life's work to you and he must've thought you would make it your own. What have you done? You have even avoided calling it your own shop! Your Uncle is long dead and that shop now belongs to you. You are the owner and you have to manage it like one. *You* need to ask *me* what I would want to do after our marriage. Do I want to work in this stressful job? *Should* I work in this stressful job? You have to take that decision and tell me about it. What have you done? You don't even mention it!'

She stopped talking to curse a scooterist who had veered too close to the bonnet of the car. I was shocked. It wouldn't have hurt more if she had picked up an axe and chopped off one of my limbs. She glanced at me and must've seen something in my expression that prompted her to lower her tone down by several notches.

'I love you Sam, and I care for you in a way you might never understand,' she said, 'but there are these elephants in the room we need to look at and talk about.'

'What are you saying? If I don't look at the elephants, we are not going to have this relationship?'

'No. We have come too far now. I can live with the elephants, but it would be just living. I know you don't want that,' she said.

We were quiet for the rest of the journey home. When she turned the car towards her flat, I asked her to let me out. She said I didn't have to stage a childish tantrum. I told her to stop telling me what to do. She stopped the car. I got out, banged the door and walked away from her without saying goodbye or even looking at her. When I told Jai what had happened, he had said that I had showed exceptional maturity, especially when I walked away without saying a word.

I had never done any skydiving in my life but I had the feeling of being in freefall after that. Everything was so cozy and wonderful and familiar when we were in the airplane. And now suddenly I had jumped from some unknown altitude without even ascertaining if I had the right chute or not.

✧

I dithered long and hard over what to do next after the realisation I had on the beach sunk in. Was it just my ego which made me stop from telling her about the hell I had gone through in the last seven months? Or was it anger at her for not even making an attempt to reconnect? Some memories of what happened after our break-up and how I behaved with her surged through like a bunch of balloons with mocking faces drawn on them. Well, I didn't want to go into the details of what I did then, not when I was going to die a few months later. I at least deserved a little room for sympathy from the one woman who I had felt was going to grow old with me, and not in a sad, irritating-the-hell-out-of-each-other way, but in a holding-hands-while-the-other-shook-with-arthritis sort of way.

I finally decided she was just one step away and I would be anyway going through the incredible pains of explaining everything – Babaji, my disastrous attempts at doing what he had told me to, the mess I had made of those women's lives and what I had become on the other side of this dark tunnel. This period in my life was like the transmogrifier in Calvin And Hobbbes. When Calvin enters the machine, it is only Hobbes who can actually see what he has become when he steps out of it. I wondered if

Maya would have the intelligence of Hobbes, who, incidentally was perceived by everyone as Calvin's stuffed toy tiger. But for Calvin he was much more than that. Like Maya was for me.

The next woman who I had fallen for was pretty easy to find. She was an author who sold truckloads of books in a genre that was a rage – chick lit. The protagonists in those novels were generally women struggling with major issues in their lives – weight problems, unfaithful boyfriends, backbiting in their workplaces. The thrillers section of Sathe and Sons, Booksellers, might have had unsold books, but there had been a time when these chick-lit books outsold all the others.

Although she has never admitted to it openly, (as in, the acknowledgements section in her books did not mention the names of Sameer Sathe or Sathe and Sons, Booksellers), we were largely responsible for the success of Neha Varma, the next woman in my list.

✧

'Neha Varma, the writer?' Jai asked.

'Yes,' I said.

'You never told me you had an affair with a celebrity,' he said in an accusing tone.

'She wasn't a celebrity then and we didn't have an affair.'

'So what was it?'

'It was a give-and-take relationship. I gave, she took,' I said.

'You mean she was one amongst a million people who successfully manipulated you?'

'There aren't so many, although I would love to believe it,' I said.

Baki overheard that bit and said, 'Boss, are you going to reconnect with Nehaji?'

'Unfortunately, I have to. Although I would gladly prefer Chinese torture over it.'

'Painful memories?' Jai asked.

I said nothing. There have been very few moments in my life when I have hated someone. Many people have done many nasty things to me. And I believe I have given it back to them in some way or the other, (Maya would disagree on both counts), but I have never hated anyone. Neha Varma was an exception. I hated her like she had never been hated before. Perhaps.

This was a time when I had decided my four years of engineering were an absolute waste of my already pointless life. I had travelled back to my hometown and told my parents. As expected, they were apoplectic.

'You can take up some other engineering, if you don't like the one you were doing there,' my mother said.

'No Aai, I just don't want to do engineering itself,' I said.

The only sound after that was my father sipping his tea a little too loudly.

'Baba, will you just say something instead of making those grating noises?' I said to my father.

'Have you thought about it thoroughly?' my mother interpreted his noises for me.

'Yes. And I am sorry about wasting your money,' I said.

'Are you telling the truth Sameer? Have you listened to people you shouldn't be listening to? Oh my god! Have you failed in your exams? Is that why you are quitting?' my mother said.

'Aai, don't exaggerate, please. I haven't failed. It's just that I don't like it,' I said.

'Did you hear what he just said? He doesn't like it,' my mother looked at my father. 'So what are you going to do?' my father asked.

'Take over Dadu's bookshop. He left it for me, and it has stayed shut for long,'' I said without meeting their eyes.

My father gave out a long 'hmmmm'. I had learned it generally meant he was okay with what was going on. He wasn't exactly overjoyed about it, but he wasn't going to stop it from happening either.

'Is that all you have to say? Our only son is throwing his life away just like your brother and all you have, is that sound?'

'Dadu didn't throw his life away, Aai. And Baba has said hmmm. I think we can close this topic now.'

For the next two days of my visit, my mother didn't speak to me. She woke me up in the mornings, made tea for everyone, cooked for everyone and did all the things she had been doing for decades, except talking, which, although it sounds mean, was a great relief. On the third day, I packed my bags, touched their feet and left for Mumbai. My father had a little smile on his face and he patted my back a little too hard.

It took me a couple of years to understand the business of selling books. By that time, Sathe and Sons, Booksellers, had hit a downward curve and had never experienced an upward since. I inherited my Uncle's shop, his love for books, his not bad looks (my father says), his weirdness (my mother says), but what I missed out on was his great business sense. He was one of those people for whom making money out of anything was no sweat. He made more than enough with absolutely no effort at all, and unfortunately for me, I made absolutely nothing with all the effort I could manage.

One of the things he had always done was encourage new writers. There wasn't a weekend when the bookstore didn't host a reading club meeting. Countless wannabe writers peddling downright mediocre stuff used to meet in the bookshop, gobble free snacks and coffee and read their 'creations'. I remembered being part of many such events and ninety-nine per cent of those people were pathetic writers. But my Uncle never discouraged them, always gave them a roof under which they could live out their dreams of being 'read'. I continued with that tradition. And in one such group meeting, I met Neha Varma.

One day, while we were in the middle of a reading community's meet, and I was squirming in my seat with the strain of applauding boring poetry and prose, she walked in. She wasn't exactly a beautiful girl. If Aishwarya Rai was at one extreme of the spectrum, and Tun Tun was at the other, she would be somewhere close to the middle, leaning a lot towards Aishwarya's side. What she had was great style. And it showed in the way she dressed, the frame of her glasses, the make-up she put on, the hairstyle she maintained, the way she walked, her shoes, the way she spoke. You had to peel off many layers of carefully built fake characteristics to discover her core, which was just average, really. But it took you a long time in peeling, and by the time you reached her core, it was either too late or it had ceased to matter.

She sat on one of the chairs and pulled out her pages from a folder she was carrying. I am sure everyone felt a sense of something momentous happening when she was there. She could create that magic with her sheer presence. The stupid read-meet suddenly became an event worth participating in. All the guys in the room were eager to make their introductions to her, even at the expense of interrupting the poor bastard who was reading his drivel. The girls were a little unnerved, hit by a primal feeling of being in the company of someone superior. I thought she took all the subtle chaos she had caused with an equally subtle acceptance. Something she was used to, something she had done for long.

It didn't matter what she read from those pages, everyone was enraptured. She had a voice which could hold an audience of thousands in a hypnotic trance. Later, when I tried to recall what she had read on that first day we met, I realised it was ordinary stuff.

After the torture of the read-meet was over, the group leader started profusely thanking me for the bookshop's continued support for young and bright writers and how the bookshop had changed their lives by stocking some of their self-published material that had been rejected by every publisher in the world. I had decided to tell them that I wouldn't be able to do so in the future because the business was struggling and I needed all the shelf-space I could find to stock Arundhati Roy or Vikram Seth or Jeffrey Archer, and not bad writing on bad quality paper by bad writers. But Neha's arrival changed everything.

I was wondering how to chat her up when she walked up to me and said, 'Thank you Mr Sathe for your help.'

'You're most welcome, and Mr Sathe isn't here. My name is Sameer,' I said.

She smiled and shook my hand. It was the softest, most feminine hand I had ever held.

'I am an investment banker and a writer,' she said.

'Pretty similar professions,' I replied.

'Quite. I write about all the horror stories in banking,' she said.

I liked her immensely. Like a moth likes the bright colours of a spider's web.

'I'm writing my first novel and it should be finished in a few months,' she said.

'That's nice, do banking and writing take up all your time?'

She looked at me with slightly narrowed eyes and said, 'They should, but they don't.'

'Good. You're most welcome to spend all your non-banking, non-writing time in the bookshop,' I said.

'Tempting. Thanks,' she said. And walked away.

I had a sinking feeling, and not for the first time after meeting a beautiful woman, that I had said something terrible and she had walked away laughing at my stupidity.

My social life was non-existent. All my classmates from college and school had become either doctors or executives in assorted corporations or had entered their family businesses like selling saris or household goods. If I were to take a sample of all the kids in my school and college for the last ten years, I was sure I wouldn't find a single person who was the owner of a bookshop. I had learnt the hard way that uniqueness isn't always exotic or appealing to the opposite sex. If all the male monkeys could jump from one tree to another without breaking a limb, and one of them decided it was better to climb down one tree and climb up the next, it didn't exactly endear him to female monkeys.

I lived in a house once owned by my Uncle. It was a little hop from the bookshop and considering the miserable time people spent in travelling in Mumbai, it was a divine gift. But it also made me hate travelling. For the first few years, my classmates never forgot to try and rope me into their annual holiday trips. I did go to a few, and regretted the decision the moment we commenced the journey.

Everyone seemed to be fascinated with the technological breakthroughs in digital photography. All of them had cameras of various shapes and megapixels. And everyone had to take pictures of everything. Half of them looked at the place we were in through their camera lenses. If we were in a place that had an ancient statue of a bull, first we would have taken a group photo. Then the guy or girl who had clicked the photo had to join the group so someone had to take one more photo. Then some innocent passer by was harassed to take the picture of the entire group. Then, everyone had to take individual photographs making psychotic faces next to the bull. It was just unbearable. For me and for the bull. I stopped going for these trips.

A week had gone by since I had met Neha and I was sure she would never again visit the bookshop because of my inane comments. Then, I did something which would have been unfathomable just a week before. I called the coordinator of the reading group and told her that if they wanted to make their read-meet a weekly affair, I wouldn't mind it. After all, what was one evening's worth of sales when it was a question of the lives of the aspiring writers. I could sense she was a little surprised, because I had been a reluctant supporter till then. She thanked me and said she would be delighted to rally her troops. Perhaps sensing her sudden good luck, she also asked me if I would be interested in stocking a book one of the members had recently published. In the heat of the moment, I agreed, something I regretted immediately.

The read-meet happened the next Saturday and Neha didn't turn up. I clenched my teeth and sat through the pain. She wasn't there the following week either, and I had decided enough was enough when in the next meet, she walked in. The scenes from the earlier one were repeated, with one exception, she left midway, without even looking at me. I was miserable for the next few days. I hated my big mouth for saying those stupid things and wondered when I was going to learn.

So it was a great surprise when a few days later she walked into the bookshop.

'I've been wanting to come here for a long time, just didn't get the time,' she said with a smile that could stop wars.

'No problem. We managed to live without you,' I said.

She laughed.

'How's the book coming along?' I asked.

'Struggling,' she said with a sigh.

'What's it about?'

'This might shock you, but it is about an investment banker and her problems at work,' she said.

'Rather alien stuff for you.'

'Very.' We both smiled.

'I haven't told this to anyone, and I hope you can keep a secret,' I said.

'Try me,' she said tilting her head.

I told her about the editor-in-chief I knew. He headed the biggest publishing house in the country, was the Bill Gates of the publishing world, and he had said that there was a dearth of great new writers. She was stunned.

'How come you know him?' she asked, 'I mean that in a curious and not disparaging way.'

'I know,' I said. 'He was a childhood friend of my Uncle's and when I was a kid we three used to sit in this shop for hours discussing books. This is not an attempt to show how arty I am.'

'That's wonderful,' she said.

'You keep up with that book. I have heard you in those read-meets, I think it is great,' I said.

'You really think so?' she said.

I nodded.

'I would give anything to leave this shitty job and do something with my writing,' she said.

'You should and you can,' I said.

'Can I send you the chapters of my manuscript? It would be lovely to get your views on it,' she said, actually fluttering her eyelashes.

'I would be delighted to,' I said. And given the circumstances, there was very little else I could have said.

Since that day, she started sending me the manuscript, chapter by chapter. I don't think I did anything spectacular with it, or changed it in any fundamental way (after all it was just popular fiction and not Shakespeare we were talking about), but I believe that in those two months there were moments when she was going through spells of deep doubt about the quality of her writing and needed someone to tell her constantly that she was good, which I did.

We met every three days or so, discussing books and authors over coffee. After the many meetings, I gathered the courage to ask her for a dinner date and to my great surprise, she agreed.

She was great company. She seemed to know everything about everything or at least something about everything. To a guy who knew something about something, that was a very fascinating experience. Later when I thought about it, I realised it could have been palmed off Wikipedia, but the sheer range of her topics made me dizzy. There must've been a very big red alarm going off somewhere deep inside me, but I ignored it completely. I was in the middle of a freefall and all I could do was to enjoy the view. As Maya would say, I was a guy with messed-up priorities, someone who brushed his teeth for ten minutes and finished his bath in two.

Bizarrely, it was Neha who introduced me to Maya. They were colleagues and apparently Neha had been telling her a lot about me. I was all misty-eyed and puppy-faced when I heard that she talked about me to people. In fact I was so dazzled by what she had said that I barely noticed Maya the first time I met her.

One fine day, we finished her novel. And when I say 'we', I really mean it even though she eventually attributed all her ideas and inspiration to the likes of Helen Fielding and believe it or not, Jane Austen.

And one day, she asked me the question. It was only much later that I saw that all the time she had spent with me, all those coffees and dinners, were perhaps all about that one question. I remember it verbatim, because later I analysed it for days and weeks and wanted to kick myself for not understanding something so obvious. She asked me – 'Will you send my book to the editor-in-chief?' 'Of course,' I said. She held my hand in her warm, soft, most feminine hand and rubbed my calluses. We were having dinner at a Versova restaurant and I had this amazing urge to clear the table and take her then and there.

'I like where this thing we have is going,' she said.

'Me too,' I said.

The next day, before I could contact Ramesh Uncle, the editor-in-chief, I had my twenty-second accident. A man driving a car decided he didn't like the way I was riding my bike. So he crashed his big SUV into it. It was like a Sumo wrestler colliding with a malnourished man. Jai later told this story to everyone who cared to listen – apparently, in a drug-induced haze, I was blabbering about being hit by Shahrukh Khan's car. Some people told me in the hospital that it was a privilege to meet Shahrukh Khan's victim.

It was during my spell in hospital that the first doubts about Neha Varma were sowed. There was a big scar on her forehead which I mistook for a worry-line, but later I realised it was her scowling line.

'Couldn't you ride safely?' she said in a voice surprisingly devoid of sympathy. Gangubai, my maid, had shown more concern when she had visited me in the hospital.

'I did. It was the driver of the car who didn't,' I said.

'Your crazy friend is telling everyone that it was Shahrukh Khan.'

'Well, he means no harm,' I said.

'What's the doctor saying, when are you recovering?'

I had a fractured rib, my neck had suffered some trauma. There was a bad head wound.

'Don't know.'

She paused for a while, and I like to think some part of her that wasn't yet entirely evil, made her stop and question what she was going to say next.

'Samir, would it be possible to send the editor-in-chief my novel?' she asked with a sudden smile. 'I know it will be very inconvenient to you, but it would mean a lot to me.'

Of course, I said yes, I would. She dialled Ramesh Uncle's number on her mobile and gave it to me. I spoke to him for a few minutes, told him about my accident, assured him that I was on the path to recovery and in response to Neha's fidgeting, told him about her manuscript. He agreed to look at it. My accident helped her, because Ramesh Uncle said he couldn't refuse Dadu's nephew, especially when he was lying on a hospital bed. He then asked me if it was someone special in my life. The red alarm exploded inside me when he said it, but I ignored it again, laughed sheepishly and said yes. Nobody else heard it, but I thought Neha knew what the last bit of conversation was about.

After that day in the hospital, she met me once. It was to make sure that I had stocked my display shelf with her novel, which, shamefully enough, I had.

✧

'If it ended that badly, why do you think she could be a potential saviour?' Jai asked.

'I have no clue. You need to ask Babaji,' I said. I was a little irritated with the prospect of meeting Neha Varma again.

A while after she dumped me, I heard she had hitched up with some long-haired painter who smoked what looked like weed cigarettes. It took me longer to recover from Neha Varma than from the twenty-second accident.

There were moments during my convalescence when I had decided to call up Ramesh Uncle and tell him to trash the bloody manuscript and that I was sorry to have sent him something so terrible. To my bitter surprise, I got a call from him one day and he was totally gungho about the manuscript. He went to the extent of calling it the best writing and ideas he had seen in the last five years. For the briefest of moments, I thought of invoking the relationship he had had with my uncle and asking him to discard the manuscript and the writer, but I couldn't bring myself to do it. What she had said reverberated in my head – it was her dream to get out of the shitty job and do something with her writing. To my mind, there isn't a bigger crime in the world than trampling on someone's dreams, so, feeling like a creep, I made the right, excited noises while Ramesh Uncle was going on and on about what a great discovery I had made.

I had also decided to confront Neha and ask her why she had messed me up. But when I thought about it a little deeply, I realised there was nothing she had done which could be classified as a crime. There are countless laws for all kinds of crimes. You do a little shoplifting or break a traffic signal you end up paying a heavy price for it, but there is no law that punishes people who break others' hearts. If they analysed the true reasons behind suicides, I am sure they would discover broken hearts. And to think that it was a crime committed by every other person in this world, was staggering. That was when I remembered Devi Mathur the most, because I was the criminal then and I had lived happily, without feeling the slightest remorse about walking away from her. Maybe there was some kind of divine justice in the way it was playing out: A heart for a heart.

One day I bumped into her on the beach. She had rolled up her jeans, had her sandals in one hand and the weed-smoker's hand in the other. It was a beautiful picture, and I wanted to kill them both in the most horrible manner possible. To add to it, she looked right through me. As if I was as non-descript as the trash floating on the surface of the sea. I felt the blinding pain in my left leg. I limped my way back home.

For weeks after, I imagined torturing them, making crank calls, wearing a hooded T-Shirt and stalking her, tripping the weed-smoker, or some such. The worst part of all my imagined revenge was that it was always preceded by an image of Neha and the weed-smoker in the throes of passion.

Jai was saying something. I shook my head and brought myself back to the present.

'I said I understand you are all cranked up with the prospect of meeting her, but do you have a plan?' Jai repeated.

'I think she's going to call the police the moment she sees me,' I said.

Neha Varma had become a big name in the world of publishing. Her books were outselling Jhumpa Lahiri's by a ratio of fifty to one. A couple of awful movies had also been made based on her books, although everyone, including Maya, seemed to disagree with me. They pointed out the super-hit status of those movies which was hard to argue with. There was even talk about a third film starring Aishwarya Rai and Hrithik Roshan. To my great dismay, her books were a rage outside the country too. In the West, she was considered the first true commercial success from India in a long, long time.

'I have an idea,' Jai said to me the next day. 'I found out she's going to be at Wordlovers in Andheri for a book-signing session. Why don't you corner her there?'

If the intention of the curse on me was to make me go through hell, it had already been accomplished. I was faced with the ordeal of meeting my most hated person in my most hated place. Wordlovers was the biggest bookshop chain in India and they were partly responsible for bookshops like my Uncle's losing a large chunk of their business. Apart from my own ineptitude, of course.

✧

'What are you wearing?' Jai asked me when we hailed an autorickshaw to go to Wordlovers the next day.

I was wearing the only hooded T-shirt I owned.

'I've never seen you wear this rag. What is it? Your slasher costume?'

I said nothing.

'You are going to behave, right? Focus, Sam, focus.'

'Can we please get moving now?' I said with an anger that surprised me.

'Yup, the man is coiled like a snake. Let's go,' Jai said.

When we reached the Wordlovers bookshop, there was already a considerable crowd inside, largely made up of girls – adolescent girls, teenaged girls, girls in their twenties, girls in their thirties, girls in their forties and some girls in their fifties and beyond. They were all holding copies of her latest book in their hands. The shop was abuzz with excited chatter. There was a large banner that said 'Wordlovers welcomes Neha Varma – the "bestest-selling" author of India'. I wanted to shoot the man who had created it.

'You're getting that look, Sam,' Jai warned.

'Don't worry, I'm fine,' I said.

'I've got a bottle of water, do you want some?' he said.

I nodded. He uncorked the bottle and gave it to me. I drank as if I hadn't had water for days.

Then I saw her. She was sitting at a table in front of a pile of her books. She was signing the books offered her by tongue-tied girls. There was a smile on her face, and I couldn't help wonder how the hundreds of people in the bookshop could not see that it was a fake.

'We'll have to buy it,' Jai said.

'You don't have to buy it,' I said.

'What? And miss all the action when she looks at you?'

We picked up a copy each and got in the queue. There were fifty girls in front of us, talking relentlessly. All her books had a recurring character of a woman in her early thirties, an investment banker in her day-job. I thought it was a great idea when she came up with the first couple of books, but from the third onwards it had become stale and now I thought she was flogging a dead horse. But the girls were loving it, the film producers were loving it, *Maya* was loving it. It was like this great universal joke that everyone was part of and I was the only doofus who was yet to get it. It must've showed on my face, because a few girls looked at me and whispered something in each other's ears. Later when I asked Jai about it, he said it could've been because my face had had the expression of a diabetic patient having a stroke.

My heart hammered away as she disposed off one girl after another. She had great flair, the way she opened the first page of the book, the way she fluttered her fake eyelashes, said something cutesy to the simpering girl and wrote 'With Love' on each book before signing it – an act developed with great practice. There were countless scenarios running in my head. Many of them had her proclaiming that this man, Sameer Sathe, was responsible for all the success she had achieved. Some less intense ones had her losing her bearings, making some mumbling sounds of apology and running away from the place. Penitence was the common emotion in all the scenarios. All of them ended with me smugly throwing the book in the dustbin and stepping out of the shop while stunned people wondered who I was.

The way the scenario actually panned out couldn't have been more anti-climactic.

After she had packed off the girl in front of me, she looked at me. I was ready to bask in the 'gotcha' feeling and I almost made that face with the humourless smile.

'Well, hi! How are you?' she said chirpily.

When I thought about it, I felt sure that there was a tiny moment when her façade had slipped. Jai disagreed.

'Uh . . . good,' I mumbled. I wasn't prepared for this.

She took the book from my hand and opened the first page with the same flourish.

'What's your name?' she asked.

Throughout my life, I have been either speechless or I have talked too much. I have never stuttered. The state I was in after she asked me my name can be safely called stuttering. Neha Varma was responsible for many firsts in my life.

After a few moments of listening to my serial gasps, she dropped her eyes to the book, signed her name and handed it back to me.

'All the best!' she said and dismissed me with her eyes.

Jai tapped me on my shoulder. When I didn't move, he pushed me a little. We moved on in the line.

'What the hell happened to you in there?' he asked me when we stepped out of the bookstore.

'I . . . I . . . she asked me my name,' I said as though it was the most amazing sentence I had ever uttered.

'I saw that. I thought you guys were close once,' he said and looked at my face, 'Oh shit. Okay, don't say it. I don't want to hear. She has already *forgotten* you.'

'Forgotten me?' I said.

Jai snapped his fingers in front of my eyes.

'Your eyes have officially glazed over,' he said.

It took me several minutes to recover. And when I did, the overwhelming feeling was of anger. Intense and I hated to admit it, impotent. I looked at the book in my hand and flipped to the first page where she had signed her name. I wanted to tear every page of the book. Cut each one of them into a thousand pieces. Burn them all and piss on the ashes.

'I am throwing these books in the dustbin,' I said.

'What? No way. We paid 300 bucks each for these,' Jai said.

'Jai, it's either me or the book,' I said.

'Oh, come on! I know you. I don't know the book yet to make a fair judgment.'

I looked at him with clenched teeth, snatched the book from his hands, stormed back into the shop and made a big show of throwing them both into the dustbin. I stepped out of the shop and took a deep breath to calm myself.

'Are you through with the reality show called child's play, or are there any more episodes remaining?' Jai asked.

'Shut your bloody mouth and let's get the hell out of here,' I said.

'Yeah, okay. This episode is called "The Ignoble Exit."'

I started walking down the street. After ten minutes of walking, two things hit me. The first was that she had not written 'Love' above the signature. That could only mean one thing – she *had* recognised me. The second was that I was walking in the wrong direction.

✧

'I think you are reading too much into it,' Jai said.

'Right. She wrote the word 'love' on roughly five hundred books today, but not on mine. I think the odds are in my favour,' I said.

'If you were in her place, you would have done the same thing to a man who seemed to be having an epileptic seizure. And will you please stop that human-pendulum-like walking?' he said.

'Jai, are you on my army or hers?' I said.

'There is no war going on here. Our objective has to be how to make her allow you to spend two weeks in her house. There is no point in discussing for hours what she meant when she didn't write one damned word,' he said.

I said, 'I think you have a point.'

'Great. Now let's evaluate what our options are,' he said.

Before we could go any further, Baki walked up to me and said, 'Boss, do you promise not to kill me if I tell you something?'

'What is it, Baki?' I said.

'I have her bracelet,' he said.

'Her what?' I said.

'Nehaji's bracelet. You remember?'

The memory of 'the bracelet' came back to me in a flash.

I got up from the chair and walked up to Baki who cowered as though I was going to lash out at him.

'Baki, my dear, you have just given me the only bright moment in the last so many days.' I almost hugged him.

✧

The story of the bracelet went back to the time when I was seriously toying with the idea of taking the names Sameer and Neha in the same breath. There was a beautiful rhythm to it, especially when I said it aloud in the confines of my bedroom. Like the way your friends talked about a happily together couple – '*You know, the other day I just bumped into Sameer-and-Neha. He was smiling and she was glowing.*' Or '*The other day I saw Sameer-and-Neha hold each other's hands. He whispered something to her and she laughed. It was so lovely.*'

Some of my regular customers, who were in fact my Uncle's regular customers, told me I was suddenly smiling a lot, that I was asking them about things I had never bothered to in the past. There was some kind of a positive, happy aura around me. I just told them I had started doing yoga.

I called up my folks and I actually told my mother I loved her. She was a little nonplussed about what I had said and was rattled when I told her to tell my father that I loved him too. She pestered me for a long time, asking whether I was all right.

One day Neha barged into the shop and screamed my name. The customers were stunned to see a sobbing woman with her mascara splotched all over her cheeks. I ran to her and held her.

'What happened?' I said.

Interspersed with wretched sobs, she said, 'I lost the bracelet.'

She had lost her mother to a prolonged and extremely painful battle against cancer. There were moments when I had thought all her values, her beliefs, her whole being even, were the subset of her mother. And when she had died a few years back, it was as if Neha had lost her soul. The bracelet was a gift her mother had given her just before she died. Apparently, it was an antique, and was believed to have been custom-made for Neha's great-great-great grandmother, more than a century-and-a-half ago.

I gently pulled her to the little store room I had in the shop. She hugged me. I patted her. She raised her face and kissed me. It was the most intense kiss of my life. I felt her grief, her desperate desire to be comforted, and it made me incredibly happy to know she had chosen me to do it.

'Will you help me find it? I was here yesterday,' she said.

She wore the bracelet a week before every anniversary of her mother's death.

'Of course I will,' I said.

We started from the front of the bookshop. There wasn't a shelf, a corner, heck there wasn't a book I didn't turn over to find the bracelet. When we couldn't find it, we traced back her day and searched every place she had been to. We still couldn't find it. When I dropped her back home, she had walked away without even looking at me. I had theorised then that the grief had finally made her angry at losing the heirloom, and she was taking out her anger on the person she loved. I had forgotten that I was never good at theorising.

'So you are not going to kill me?' Baki said.

'You have given me the opening I wanted, Baki. But how do you have it?'

'You remember you had messed up the bookshop completely when you were trying to find it?' he said.

It wasn't a proud moment in my life, but I hated to admit I was ready to do anything to find the bracelet, including shaking up my Uncle's bookshop.

Baki looked at my face and hastily said, 'But you forgot to look in one place. The water cooler. Nehaji must've gone to the water cooler to drink some water, the bracelet must've got loose.'

'But why did you wait all these years for this show and tell?'

'I found it two weeks after you had your accident and somehow, you always seemed to get very angry whenever someone mentioned her name...'

Baki smiled and pulled out the bracelet from his pocket.

'By the power of castle grace skull,' Jai said. It was a line from the television series HeMan, we'd been crazy about it as kids.

'It's time to call Miss Varma,' I said.

'Look, Sam. Just think about it for a while, will you? You see, this bracelet meant something important to her. It was gifted to the poor girl by her dying mother. Do you think you can use it for leverage?' Jai said.

It made me stop my gleeful dialling of her number. Jai looked at me and shrugged.

'Let me get this straight. Are you suggesting that I do not use this,' I said lifting the bracelet, 'to make the woman responsible for the worst phase of my life, the woman who altered my life forever and not in a nice way, do one tiny thing for me?'

'When you put it that way, it seems fair. But look at it in isolation. You aren't the same lovelorn, miserable wreck anymore and perhaps she isn't the same heartbreaking vamp,' he said.

I thought about it for a few long moments.

'You are wrong about one of those things. She is still the heartbreaking vamp,' I said.

I dialled her number and said to Jai, 'Thanks.'

'You are welcome.'

It was picked up by her voicemail. Listening to her recorded voice made the hair on the back of my neck stand on end.

'Neha, this is Sameer,' I said. My brain overloaded with many options for the next sentence. All of them started with 'You fucking bitch . . .'

Instead I said, 'I've found your bracelet. Let me know how I can give it back to you.'

I disconnected the phone and said to Baki, 'You should've told me, Baki.'

Biting his finger he said, 'Is that thing so valuable, boss? I had no clue it meant so much to her. I hated her for making your life so miserable then. And I have never told this to you, but while you were searching for it, she had accused me of stealing it.'

I looked at him. There were tears in his eyes.

'It's okay,' I said. 'In some warped way, I think I understand.'

I got a call from her five minutes later.

✧

'Is this a joke?' she said in the form of greeting. 'I don't have time for this nonsense, Sameer. If you are trying to reconnect because Maya kicked you out, I am telling you it's not going to work.'

I was pissed. It told me two things. First, my ex-fiancée was in touch with my-ex (almost) girlfriend. They had been colleagues and friends. Second, I was proved right; she still thought I was a lovelorn miserable wreck.

'Neha, don't mention Maya in the same sentence as you. I think you are insulting her,' I said.

'Whatever,' she said.

This was her 'fuck-you' word. She said it whenever she was in a corner.

'Here's the deal. I have the bracelet and I want you to have it. You just tell me how I can hand it over and we'll part ways with the promise that we will never talk to each other again,' I said.

She was quiet for a few moments before saying, 'I will have someone come over to pick it up. Are you *still* working at the bookshop?'

'Some of us have learned to make an honest living,' I said and hung up.

'On second thoughts, maybe you should have used it as leverage and made her grovel – a little, at least,' Jai said.

'It wouldn't have been worth it,' I said.

To my great surprise, I saw her standing at the entrance of the bookshop a little while later. She wore large black glasses, hiding most of her face. I wanted to tell her that she *wasn't that* famous. She paused at the entrance for a few seconds, saw me fiddling around with a shelf and walked up to me. Many customers turned their heads towards her. I saw the surprise in the eyes of all the girls and they started whispering something to each other. Well, maybe she was *somewhat* famous after all.

'Hi,' I said as she came close to me.

'Where is it?' she said.

I handed it to her. I couldn't say what she felt because of the black sunglasses covering her eyes. But I thought her lips quivered.

'Why did you hide it from me all these years?' she said.

'Remember the promise? Not a word. Ever. Goodbye, Neha,' I said, turning my back to her and resuming my fiddling with the books.

'Answer me,' she said.

I ignored her.

'Answer me, you bastard!' she screamed.

There was a sudden silence in the bookshop. I still ignored her. She clutched my shoulder and spun me around with surprising force.

'Was this your idea of revenge, you son of a bitch?' she said and removed her glasses. Her eyes were red and there were large tears about to begin their journey down her cheeks.

'Great to know you acknowledge doing something worth avenging,' I said.

She slapped me hard on my face and walked out of the shop.

'Sorry for the interruption.' I said to the stunned customers. 'Kindly continue your shopping experience,'

'Women,' an elderly man said to me.

'Yup,' I said, trying hard not to rub my stinging cheek.

After listening to my phone conversation with Neha, Jai had stepped out of the shop. When he returned, Baki told him what had happened. By that time, Baki was crying like a baby. Many customers walked out of the shop, embarrassed. The ones who remained were curious to know what had happened. This was turning out to be one big melodrama at my expense.

'She actually slapped you?' Jai said peering at my face.

'Don't you see the red welt on my cheek?' I said.

'And what did you do?'

'What can one do when a girl slaps you? Slap her back?'

'Shooting her is closer to what I had in mind,' he said.

'Boss . . . boss . . .' Baki said.

'I'll listen to you if you stop crying, blow your nose and wipe those tears,' I said to him.

He walked to the little washroom in the store.

'What happens if she is your saviour?' Jai said.

'To be saved by Neha Varma is worse than death,' I said.

'I know it irritates the hell out of you when I say this, but – focus, Sam, focus. People spend millions to save their lives,' he said.

'Forget it, Jai. I am not going to live in humiliation, even if I had millions.'

He thought about it for a while.

'Let's consult Babaji and tell him there's a problem with one woman,' he said.

'There is something I need to tell you,' I said.

Jai stood still. 'Okay, that's the line you use when you want to confess something bad. What is it?'

'I have been having these weird dreams in which Babaji visits me, very regularly. We have long debates about things like life and death,' I said.

'Well, I think those are the two hot topics in your case right now, so no surprises there,' he said.

'The point is, I have a feeling Babaji knows everything about me. I think he knows the woman who is going to save me, *if* I am going to be saved at all,' I said.

'Is that so? I think there's a simpler way of going about this, then – why doesn't he just bloody tell us who that woman is!'

'Now this is the weird part. Many times he refers to death, as though it were some rival entity to Babaji. So that makes Babaji sort of anti-death.'

'I think you're forgetting that all those conversations never actually happened,' he said.

'I know it might sound crazy, but I think they did. Babaji did come to meet me. Only I think they are dreams,' I said.

'Anti-death,' he said as though trying the word on his tongue to know how it tastes.

'It isn't making any sense right now, I know, but I'll soon have some answers. We keep having many discussions,' I said.

He nodded.

'So what now? We go to the next one on the list?'

'No, we wait for her to come back. Believe it or not, Babaji had told me she would slap me today,' I said.

✧

Two days later, as Babaji had predicted, she called me.

'Can we talk about what happened?' she said.

'Yes, unless your true intention is to assault me again,' I said.

'I'm sorry about that,' she said. I could hear the pain it was causing her to say it. And the very next instant, she revealed why she was putting on the garb of penitence.

'Looks like someone shot the entire scene on the phone video camera,' she said.

I wanted to laugh, and after a few moments of herculean effort to control myself, I did. I laughed till my eyes watered and my throat hurt. I heard her angry voice saying my name repeatedly, but I just couldn't stop.

'Now, I'm sorry,' I said, just before a second wave of laughter hit me.

'I get a feeling you planned it all,' she said.

'That's a compliment, but quite undeserved. If I could plan something to perfection like that, I'd be a millionaire,' I said.

'The stupid video clip is all over the internet. Bastards,' she muttered.

'I think you're taking all this too seriously,' I said.

'You want to know what I think? I think you don't take anything seriously enough. You never did,' she said.

My smile froze on my face. It was as if she had hit me with a sucker punch. It was so out of the blue I couldn't think of a comeback line.

'Looks like something has hit home, right Sameer?' she said.

'I have no idea what you are talking about,' I said.

'Four o' clock at the usual coffee shop.' She disconnected.

I stood there holding the phone to my ear.

I couldn't stop thinking about what she had said. Didn't take her seriously? What the hell was that supposed to mean? I took her as seriously as a fucking heart attack! I wanted to spend my life with her. I had even imagined the wedding photograph of our families together and the expressions of each one of them (my mother – excited, my father – bored, her aunt who raised her – angry, her father – surprised, me – happy, she – happy). For the next one hour, I was irritated. The hour after, I was angry, and by the time it was four, I was downright furious.

I stormed to the coffee shop at 4.15, purposely deciding to be late to make her wait. She wasn't in the coffee shop. For a very brief moment I thought she had left and cursed myself for overdoing it. Since I was in the coffee shop where we had had some of the happiest times together discussing her books, her dreams, her likes, her dislikes, her family, I decided to have a cup and curse those memories for a while. Just as I ordered coffee, I saw her walking towards me. She put her purse on the table, sat down (oh so elegantly) and crossed her stunning legs (oh so sexily).

'Can I see the videoclip?' I said.

She stared at me without blinking.

'Okay, wrong question,' I said.

'I want you to hold a press conference and tell the press it wasn't me,' she said.

'Pardon me for being repetitive, but I think you are taking a stupid prank way too seriously,' I said.

'Sameer, if you stepped out of your fanciful little world, you would see there are things people get hurt by. This videoclip is on every news channel and the assholes have been replaying it non-stop,' she said.

I was stunned. Maybe she was *very* famous. I wondered how she became so without me even knowing about it. It was as if she inhabited some parallel universe where faking was considered a virtue and the better a faker you were, the more people loved you.

'I will call the reporters I know and you can tell them it wasn't me who slapped you,' she said.

'You mean I should acknowledge in front of the whole world that I was slapped by some unknown woman?'

'No one will remember you, Sameer. They'll just remember what you said.' I looked at her as if seeing her for the first time and wondered what I had ever loved in this woman.

'You see, Neha, every person in this city might know you, but there are some little people in my little world who know me and they wouldn't want to see me making a fool of myself,' I said.

The waiter came to us and asked if she wanted something. She ignored him. He walked away. I called him back, pulled out the little notebook and pen from my pocket and said to him, 'Can I have your autograph?'

He was a little flustered.

'You are the only one in the world who doesn't know this woman,' I said. 'That makes you special.'

'Leave us,' she said to the waiter who walked away with a totally bewildered face. We were simply great together, Sameer and Neha.

'I can give you something in return if you want,' she said.

'Well, there is one thing.'.

She rolled her eyes.

'Don't worry, my world is far too little for you,' I said.

I told her the story. Her expression changed from wary, to mildly interested, to amused, to downright amazed.

'This has to be the longest running joke I have ever heard,' she said.

'If I were telling you a joke, I would say . . .'

'Okay, okay, just bottle that up,' she said. 'You do the press conference and I'll do this.'

'Neha, we have a history together where trust was a dirty word,' I said.

She looked at me and for a little moment I thought she was going to lash out at me again. But the moment passed, and her shoulders drooped.

'Okay, you do the press conference a week later then,' she said.

'Deal,' I said.

'Wait,' she said, frowning. 'If we are seen together for the next two weeks, it will kind of defeat the purpose of the press conference, don't you think?'

'So I guess we will have to stay indoors for a while,' I said. It came out completely wrong.

'No, what I meant was, we should not be seen together, I mean . . .'

'Yeah, I know what you mean,' she said in a very tired voice. 'I have a guest house in Lonavala. I was anyway planning to go there for some peace to write in.'

'Okay,' I said.

'And you have to promise me. We will not speak to each other. If you need something, I have maids and servants over there who will give it to you. I would prefer not to see your face. One week later you will come back to Mumbai and have the press conference. I would love it if you didn't come back, but I promise to keep my end of the deal,' she said and got up. 'I leave tomorrow five o'clock, in the morning. I'll meet you at the guest house.'

She picked up my pen and notebook, wrote down the address of her guest house, put on her face-obliterating glasses and walked away.

I had the feeling that the next two weeks were going to be the longest and loneliest of my life.

✧

When I reached the guest house at nine in the morning, I had expected her to at least have informed the servants I was expected. They refused to let me in. I told them I was her friend. They said this wasn't the first time someone came and claimed that. I told them to call her up to confirm. They said they couldn't be bothering 'madam'. Utterly frustrated, I called her mobile. It was switched off. I ran out of options. I stood outside the gate of her guest house. A thin, stick-like servant whose name was Tukaram kept a constant watch on me. He looked like a brown skeleton. Being watched by a creature like that wasn't the most comfortable experience.

'Madam' stood me up for close to three hours. Tukaram didn't move a limb and after a while I was convinced he actually was a skeleton. When her car arrived at the guest house, I was ready to pounce on her and give her back in kind. She stepped out of the car and without even acknowledging my presence walked inside, telling Tukaram that I was a guest and that I should be shown my room.

Tukaram opened the gate giving me a guilty smile.

'I am sorry saheb,' he said.

'I am too,' I said.

'Why are you sorry, saheb?' he said.

'I generally am,' I said.

He rubbed his chin.

'Forget it, can you please show me my room?' I said.

◇

The room was wonderful. King-sized bed, lush carpet, wall mounted flat screen television, the works. I had no clue being a novelist in India had become such a big deal.

I plopped down on the bed and wondered how I was going to spend the next two weeks alone. I had packed two bags, one of which was full of books. I had finished half of *Neuromancer* by William Gibson and I was on the verge of going to the dark side – the side where people loved sci-fi and fantasy, when I heard a knock on the door. It was Tukaram with a piping hot plate of breakfast.

'I have made it saheb. Please tell me how it is,' he said.

It was delicious.

'It's wonderful, Tukaram,' I said.

That was the routine for me for the next three days. Tukaram asking me how it was and I telling him it was delicious. When she had said she didn't want to see my face, I hadn't thought that she meant it literally. On the third night, after I had finished *Snowcrash* by Neil Stephenson, I stayed awake for a long time. I wondered what the point of it all was. If Babaji wanted me to accomplish some higher objective by being with Neha Varma, I was sure it couldn't be achieved without us even meeting each other.

That night I also finished Baki's pages. I closed my eyes for a few minutes and visualised Baki. It was as if I had not known him at all. He was my first employee. (Maya of course said I had hired just two 'employees' in my entire life. And Pinky Patel didn't want a salary, so technically, Baki was the first and the last employee I ever hired.) Managing the bookshop on my own for the first three years had been nightmarish. It was like cooking ten dishes together. If you paid even a little more attention to one, at least one of the nine others burned. I decided I needed one more pair of hands and put up a poster saying *'Need someone who shares the same passion. Don't get any ideas – it's just for the books. Good salary.'* A grand total of one-and-a-half people applied for the lucrative position with Sathe and Sons, Booksellers. The 'half' was a twelve-year-old kid who informed me he would definitely consider it if I was ready to pay him ₹50,000 a month. I told him child labour was banned in India and cheap child labour was an even bigger crime. The other person to enquire about the job was Baki. It was on the day I had decided I would remove the poster as nobody else had bothered to apply. The interview lasted roughly five minutes. All the while, Baki sweated as though he was in the middle of the Sahara. He never met my eyes and spoke in a voice I had to strain my ears to hear. What clinched the deal was when he told me he had read *Gravity's Rainbow* by Thomas Pynchon in two days. You had to respect that.

The pages Baki had given me to read were pure gold. It was as if this wholly different persona inhabited the shy elf's body.

I was thinking about calling Baki and telling him what I felt about the book when there was a knock on the door. Thinking it was Tukaram the skeleton, I opened the door intending to tell him to leave me alone. Instead I saw Neha standing there with folded arms.

'How are you?' she said.

'Wonderful! I've met so many creatures here. Meet Mr Mahogany,' I said pointing to the shiny centre table. 'We met just three days ago, but it feels like we're old friends!'

Sighing exasperatedly she said, 'I thought I was being rude to a guest in my house by not talking to him, however unwelcome he may be.'

'The guest must be a miserable wreck by now,' I said.

'Would you like to have a cup of tea?'

'Yup,' I said and followed her.

I leaned against the refrigerator while she made the tea. It was a surreal scene. I had once dreamt of a life in which we did this every day. The only thing missing was her being naked.

'How is the writing going on?' I asked.

She didn't answer. I didn't ask again. She handed me a cup of piping hot tea and we sat down at the dining table.

Then she said: 'Why do you care?'

'Just making conversation,' I said.

We sipped the tea in silence for a while.

'I am quitting writing,' she said.

As far as bolts from the blue go, this one had the highest voltage.

'Do you promise not to say why do I care if I ask about it?'

She thought for a few moments before saying, 'I think you know why. This idea, this character has had her run. Perhaps I have dragged her beyond the finish line for a while now. My publisher tells me the sales of the new novel are slow.'

'Why don't you create a new series? A new character?'

'I've thought about it for the last two years. I have roughly five unfinished novels. And they're all bad,' she said.

The easiest thing to do would've been telling her to keep at it, to not give up yet. But there was something in her voice which told me she had thought about it very deeply.

'I've been trying to write for the last three days. I've stared at the damned laptop for hours together, but nothing has come out,' she said.

I should've felt some kind of vindication. I had fantasised about this scenario in which Neha Varma, the most successful Indian novelist, admitted she couldn't write. But all I felt was a hollow saddness. I still hated her, right? The tea suddenly tasted bitter. When I looked at her staring vacantly into her cup, I thought I saw the real Neha Varma, minus the façade she had so carefully built. We were quiet for a long time.

'What are your ideas?' I asked again.

'One is writing about a fashion model. I researched a lot about it. But when it came to writing, it was so bland, so boring. Then I thought about a TV journalist who turns thirty-five and suddenly realises life has just gone by in covering a series of events without her ever pausing and learning something from them. I spent days with a TV reporter friend trying to get into her head, but nothing good came out of that either,' she said.

'Most of them have been done before. I guess your novel would end up sounding like another wannabe,' I said.

She nodded.

'Why don't you write about a female Private Investigator?' I said.

She looked up at me with her head tilted to the right. I recognised it as her deep thought pose.

'The private investigator could be a recently thirty-plus woman, not able to find any worthwhile men, struggling in her business. What if one fine day, this incredibly good-looking man walks into her office with a problem she thinks she can solve in a few days but doesn't because she wants to be with him?' I ploughed in.

I knew it had got her excited – she was biting her lower lip.

'It could be interesting,' she said finally. 'I'll have to do some research.'

✧

For the next two days, we discussed what could potentially become her next series. By the end of the second day, she had the sparkle back in her eyes. I had a sinking feeling of déjà-vu, but I couldn't care less. The feeling of being with her, talking about books and writing was like some kind of old addiction revisited: You know it's dangerous and it will end very badly, but you just can't stop yourself from jumping headlong into it. When she was with you, Neha Varma could make you feel like the most special man in the whole world. She made the rest of the world irrelevant.

A few more days and I had forgotten the names I had given to the furniture in my room.

On the seventh day, I told her I would be heading back to Mumbai to keep my promise. She could round up her journalist friends and I would tell them she hadn't slapped me.

'There's no need,' she said. 'They aren't showing it anymore on TV and the hits on the internet have come down.'

'Is that the only reason?'

'What else could there be?'

We were just terrific together, Sameer and Neha.

Two days later, Maya came to know that I was living with Neha.

✧

On the tenth day of Sameer and Neha Part II, I got a call from Pinky after which I couldn't breathe for a long time.

'Maya had come to the store today,' she said.

I thought she was as usual having fun at my expense. She had this habit of saying the most shocking things, like when she told me she was thinking of piercing her clitoris.

'Okay, and was she 50kg overweight and bought How to Reduce 5kgs a Day?' I said.

'Boss, I am serious,' she said.

'Yes, so am I,' I replied.

She was quiet which gave me an opportunity to understand the full impact of what it could mean if it were true.

'She asked Baki where you were. The combination of Baki currently behaving like a human faucet with all that crying and his chronic nervousness around pretty women have put you in a most uncomfortable position. He told her you were with the manipulative bitch,' Pinky said.

My first instinct was to tell her Neha wasn't a manipulative bitch and she hadn't even met the woman she was accusing of being such a vile thing.

'Okay, scratch the manipulative bitch bit. The point is Maya knows you are with her,' Pinky said.

'I'm going to rip Baki apart when I come back. I'm going to feed him to wild animals,' I whispered fiercely. Then calming down a little, I said, 'What was her reaction?'

'Yeah, I will join you gladly in killing Baki. Her reaction? Well, it was enigmatic. As though she was a little relieved,' she said. 'All the best boss. And oh, by the way, that Neha woman isn't *just* a manipulative bitch. She is a self-centred, man-eating, exploiting, manipulative bitch.'

She disconnected the phone before I could say anything.

Neha saw the expression on my face and said, 'Has anyone died?'

'Maya knows I am here.'

'So?'

'I hadn't told her,' I said.

'Last I heard from her, you guys had broken up, right?'

'Yes, we did,' I said.

'If I remember correctly, she dumped you,' she said.

'Your memory is perfect,' I said.

'So . . .?' she said.

I debated with myself. If there were two of me, we would both be sprawled on the floor with grievous injuries. Should I call her or not? And tell her what? *'Maya, I am sorry I should've told you I was with Neha. But it's just a temporary thing.'* I was sure she would never talk to me if I said that. *'Maya, this is far bigger than what you think. I would be dead if didn't live with Neha for a while.'* That was sure to make her claw my face to ribbons the next time she saw me.

Everyone dithers differently and mine went on for a whole day. At night, I had a dream in which Babaji took me to my favourite place – the beach. Like in all dreams, the sand seemed to be made of gold and it was sticking to my body like a second skin and the sea was shiny and silvery. As always Babaji made his grand entry by doing something awesome. He appeared on the horizon and walked on the shiny sea towards me. In no time at all he was sitting down next to me. His shoes seemed to be covered in liquid silver. I knew it was a dream because of the downright hokeyness of it all. Golden beach and silver sea. Standard bizarre dream setting.

'Long day, huh?' Babaji said.

'The longest and the slowest of all,' I said.

'It's all coming very near, isn't it?'

'What? My death?'

He smiled a little. I felt like kicking him.

'That and some kind of realisation about what you are and what you are going to be?'

'I have no bloody clue, as always, what you're talking about,' I said.

'Oh you do. There were moments in the last ten days when you were trying to get back to your discarded version,' he said. 'The version which you had always fantasised about. The version with Neha Varma, that was perfect, happy, so much in love. You seemed to forget it was fictitious, it existed in your imagination. Even you didn't believe it.'

'What are you? Part-time soothsayer, part-time my conscience?'

'No, I am the boatman,' he said and laughed.

'Oh yes, you tell me the boatman and river story once more and I will break your teeth,' I said.

'You will have to snap out of this discarded version and realise it was not what you ever wanted,' he said.

'I am no fucking software to have versions. And what if I liked it?'

'You liked it three years back too. Look where it got you.'

'Where did it get me?'

'That's the problem, Sameer. You don't even know where it got you. Neha Varma is the constriction in the flow of your life. It stopped you for years last time. Don't let it happen again,' he said.

I looked at the sea for a moment and when I turned back, he was gone, as I had expected him to be. By the end of the dream I had decided to call Maya the next day.

✧

When the morning dawned, my hands were sweaty. I had not slept for the better part of the night. The pain in the left leg didn't allow me to. I regretted deciding to call Maya at nine in the morning. My logic was that she started for work at eight fifteen and she was generally very cranky in the mornings before she got into her car. She was a lifelong fan of punk rock, jazz and Kishore Kumar – that was one of the reasons I fell for her. Who wouldn't love a woman who liked the combination of Greenday, Billie Holliday and Kishore Kumar? It was like asking for a single scoop of your favourite ice cream and getting a triple sundae made of three of your top choices. She would in all likelihood put 'Boulevard of Broken Dreams' or 'Missed Train' or 'Yeh Jo Mohabbat hain' on her car stereo and reach the swanky offices of her company at eight fifty. She would climb up the stairs, because she hated closed spaces, especially lifts, and be at her desk at eight fifty-nine. Nine o' clock she would get my call. But I regretted waiting so long. I should've called her at five in the morning.

When the watch told me it was eight fifty nine, I said to myself to hell with it and called her desk number. It was picked up by an unknown voice.

'Uh . . . may I speak to Maya please?' I said.

'She isn't in her cabin yet,' said the male voice.

'Cabin?' I said.

'Yup, cabin,' the man said. 'Who is this?'

'Never mind.' I disconnected.

Cabin? That meant Maya had got promoted. It paralysed me for a long time. I had never formulated a clear picture of what she had done after we broke up, but I had a vague expectation that she would be quite despondent for a long stretch of time. My definition of a 'long stretch' was at least one year, if not two. And she had had the time and energy to not only move on, but move up! To hell with it, she didn't deserve me calling her. If she could get promoted, I could spend two weeks with Neha Varma. Heck I could spend two weeks with a prostitute. After all it was just a difference of degrees of randomness, right? Five minutes later, I called her again.

If someone had told me a year back that the first sentence I would say to Maya after a long hiatus would be 'So are you all happy sitting in your own bloody cabin?' I would have thought it to be a ridiculous, insulting joke, but that's precisely what I said to her.

'What were you expecting? That I would be in some mental hospital weeping the whole day?' she snapped.

I was thrilled to hear her voice. If someone gave me a choice between Aishwarya Rai calling me and saying the most romantic thing ever and Maya calling me and saying I was an asshole, I would blindly choose Maya's voice.

'Not the whole day. Sometimes you would laugh too, while remembering what we did when we were together,' I said.

'Sameer, I have a meeting in five minutes and I don't want to spoil my mood before it.'

'So it's *Sameer* now, is it? What all has changed in your heart, apart from my name? And when did some bullshit meeting become more important to you?'

'You're talking like your mother now. Asking rapid-fire questions.'

'Don't get my mother involved. I need to talk to you about the way you are treating her too,' I said. I was talking into a dead line.

For a while I was pissed off, but there was this tiny voice that told me I was incredibly happy about talking to her. I was so happy I called up Jai and told him.

'Guess what happened today? I spoke to her Jai! She actually took my call. And we spoke for a while,' I said.

'Let's roll it back a bit now, shall we? You called her up for what exactly?'

'It's not important. Didn't you hear me? She spoke to me,' I said.

'Okay, don't say it. I don't want to hear it. You called up and said something stupid to her like how could you be so happy or something equally rotten, right?'

When I didn't reply, he said, 'Sam, you are the biggest ass I have ever met in my life.'

'Now that is just an exaggeration,' I said.

'For once, I am not exaggerating,' he said and hung up.

I wondered what the hell was wrong with everyone. Why were they all hanging up on me?

When I met Neha in the afternoon she asked me if I had spoken to Maya.

'I did. But we couldn't talk much. She had a meeting in the next two minutes,' I said not looking at her.

She laughed and said, 'She asked you to take a hike, didn't she?'

'None of your business,' I said.

'Yes, I agree. So are you going to run from here, back to her, to apologise? Doesn't it go against the rules of the two-week stay?' she said.

'Neha, I have news for you. If I had to choose between Maya and my life, I wouldn't have to think much. But I guess making a choice between something like that and something like getting your next book published would be a tough choice for you. You would negotiate for more than one book, won't you?'

'What are you bitter about, Sameer? That I broke your heart? It wouldn't have worked between us, and you know it.'

'No, I am not bitter about it. I was for a long time but I'm not now. In fact, I'm really glad about it. Sometimes what seems like terrible misfortune, is actually a lucky break,' I said.

She was quiet for a while.

'I guess that closes the chapter then, doesn't it? We really part ways three days later with no hard feelings, knowing exactly what each one of us wants in life.'

'Yes, we do,' I said.

This might sound incredible, but me and Neha got along just fine for the remainder of my stay with her. Perhaps we both understood that there was no point in being bitter about something, a relationship, that was never meant to be.

Three days later, when I was travelling back to Mumbai, I felt a strange kind of lightness. I wanted to fly. I again wanted to sing. I wanted to dance. I wanted to tell my parents I loved them. Tell Jai how much I loved him. Tell Pinky and Baki how much they have enriched my life. After all, I was going to meet Maya and see if she could let me live in her house for a couple of weeks.

✧

Chapter 8

I HAD NOTHING AGAINST PEOPLE PIERCING THEIR BODIES, but I loved it when I saw Pinky minus all the metal. Though she still had the weird hairdo, she looked lovely.

'Do I know you?' I said to her.

'You might've if you had paid some attention,' she said putting a few books back where they belonged. She was smiling a little.

'I've been accused of that before,' I said.

'Are you going to Maya's place?' she asked.

'Have to, no other option,' I said.

'If it was such a forced choice, why do you have a goofy smile on your face?'

'Some facial muscles work from memory,' I said.

'It's nice to see you smile, boss.'

'This is the "flame burning brightest before extinguishing" nonsense,' I said.

'You've done the tough bit now,' she said. 'I think you'll be all right.'

'You promise you'll be all right if I am gone?' I said.

'I think you are talking crap now. And by the way, I was always all right,' she said and walked away.

I told Jai what had happened in Lonavala.

'So that little unpleasant episode in your sordid story is over,' he said.

'Yeah, it is,' I said.

'When are you going to talk to Maya?'

'In a day or two,' I said.

'Okay, that's good. Make it a month or two. In fact a year or two. Wait a minute . . . you'll be dead by then!'

'You are being a fatalist,' I said.

I dialled her number. There was no answer. That left me with just one option – visit her home.

✧

There are things you hope you never have to do. For example, you wouldn't want to go back to an office, begging for a job, because you had left after telling the employers they were a bunch of morons and you were too good for them. You don't really want to see the smug faces of the people snickering at your expense. In a relationship there is nothing more pathetic than going to your ex to ask for a favour. It is humiliating, and you have to eat your own words, the ones that were bitter when you first spat them out during your break-up. The only consolation I had was that we had not officially broken up. While I was on my way to her place, it struck me that there is nothing like an 'official' break-up. We were engaged and the engagement was attended by hundreds of people. What do you do in such situations? Send all the people a card that says, *'Please come to grace the solemn occasion of Sameer and Maya's dis-engagement?'*

I stood in front of her apartment complex pondering if my life was worth my ego. My old friend Zia looked at me from the gate house with the same suspicious eyes. I wanted to tell him his tough guy act couldn't scare a mangy dog.

'You're back again?' he said, stepping out of his little booth.

'I'm like the irritating soap commercial that never really leaves the television,' I said.

He stared at me, wondering what kind of sins he had done to deserve this job.

'I told Ms Saxena you had come here the other night,' he said.

The man did his job all right.

'You what? How could you?' I said.

'I thought I should warn her, to be wary against your next intrusion,' he said defensively, as though he had broken some ancient pact we had.

'What did she say?' I asked, hating my excited voice.

'She laughed and said you were harmless,' he said, rubbing his chin.

Harmless?. From being the cynosure of her eyes to becoming harmless! Nobody could have predicted such a fall.

'She actually used the word harmless?' I said.

I think Zia sensed something frightening in my voice and said, 'Well, my memory isn't what it used to be once. So I might be completely wrong.'

I nodded. We both knew he was being nice and we smiled at each other.

'The other guard told me you and Maya Madam are engaged. I'm sorry for being rude to you earlier. Please forgive me,' he said, with a sheepish smile.

'Oh, no, you are the nicest of rude people,' I said.

He smiled.

'Is Maya Madam at home?' I asked.

'I think she is,' he said.

'Is the drunken Mercedes man with her?' I asked.

'No. I never saw him again,' he said.

Maya had taken to one night stands? (Mean! Mean!)

'Thanks,' I said and started walking towards her apartment.

'Sir, one more thing,' he said.

I stopped and turned warily. Was there someone else with her?

'She smiled when she said that word. Harmless. I know a loving smile when I see one, sir,' he said.

Everyone's a philosopher.

✧

When she opened the door, and honestly I hadn't expected her to, she had a curious smile on her face. I was thrown completely off-guard. First, I didn't think she would want to see me, and if she did it would be to grow up and stop stalking her and not trouble her security guard at night. The smile gave me a strange thrill, the kind you get after you've won ₹10,000 in a lucky draw. Ten thousand bucks won't make you a rich man, but it could make you *feel* rich for a split second.

'I was wondering when my turn would be up,' she said.

'So you know about it?' I asked.

'You assumed I didn't know?' she said, opening the door and turning away from me.

I walked in. I had so many fond memories of the place. I could see a lot of changes. They weren't very obvious, but if you looked closely or if you had obsessive memories about how it looked a while ago, you could spot the differences: The couch had brand new covers. They were burgundy in colour. I hated burgundy. The beautiful table lamp we had bought wasn't there. The painting of a stunning sunrise we had purchased from Jehangir Art Gallery was still there, but it was accompanied by a landscape, and I wasn't a great fan of landscapes. Like I said, subtle.

'You've changed things,' I said.

'Just a little. Here and there,' she said dismissively.

I was quiet for a long moment.

'What's my number, Sameer?' she said.

We were still on Sameer.

'You're number seven,' I said.

'The last?'

It was like she had blindsided me. It was her most lethal move. Perhaps she had practised it for days, imagining what I would say. Anything I said would be a big victory for her. I wished I had come to her better prepared. I hadn't bothered to rehearse before the finale.

'Yes,' I said.

She leaned back on the couch with a little smile of victory. I didn't want to ask her the same question. It would've sounded desperate.

'How do you know?' I said.

'Jai told me.'

'When you had finally decided to check if I was alive a few days back?' I said, with a nasty smile.

'No, a few months back,' she said. 'When . . . when I told him about Rajesh.'

'What about Rajesh?' I asked.

There was surprise on her face, which immediately turned to dread.

'Hasn't he told you?'

'No,' I said.

'That Rajesh and me . . . we were involved.'

I now knew what it felt like when your worst fears came true. All the reactions that accompany this realisation were there.

Smile freezing on my face? *Check*. Numbness of the tongue? *Yup*. Actually seeing red and feeling dizzy? *Bingo*.

She must've seen all these on my face. She stood up, knelt in front of me and said, 'But it's . . . it's over, Sam. I couldn't imagine living with anyone else but you.'

'Lucky me,' I said. It was as if someone else, someone who was a few blocks away, had whispered the words.

'Will you at least look at me?' she said.

'*Rajesh*? That schmuck? Of *all* the people?'

She looked away, bit her lip and said, 'Why is he a schmuck? He didn't run away when I spoke to him about planning a holiday.'

'How many babies were you guys planning to have?' I said, and didn't even regret saying it.

She looked at me. There were tears in her eyes.

'You bastard! How dare you? There are things I have never ever spoken to anyone about. Except you,' she said.

I stood up.

'I think I need to leave now,' I said.

She sounded panicky.

'Sameer, did you ever wonder why I still have so many of my things in your house?'

I stood there, trying to make some sense of what she was asking me.

'I never wanted to leave you. Ever. Even when I was with Rajesh. And if it gives you any satisfaction, he is a schmuck. The biggest I have ever known. I mean it,' she said.

'I need the keys of my house,' I said.

'Why didn't you tell me about your curse?' she said, ignoring what I had said.

'It's my curse to bear,' I said.

'That's the thing. My books. But not my bookshop. My life, but not our life. My curse but not our curse,' she said, her voice rising. I could sense anger boiling inside her. It was making her choke on her words. .

'I would never have been able to fulfil your dreams, Maya,' I said. I had never been able to shrug off the feeling that I was going to die young. Babaji, did tell me about the curse, but I think somewhere deep inside me, I had already figured it out years ago. And the first casualty of this realisation had been the conventional dreaming about your future part.

'It was never about me, was it! It was about you, you fool. You never *had* any dreams. You used those accidents to hide that. And you were scared when you were with me, because for the first time ever, you thought you could dream. But then you would've had to quit the accident-to-accident cycle, right? Read as many books as possible before the next one. Listen to as much music. And keep waiting.'

She was shaking, and by the last sentence, she was sobbing. Every single cell in my body wanted to hug her. Tell her that we should start a new life together, forgetting everything else. But I couldn't. I knew this accident was going to be the last.

I walked out of her house without saying another word.

I had no idea what made me do it. If I could rewind my life it wouldn't have panned out like that. If something we said could've been altered, even one lousy sentence, maybe I wouldn't have walked out of her house, walked on the crowded streets of Mumbai and stopped in the middle of the road wondering what the hell had just happened. If someone had told me in the morning that Maya knew all along about the last eight months and was willing to have me over for two weeks, I would've jumped at the chance.

✧

I invited Jai to Harish Bar. When he arrived, I ignored him. I was sipping beer.

'You've already ordered? What the hell is this?' he said.

'Why didn't you tell me?' I said.

'So she told you about it. Look, Sam, you knew what I always thought about you guys being together, didn't you?'

When I had told him about Maya for the first time, he had asked me some stupid questions. First – what was her favourite band? When I said Greenday, he had laughed as though I had told him a sick joke. The next question was about her job. When I told him about her investment banking job he was quiet for a while and then had said okay. I had asked him many times about that 'okay' because I thought he wanted to say that I was better off without her.

'I always thought of her as too perfect. It's like you went to some futuristic shop and got a configured person,' he said.

'I have no clue what you are talking about,' I said, although I knew exactly what he meant.

'Okay, let me try again. I heard you talking about her and I *thought* she was this perfect superwoman who had a great job, was beautiful, read books, listened to Greenday and did everything you ever wanted a woman to do. I heard your soppy voice on the phone and I knew what had happened. *You* had seen it all, but she wasn't just that, Sam. You had superimposed your idea of some dream woman onto her. There were many things about her you chose to ignore.'

When I said nothing he continued, 'Didn't you ever see that beneath all that sophisticated charm she was just an ordinary girl, with ordinary choices to make and ordinary dreams about her life with you? I think you chose not to see her ordinariness. I think you took your fascination for all the things Neha was and added to it to all the things you *wanted* Neha to be and made up some mutated version and imposed it on Maya.' He was right.

Maya was an incredible woman, but I had imagined her to be this goddess who had acquiesced to my prayers.

'When you guys broke up, what was she supposed to do? Mope for you for the rest of her life? That happens only in bad movies, Sam.'

'I want you to go away, Jai,' I said.

'Sam, I think you're drunk,' he said and called Harishbhai.

'What have you given him?' Jai asked the corpulent owner of the bar.

'He wanted a few pegs of whiskey,' Harishbhai said.

'Harishbhai, you are the biggest asshole I've seen in my life,' Jai said. 'This is the last time I'm coming here.'

'You bet your fucking, intrusive ass,' I said. 'You're out of here.'

'Fine. I'll be around. You won't see me, but I will see you,' he said and got up.

'You better not be around, Jai,' I said.

'Who the hell are you to decide what I do?' he said, and walked out of the bar.

I felt worse than I had ever felt when he left. I had selfishly dragged him into the mess of my life and we had been together in it for a long time. It was better this way, I guessed. I wouldn't have to say a long goodbye to him when the time came.

✧

Chapter 9

I HAD NOT FOLLOWED WHAT BABAJI HAD TOLD ME TO DO completely. I had not stayed with Maya for two weeks. But if she was going to be my saviour, I believed those two weeks were irrelevant. If the purpose of living together for two weeks was to make sure every woman realised I was worth saving, I guessed she didn't need that conclusion.

As if on cue, the Babaji-dream visited me again. This time, we were sitting in Maya's house, the way it was when we were happiest together, when there was no burgundy sofa to spoil the view.

'Is it so difficult to change?' Babaji said.

'She got a *landscape*! Can there be any more emphatic statement?' I asked.

'What if she always liked landscapes and never told you because she didn't want to hurt you?'

'Are you serious? Who'd bother so much about a landscape?'

'You,' he said with a smile.

He had this ability to trap me in my own web of words.

'Look, it's not just the painting. She isn't the same anymore. She is . . . she has outgrown me,' I said.

'Just because she doesn't talk about Ernest Hemmingway or William Faulkner any more as much as she used to?'

'I'm not going to answer your bloody questions. Are you my soothsayer or my relationship counsellor?'

He laughed and before he could say it I shouted, 'And don't you tell me that you're a bloody boatman!'

'No, I was going to say I am your soothsayer. Counselling you is a waste of time,' he said.

'So what happens now?' I said, dreading his answer.

'We wait for the day. Perhaps I will see death defeated,' he said.

I felt like crying.

'Have you ever seen death defeated before?'

'I wouldn't be so curious if I had,' he said.

It was the last time I saw Babaji.

✧

'I am going to publish your book,' I said to Baki the next morning when he walked in with the latest consignment of paperbacks I had ordered. He was so stunned that he dropped the bundle.

'And if any of those books are messed up, I am going to change my mind.'

'I am so sorry boss, I am extremely sorry. I will not let anything happen to these books. If anything has happened, and I am not saying anything has, then you can reduce the amount from my salary.'

'That's okay, Baki. You have to excuse my morbid sense of humour nowadays,' I said.

'Were you joking boss?'

'Yes, I was,' I said and realised he wasn't asking about the books. 'But not about publishing your book,' I reassured him.

He looked like he was going to cry.

'I *will* change my mind if you shed one more tear,' I warned.

'No boss. No more tears. If they do appear, they will be happy tears,' he said.

I smiled. I had sent the script to Ramesh Uncle a few days back, called him up and told him he would be blown away. Thanks to my record of 'discovering' Neha, my credibility was high. He had said that he would definitely read it. That morning, he had called me back saying that I had discovered another gem and that he wanted to talk to the author. I handed Ramesh Uncle's name and number to Baki and told him to get in touch.

He cried. For the first time, I didn't feel like kicking him for it.

There was one last thing to do before the day arrived. Something I had promised Devi I would do. I didn't want to die with a broken promise on my head.

It was time to visit Usmanbhai again.

✧

'Is that all?' Usmanbhai gave me a surprised look.

'Yes, Usmanbhai,' I said.

'I would have thought you would want something more materialistic,' he said.

'I was tempted, but I guess I may not need it,' I said.

'Why do you say so? Is everything all right?'

'No, everything is all right, bhai. I will be forever indebted to you if you do this for me,' I said.

'Are you joking? This is nothing compared to what you have done for me. I can never repay your debts. You just have to command. I will do what you want.'

I felt as though I had discovered Alladin's lamp and a malevolent genie was at my disposal now. The temptation of summoning the genie was overwhelming and I was glad I wouldn't have to worry about it too much. Perhaps...

'Do you want to watch it happen?' he said.

'I would love to,' I said.

It turned out to be the last big mistake I had made in my crazy quest.

✧

It was four in the morning when I knocked on Devi Mathur's door. When she opened it, there was a glimpse of stark fear in her eyes, as though she had been awake all along.

'I'm here to keep my promise,' I said and gently pushed the door open. She looked behind me and a little sob escaped her throat.

Behind me stood Patil and his goons, bound by ropes, like common thieves. They were under the supervision of a battalion of policemen.

'These people won't trouble you again, Devi,' I said and held her hand.

She walked out of the house with me and looked at the men who had bruises all over their faces and bodies. Patil couldn't even look at her.

'Are these the men who have been harassing you?' asked the superintendent of police who had accompanied me all the way from Mumbai to carry out what I thought was a bizarre 'operation'.

At the behest of an underworld don, the police were out to wipe out a village gang. It was like bringing a bazooka for an ant, but I thought it was Usmanbhai's style. I had asked the SP while we were heading towards the village what he thought about it all. He had laughed and said he could do with a hundred such bizarre requests from Usmanbhai. I thought there was a sound, but warped logic, in the way he perceived it. I guessed all of us have our own way of processing the realities of our lives.

Devi nodded. The superintendent smiled and slapped Patil hard on his face.

'Load these bastards in the van,' he barked at the battalion.

The policemen hauled the goons into their vehicles. Like most of life's dramatic moments, it was over in minutes.

'Thank you,' she whispered.

'No, thank *you*,' I said and held her hand. We stood outside her house for a long time without saying a word.

I hadn't liked the way Patil had stared at me while he was pushed into the vehicle. But I shrugged the image away, telling myself he wouldn't be able to do much while he rotted in a dungeon.

✧

The worst part of this 'wrapping up your life' thing is that you start questioning everything that you have achieved. I was sure I was kind of unique, not many people would know exactly when they were going to die. It is an especially terrible position to be in at the age of thirty. Apart from the likes of Sachin Tendulkar or Christopher Paolini about 99.9 per cent people have achieved close to zero in their lives by thirty. I couldn't bat like Tendulkar or write like Paolini or compose like Beethoven. So it was a lot tougher to be in my position of 'taking-stock-of-my-life' and deciding whether I was a 'loser' or worth something.

I knew what Maya would say 'you think someone who hasn't read Conrad or doesn't listen to Bhimsen Joshi or Aretha Franklin is a loser too.' Eevryone is entitled to their own definition of a loser.

I doubted anyone apart from Jai took my impending death scenario too seriously. Madhuri, Anjali, Devi, Mrs Jacobs and Neha – I was sure those women were questioning their sanity in allowing me to stay with them for two whole weeks and messing up their lives. Maya would think of it as a crackpot idea someone had put in my head and that, as usual, I had jumped into it headlong. I was sure Baki and Pinky were being indulgent when they said they understood what I was doing. I hadn't told my parents or any of my other friends. My Uncle, who had taken everything I said seriously even when I was eight years old, was dead. That left me with Jai, whom I had asked not to interfere with my life anymore. I finally understood what it meant to be lonely. Some words are used too liberally. When you're waiting for a friend at the movies you say you feel lonely. Nothing could be farther from the truth. You're not lonely, you are alone. For the first time in my life, I felt a wretched sadness that could only be a result of understanding the profound meaning of loneliness – to die with nobody around you.

✧

A week before the day, I had decided I would blank it out, just not think about it. But it was impossible. Bizarrely, I was missing Babaji's calm voice in my dreams. Through our conversations, he had almost made death human, an entity that was beatable. I still hated the bastard for what he had done to me in the last year, but I thought he would've been a good man to have by my side when death decided to finally visit me.

I hadn't called up Jai for the last month or so, but I felt his presence around me, as though he was watching over me, making sure I was all right and when the moment came, he would step between me and death like the sidekick in Hindi movies. I attributed that feeling to my fast deteriorating sense of reality and my heightened sense of guilt for doing certain things to people close to me.

I had decided not to call my parents every day, lest they got too worried and came over to Mumbai on D-day. I had vowed to save them from the shadow of my death. As the day came closer I regretted making that vow. I believe home is where you feel the safest. If someone showed us our childhood like a movie, especially between the ages nine to sixteen, I think we would find many more sad moments than happy ones. Perhaps a majority of those fucked up moments would have happened in our homes. Strangely, when we grow up, the same place becomes this cozy, warm, safe place where everything is all right. I wept.

✧

Technically, the day had started at one second past twelve. I remembered what Jai had said all those months ago. *Don't step out of your house.* I had mocked him then, but I couldn't step out of bed. I stared blankly at the overhead fan and wondered when its bearings would break and the blades would sever my head. I shivered at the thought and closed my eyes.

My cellphone rang. I ignored it. But it refused to shut up. I grabbed it and was about to switch it off when I saw Jai's name flashing on the screen. I disconnected. The phone rang again.

'Jai, the fan is making creaking noises,' I said into the phone.

'Your friend will soon be dead you bastard,' said a voice which was not Jai's.

It was Patil's voice. A strange calmness took over me. Perhaps it was the relentless obsession about something horrible the future held, all that talk of death as my reality that made Patil's phone call a big letdown. If death came in the shape of Patil, the bastard was an idiot.

'What happened to Jai?' I asked.

I thought he was surprised by my unruffled voice.

'He is on the floor in front of me screaming like a pig.'

'Listen, Patil. I know you want to pull off some kind of filmy-style revenge drama, in which you make me beg for the life of my friend,' I said in the same cool voice. 'But that's a waste of my time. You let him go and you can have me in return. You hurt him even a little more, I promise you I won't need Usmanbhai to help me. I may not be able to kill you, but I am ready to die trying.' There was silence for a few agonising moments. It was pierced by Jai's painful screams.

'Okay, you have to come alone,' he said and gave me directions to a dumping yard in the industrial area on the outskirts of Mumbai. I disconnected the phone before he could say anything else.

For the first time in my life, I felt in control. It was as if I was reborn as a man. Too bad it had to happen on the day of my death!

◇

When I reached the dumping yard, I expected to see Patil surrounded by his men. I also imagined that Jai would have his limbs bound, his mouth covered with a dirty cloth and he would be bawling. Patil would laugh like a hyena and beat us up before killing me. I had no plan for tackling this situation. I didn't own a gun, and I had no time to shop for one. Anyway, guns weren't available like loaves of bread at the local kiraana-shop. The only thing I could bargain for was a swap between me and Jai.

The scene at the scrap yard was not even close to what I had imagined.

It was a scrap yard, but that's where the similarity between my imagination and reality ended. Jai was sitting with his back to the wall, his limbs free. He had a bored expression on his face. There were no goons scattered around holding menacing guns. And the man in charge, Patil, was alone. He had a large sickle in his hand, the kind with which my grandfather used to remove pesky weeds from his garden.

'Are you all right?' asked Jai.

'Apart from a psycho trying to chop off my head, yup, I am hale and hearty,' he said, sullenly.

'Why were you screaming a while ago?' I asked.

'Because the bastard wanted me to. He said he would chop off my finger if I didn't.'

'Keep your mouths shut, both of you!' Patil screamed like a petulant child.

'Patil, let him go,' I said. This wasn't what I had hoped for. It seemed too easy.

'Can you get Usmanbhai off my back?' Patil said. There was desperation in his voice and it almost made me laugh.

'Tell him I will not trouble that woman anymore. Please? I have paid ₹1,00,000 just to get out of jail for a day! I promise I won't bother that woman.'

I couldn't help but laugh. This man, who had acted so bloody tough just a few months back, was threatening me to save his own life. Nothing could be more bizarre.

'There is nothing to laugh about!' he said.

I couldn't stop.

But I should've.

He threw the sickle at me. I remember it hitting me on my neck. I remember touching my neck and being surprised by the blood on my hand.

Everything went dark after that.

✧

Chapter 10

I FINALLY SAW DEATH. IT *WAS* A MAN.

A big, bearded man who sat on a mighty throne. There were scores of people in front of me. We all stood silently, with our heads bowed, as though we were a bunch of errant schoolchildren who were going to be spanked. When I looked down, I saw a sight that should have shaken me. We were standing thousands of feet above the ground. I could see the earth the way I remember seeing it on Discovery Channel. But this sight just made me curious. There was nothing under our feet. I lifted my left leg and put it down again. There was no ache. I kind of missed that pain.

The line was moving very slowly. To some people, Death was totally dismissive. He didn't even look at them and they just disappeared. Others got a big dressing down from him. The victims cowered. After the ranting, Death made them disappear too. For some others, he actually had a smile -- I could see his big, bushy beard wiggling in glee, as though he was truly looking forward to killing those people. I wondered what he would do to me.

After what felt like an eternity, I stepped in front of him.

'Oh you,' he said and was about to dismiss me.

'Hold on!' I shouted.

He looked at me, both surprised and annoyed.

'Don't just dismiss me,' I said. 'I think I deserve more than that.'

His eyebrows scrunched and he looked at me with narrowed eyes, as though I was a little dog who had pulled off a great trick.

'Why was my death so pointless?' I demanded.

'I thought you were going to ask me something much more profound,' he sneered.

'This is the most profound question I have asked in my life. Too bad, I had to die for it,' I said.

'What were you expecting?' he said, leaning back on his throne.

'Couldn't you have given me death after I had achieved something meaningful?' I said, hating my pleading voice.

'Like what?'

'Like calling my Uncle's bookshop my own? Or fulfilling *my* dream of seeing it grow, maybe opening two more branches? Or telling Maya how much I loved her and what a fool I was to think that she would stay the same person forever? Or telling Jai I am sorry to have hurt him? Maybe after I had seen some glimmer of happiness in the eyes of my parents about what their son was doing with his life?'

He nodded and sighed.

'You aren't the first to ask me that question. It makes me sad every time I hear it. I used to console people earlier, but now I just say, tough luck.'

'That's it?'

'Yes,' he said.

'One last question.'

'You are irritating me now,' he said in a bored tone.

'Only one, promise. Do you know Babaji?'

Death laughed, as though I had told him the funniest joke he had ever heard.

'Don't worry, I'll pass on the message to him. He lost this time too!'

I closed my eyes and knew I was going to disappear.

✧

When I opened them again, the first feeling I had was of disappointment.

I wasn't dead after all.

I was in a hospital. *After all.*

I heard cheering and saw familiar faces.

My mother who was crying copiously. My father, who rubbed his eye with his thumb and forefinger (the first time I saw him cry). Jai, who had a stupid grin on his face. Baki who ran out of the room hollering and Pinky who made a big O of her lips, blew out air and nodded.

I felt Maya's hand in mine. I looked at her and saw the most beautiful smile I had ever seen.

'Hello,' she said.

'Hi,' I whispered back.

✧

Epilogue

I WOULD LOVE TO SAY THAT EVERY SINGLE WOMAN I HAD stayed with in the last one year was there in the hospital room, waiting with bated breath for me to open my eyes. They weren't. But they did visit me in the hospital. Madhuri, Anjali, Mrs Jacobs, Devi. And even Neha. They all said the right things, made concerned noises, told me how relieved they were that I was alive. I told them I was grateful for the visits. I thought I saw some kind of guilt in their eyes, for not taking what I had told them seriously. But it could well be something my medicated brain wanted me to see. Honestly, it doesn't really matter.

As it turned out, Maya had saved me. She had parked herself in her car outside my house from the night before the fateful meeting with Patil. When I had stepped out, she had followed me. She had called up Pinky and told her I that I looked flustered and tense. (I had thought I was in complete control!) Pinky, for the first time in months, had called up her father and told him about it. He had sent his men to the scrap yard. But they were following Maya's instructions to get there. All this coordination took time – enough time for Patil to sever my vein.

When Usmanbhai's men had reached the scrap yard, the sickle had already hit me. Apparently, Jai had tripped Patil while he was throwing the blade at me. I told Jai that I didn't believe him. He called me a thankless bastard. I didn't argue. Shetty and Curly had overpowered Patil before he could do any more damage.

I was taken to the hospital. The familiar last step in all my accidents.

'That's some story,' I said to Maya as we sipped coffee in her house. The burgundy sofa was gone. I had asked her about it. She said she had never liked it. I said she shouldn't have disposed off the sofa, the covers would have been enough. To that she shrugged. I liked the shrug.

'Have you met Babaji?' she asked.

'No. And I don't want to,' I said.

She nodded as though she understood.

'So, what next?' she said, holding my hand.

'Is there a next even now?' Jai quipped from across the room.

Devi laughed. Jai and Devi had plans to get engaged soon. I thought it was great. A little weird, but great nonetheless. He had even asked me if I was okay with it. I had told him I had no right to be otherwise.

'Next, I do everything I told Death I would do,' I said.

'Like what?' Maya asked. She was smiling but there was a cloud of concern in her eyes, as if she was still worried that I had suffered some kind of irreparable brain damage.

'Now *that* would be telling, wouldn't it?' I said.